Lost & Found

By Jacqueline Sheehan

LOST & FOUND
TRUTH

Lost & Found

Jacqueline Sheehan

AVON

An Imprint of HarperCollins*Publishers*

HarperCollins books may be purchased for educational, business, or sales promotional use. For information please write: Special Markets Department, HarperCollins Publishers, 10 East 53rd Street, New York, NY 10022.

FIRST EDITION

Designed by Elizabeth M. Glover

Library of Congress Cataloging-in-Publication Data
Sheehan, Jacqueline.
    Lost & found / by Jacqueline Sheehan. – 1st ed.
        p. cm.
ISBN: 978-0-06-112864-6
ISBN-10: 0-06-112864-3
1. Animal welfare—Fiction.   2. Loss (Psychology)—Fiction.   3. Maine—Fiction.
I. Title.
PS3619.H437Y43   2007
813'.6—dc22   2006032267

07 08 09 10 11   DT/RRD 10 9 8 7 6 5 4

Rebecca Elfrieda Sheehan
1912–2005

Acknowledgments

I called on the good will and generous spirit of others for their expertise. Suzanna Choi Adams, a superb psychotherapist, read for clinical accuracy. Joann Berns and Joanne Blanchard, both physical therapists, offered insights into their profession. Police Chief Paul Scannell, of Westfield State College, provided information about tasers. Lee King, retired Animal Control Warden of Woodbury, Connecticut, and Carol Hepburn, Animal Welfare Officer of Amherst, Massachusetts, shed light on animal care. Tom Dussault, Agawam Sportsman Club in Massachusetts, tried to give me archery lessons, and Linda Randall, DVM, Cloverleaf Animal Hospital Medina, Ohio, spent hours on the phone correcting my mistakes about dog anatomy. I take all the credit for mistakes in each area.

Special appreciation goes to the members of my manuscript group who read every page: Marianne Banks, Kris Holloway, Celia Jeffries, Rita Marks, Brenda Marsian, Elli Meeropol, and Lydia Nettler. The members of the Great Darkness Writing Group also listened with care: Jennifer Jacobsen, Alan and Edie Lipp, Patricia Riggs, Morgan Sheehan, and Marion VanArsdell. I thank Sharron Leighton for her encouragement and Patricia Lee Lewis for the spaciousness of her international writing retreats. Thanks to Mary Ellen and Jeffrey Zakrzewski for sharing their dog, Spud, with the rest of us. Carrie Feron and Tessa Woodward at Avon Books and Jenny Bent at Trident Media are a brilliant team of brains and heart.

Chapter 1

Bob had left the waxed food carton on the counter the night before and it now smelled of grease and fish. Rocky picked up the box and a puddle of oil pooled beneath it. Her husband ate deep fried food when salted fat was the only way to soothe the layers of accumulated sadness after a day telling a pet owner, "Your dog has had a good long life and this cancer won't be cured by surgery or chemo. Her kidneys are failing. What would you like me to do?" She knew from looking at the contents of the food container that Bob's day had gone badly yesterday and that his mumbled response to her as he got into bed was a result of self-medication with the worst sort of fast food. "They only change the grease in that place once every week," she warned him.

They had traveled to Ireland one year and the highlight of the trip for Bob had been learning that the Irish had a polite form of a well-worn expletive that was cleverly one letter off. The first time he heard a storekeeper in Sligo say "Oh feck!" Bob perked up. "Feck?" he asked. "Is that something you can say around your mother?"

"'Tis, as long as you don't say it about her, if you get what

I mean. But don't you dare say 'fook' around Herself," he explained, pronouncing the expletive with an Irish lilt. Ever since then, Bob said the world was fecked if he was mildly peeved. He mostly said it to his patients, cats and dogs, who came to him. "Why, that's a fecking shame, Simon, but antibiotics will clear that right up." But if he was massively indignant, the world was completely fooked. When he was sad from too many old golden retrievers looking at him with dreamy-eyed forgiveness as he injected them with death, he went to get "fooking fake fried clams at Johnny's Drive-In."

Rocky tossed the white container into the garbage. She was on her way to the university, but remembered her promise to order new socks for them to wear at night as they scuffed about the house. She was annoyed that he had been so insistent and it was only the first week of May. Why couldn't he take time to make the call? And why now? The semester would be over in ten days, then she'd have time for this, not now. She began lining up her points for the argument that she planned to have about Bob assuming that she should call. They would have the argument over dinner.

She picked up the cordless phone and punched in the 800 number for Lands' End, when she heard the thick sound from the upstairs bathroom. She pictured Bob brushing his teeth, peeing a coffee-scented stream into the toilet, shaving his face, but none of those predictable morning rituals accounted for the sound.

"Good morning. This is Priscilla. Let's start with your catalogue number," said the voice on the phone. Rocky hit the off button and climbed the stairs, head cocked to one side, listening for another sound to explain the first one. She held on to the phone in her right hand as she mounted the stairs and went through the doorway into their bedroom.

She called to her husband and the hollowness of the house hit her beneath her ribs. "Bob, are you okay in there? Did you drop something?" She tried to open the bathroom door but something was wedged against it, letting her open it only an inch. There was nothing else in the bathroom other than Bob that could provide such resistance. Had he fainted? She shoved the door open, inching his body back and wondering if she should call 911, or would she look foolish if he'd only gone dizzy for a minute? When the door was open wide enough to stick her head in, she saw his open-eyed stare and punched 911 into the phone. Then she flexed her legs and heaved all her weight against the door and entered the bathroom with such velocity that the latch of the old door caught at her pants, ripping them at her thigh, grabbing at her skin. She dropped to the floor and put two fingers of her left hand on his neck. Rocky had been a lifeguard since high school, through college and grad school. Her old bathing-suited self, ten years younger, dropped down from the white lifeguard chair. Someone answered the phone and Rocky put the phone near Bob's head so that she could shout her replies. "No, he's not breathing. Yes, I know CPR. No, I'm not going to keep listening to you. I'm doing it now; I'm doing the CPR. Just get someone here fast. Please."

She breathed into him, first tilting back his head, closing off his nose, then sealing his lips with hers and blowing air into his mouth, keeping her left eye open to see if his chest rose. She tasted mint toothpaste. There was shaving cream on his neck, the part that Bob hated shaving, so he saved it until last. Her brain stopped working except to think things like, The front door is open because I let the cat out. The ambulance guys can get in, so I won't have to stop breathing for Bob. Her body took over. She pressed the heel of her hand slightly to the left of his breastbone and met with surprising resistance. Bob's chest was suddenly unyielding and without the fluid grace of his big easiness. Rocky had never pressed this hard on him for any reason. Five compressions, another breath, was this right? She looked at her watch, how much time had gone by? She should have run up the stairs instead of walk. How long had he not been breathing? His wonderful brain needed blood. Where the hell was the ambulance? She did not want to be the one compressing his heart and breathing into his lungs, someone more experienced, more medical should be doing this. In all her summers of life guarding she had never really done CPR on a victim, and now she wondered if she ever knew how.

The young cop with closely cropped hair was the first one in.

"Good, good form," he said, straddling Bob. "I'll take over the compressions." He knelt by Bob and pressed the heel of his hand shockingly hard into Bob's chest. "How long have you been doing CPR?" He placed his hat on the bath mat. His hair was buzz cut so severely that his white scalp beckoned through.

"I don't know. Maybe ten minutes. Don't break his ribs. He's a vet and he has to go to work today." The young cop glanced at her for a moment and the morning light reflected oddly, as if she could see a tidal wave coming in his iris.

The ambulance crew arrived, and only moments later

applied the paddles that shocked him into a rag doll dance. When they loaded him into the ambulance, Rocky ran to her car and followed, going through every red light that the ambulance did. When the ER crew gave him further care, she waited for someone to say, "We got him, here he comes!" And she could live her life again just as she had before starting to order socks from Lands' End. Bob's refusal to come back into his body left Rocky stunned, frightened—and worried, that he was lost, just beyond her reach. The instinct to try and find him was overwhelming.

She watched, demanded to watch, from outside the room, as they tried again and again to electronically goad his heart into starting. They ventilated him and Rocky felt the rasp of the tube in her own throat, forcing air into her lungs. A nurse came out and said. "He's had a major heart attack. Does he take any medication? Has he been ill recently?"

"No."

"How old is he?"

"Forty-two."

Both the nurse and Rocky looked up as a man dressed in blue cotton scrubs came out of the room where Bob lay stubbornly stiff.

"Are you his wife?"

Rocky was unsteady, unaware of how much time had passed. She looked past his head at a wall clock and saw that two hours had passed since Bob had collapsed. Time had altered while waiting for Bob to come back, waiting for his heart to suddenly throb again. It occurred to her just then that they had been working on him too long.

"Yes, I'm his wife."

"Would you like to sit down?" He had an earnest face,

clear eyes, sandy-haired, with the beginnings of lines around his eyes.

"I don't want to go far away from him," Rocky said. She realized her voice was shaking and pressed her lips together to stop the vibration that ran all through her body. She wished the doctor would offer her a blanket. She felt as cold as the time they had stayed out too long cross-country skiing and darkness had slipped in around them when they were still an hour from the car. She was shaking uncontrollably by the time they made it back. This doctor was not going to offer her anything warm.

They sat in two chairs in the hallway. Rocky declined to go to the room called The Family Room because that sounded oddly ominous, and she felt safer in the hallway with the bright lights. The doctor told her everything about Bob's heart. He explained the blown-out lower left ventricle, what looked like dense scar tissue, and the length of time since any brain activity had been recorded.

"He's dead, isn't he?"

The doctor didn't blink or back away. "Yes. If we take him off the ventilator now, his heart will cease to beat. There are no further messages coming from his brain to any part of his body."

The doctor waited for Rocky to respond. It was her turn and she wanted to blast out the fluorescent lighting and hide. She waited out the doctor.

"The cop told me you were doing CPR when he came to the scene. He said you were great, that you were doing everything that you could for Bob."

"Then why is he dead if I was so damned great? This is supposed to work!"

The doctor tried not to flinch, but he looked worried about the direction that this sort of questioning could go.

"There is a sad little secret about CPR. It doesn't work most of the time. It saves lives, that's true. It's great for children who have just fallen in the pool. But with heart attacks, even when you kick-start a heart with CPR, eighty percent of the time the patient will die anyhow."

Rocky wondered why she hadn't known this. When was the last time she had taken a review class in CPR? Would it have mattered to her if she had known this?

"This is where I tell you to take him off the ventilator, isn't it?"

The doctor nodded.

A hospital chaplain slipped quietly into a chair on the other side of Rocky. She asked Rocky if she wanted to call anyone. She did not.

"But there is something that I want you to do. Will you just stay outside the door so that no one else comes in? I want to be alone with him." She stayed with Bob while the ventilator was shut down and for half an hour later, standing by him as his skin began to cool. She wanted to get on the gurney with Bob and press her body against his. But all she could do was awkwardly get one leg up and balance the other leg on tiptoe; Bob was exactly in the middle and there was not enough room for her entire body.

The cop, who had waited in the hallway, attempted to comfort her by saying, "You did a good job with the CPR; that's not why he died. I'm zero for five."

"What do you mean?"

"I've done CPR five times and no one has lived to tell about it," he said with great seriousness. Under other circumstances, his attempt at consoling her would have been funny, but now she just felt tricked.

"I thought this always worked," she said in a dazed, dry-mouthed sort of way.

She walked out of the hospital, into brilliant sunlight that made her shade her eyes. This day had started so unconsciously, so automatically and now Rocky felt the stab of every pebble beneath her feet, every twitch in the leaf of the parking lot azalea bush, as if the day had torn apart and left her bleeding. When she found her car, she got in the back seat and locked the door. She pulled into a fetal position, covered her head with the road atlas, and cried with a violence that shook the car.

Their friends and his office staff rallied around Rocky and planned the memorial service. She followed his wishes and had his body cremated.

"I just don't want him to be afraid or sad. I'm afraid he's alone. What if he doesn't know where he is?" Rocky whispered to her mother at the service. Her mother had flown in from California and she put her hands on either side of Rocky's face. "He knows where he is, sweetheart. It's the rest of us who are confused."

The container of ashes sat on the kitchen counter for several weeks until she worked up the energy to carry out the final disposal of his remains. She discovered that she didn't particularly like having his remains in the house. It did not comfort her to have Bob reduced to ashes. The stuff in the metal urn was nothing like Bob. She walked a wide path around his remains, eyeing them warily.

He had been forty-two, getting soft in all the right places, a few hairs sprouting from his ears, and a countable number of white hairs scattered on his chest. Rocky would have been content to watch these glacial changes for another thirty or forty years. She was positive that they had that much time. The doctor told her that her husband's heart was etched with a poor combination of defective genetics and the aftermath of a shotgun approach to radiation treatment when he was in his teens, long before Rocky had met him. He had gotten cancer and was blasted from here to Albany with radiation. But he was the miracle, cured from the worst thing they could think of, and all the rest of his time was supposed to be easier. He always said, "I've already done the hard part, the rest is easy."

When she finally dreamt of him, when she slept long enough to actually have a dream, she was neither sad nor afraid. In the dream, Bob was asleep in a field and Rocky was so close to him that she could see a sleepy crease along the edge of his nose. He looked like he was in a recovery place, a special death rehab unit, slowly recuperating into formless intentions. "This is what it's like after death, I've seen it," she told her mother later on the phone. She was sure she had been given a private showing of the place that people go to after death. When she woke, she pulled his pillow over her face and breathed in the scent of him, and the terror of being left behind came back in torrents.

She knew it was time to dispose of the ashes and she was sure she knew what Bob would have wanted. Or had he only meant it in jest? Even after eight years of marriage, she sometimes missed the giveaway twitch of his eyelid that meant sarcasm or irony. But she believed he was clear about cremation. He said that he had seen enough bodies: dog bodies, cats, horses, iguanas, cockatiels, all of them, and that when the spirit was gone, the body was done. He had stood in the bathroom, watching Rocky as she bathed.

"We recycle, right? We bundle up our newspapers, bring them to the recycling center where the big trucks haul them off and they get ground up and made back into some other kind of paper. Make me elemental when I die. Make me into dust, bone meal, plant food." Rocky had loved watching him orate naked, his soft penis flopping side to side as he gestured with his toothbrush.

Well, that had been clear enough and she hadn't been left to decide on her own. She knew. It was the disposal part that made her pause. Had he really meant what he said on several occasions?

"Toss me in the fooking fake fried clam vats! Wouldn't that be something? Clog up the machines. Call in the Health Inspectors! I'd be performing a public service." Bob treated the greasy restaurant like it was a drug dealer; the place was despicable, unless he craved what they offered.

Rocky drove to Johnny's Drive-In with the ashes divided into two plastic baggies in the seat next to her. It was midafternoon and the owner, a regular golfer, was just teeing off at the municipal course. It was a well-known fact that the owner rarely worked, and he had bragged to Bob, during a rabies clinic, that afternoons were meant for golfing and not working. She slipped the bags into her jacket pockets.

"I'm from the health department and I need to make an inspection," she lied and flashed her university card at the high school boy behind the counter. She walked around the counter and opened up the walk-in refrigerator.

"Looks good, everything looks fine." She scribbled notes on a legal pad. A customer came in and the boy turned his attention from Rocky. She walked directly to the deep-fry machine. She had never been this close to one before and she thought it looked dangerous. She considered that the high school kids who worked here were in peril. She pulled the two bags from her pockets and emptied the remains of Bob into the fryer.

The deep fryers flared when Bob was dropped in. The counter boy turned and looked at her.

"Everything's fine back here, just doing a fryer test," she said.

Now that the last of Bob was deep-fried, hot and salty, she didn't want Johnny to change the oil right away. Customers who came for the solace of hot, greasy food would taste the fooking, almighty sweetness of Bob. If they were sad, if their dog had been put down, if they needed the salty sweetness of a momentary cure, they had come to right place.

It was not until she walked in the side entrance of her house, stepped into the kitchen, and saw the urn on its side on the counter, that she realized what she had done. She clutched the urn to her stomach and pressed hard. Deep howls emptied out of her and jerked her body as if her tendons had sprung loose. Each blast of sound battered her until she wondered if her neck would snap. In the end, Rocky lay on the floor with the urn and saw the boundary land of madness open up before her and felt a seductive pull.

Chapter 2

When Bob had died, the brushed cotton sheets had been on their bed for one week. Only one week of precious scents left on their bed, one week of his head pressing deeply into his pillow, leaving an invisible impression. She wished she had not been so concerned about sheets needing to be laundered when Bob was still alive. They had argued about it since the day they had moved in together when Rocky was still in graduate school and for the eight years of their marriage.

"How dirty can sheets get in one week, or two weeks? We shower, we're clean people. It's not like we're sheep dogs," Bob had argued.

Over four months had passed. The new fall semester had started and this was the time of the year that Rocky had always loved. But all she could think of was preserving Bob's scent on his pillowcase. The sheets had not been the same because her scent, skin cells, and hair were mixed in; it was not pure Bob. She had reluctantly changed the sheets after a month, but Bob's pillowcase remained unwashed. She panicked at the thought of his scent evaporating completely.

Every morning, she covered the pillow with white newsprint, pulled from an unused roll she got from the local newspaper. She imagined the skin cells that Bob had rubbed off in his fitful sleep were still there, bits of his DNA, and she was desperate to keep them. She pictured tiny cells, atoms really, all spread out on the pillowcase and she wanted the newsprint to keep them safe. She had her own pillow, but Bob's pillow was placed next to hers and she chanced a stroke or two in the night, a light sniff to catch his essence during the long hours until sleep came. She dreaded the day that the pillowcase would be empty of his smell. That would be worse than his death, or like dying again.

She kept three of his flannel shirts and one gray cashmere sweater. The rest of the clothing was stuffed into black plastic bags and taken across the state line into New York. She didn't want to see any local people wearing his clothes, not that she begrudged them anything, she just didn't want to see the town suddenly dressed as her dead husband. Dead husband. Not like the live one.

The clerk at the Salvation Army store said, "Do you want a receipt for taxes?"

Rocky looked at the four black plastic bags, lumpy with Bob's clothes. "These are my husband's things. He died. His heart was bad. I didn't know about his heart."

She wanted the clerk to know all this about the clothes. That they weren't just clothes that someone got tired of, or grew too fat to wear. The world would never be the same again.

"Do you want a receipt?" the clerk asked again, with a hint of impatience. The woman shifted her weight to one hip and sighed.

"Yes I do. I want a receipt." Rocky felt the crush of the

clerk's coldness start at her brain and then descend like a thick poison throughout her body. She did not leave the house again for three days.

Fall semester started again and Rocky returned to her job at the university in western Massachusetts. She was a psychologist at the counseling center and she lasted two weeks before the director asked her to come into his office. He asked her if she needed more time. He told her that several students reported that Rocky had gotten up in the midst of a therapy session and stared out the window. One student had apparently stayed for the full fifty minutes watching Rocky's back, and then left. Rocky told him about the clerk at the Salvation Army. She did not tell him about Johnny's Drive-In.

"The strange thing about you is that you expect store clerks to understand your grief instead of opening up to people who care about you. Did you really expect a clerk at Salvation Army to be an empathetic angel? She was probably tired, horribly paid, and afraid of your sadness. We are all afraid of someone else's grief," said Ray Velasquez. He was older than Rocky, closing in on fifty.

Rocky grabbed a hunk of her long dark hair and rubbed it between her thumb and forefinger. "I thought just getting in my car and coming to work was such an accomplishment. But I can't remember why any of this matters. I can't remember how I ever did therapy. My brain has been deleted."

They agreed that the university could give her a year's leave of absence. She was guaranteed her job when she returned. "You know that work can sometimes be the best friend after a death," he said. "It can give you structure. Are you sure about this?"

"I'm not sure about anything, but I know that I can't possibly help anyone right now," she said. She did not add that she was still awake every night until two A.M. and awake again at three A.M.

She and Ray had worked together for six years. Rocky had interviewed with the University Counseling Center after floundering in private practice for the first few years after graduate school. When the HMOs started haggling with her about how long to treat a person with depression or panic attacks that turned people into prisoners in their home, she knew that she would abandon her career if she had to keep dealing with insurance companies. University counseling centers provided therapy and there was no HMO, no exchange of money between client and therapist. The university paid Rocky a salary, smaller by far than private practice, but the joy of not dealing with the HMOs was beyond price.

Cutting her hair was the last project before closing the house in the foothills of the Berkshire Mountains and heading east to the coast. She had left it long, partly in defiance of the more professional, crisper look, and partly because she and Bob loved it. It flapped like a dark curling flag when she let it loose. When she braided it, the rope of hair hung powerfully between her shoulder blades.

Without Bob her hair grew sad. The summer had always been the hardest time for her long hair; it spent most of the steamy months of July and August twisted and knotted on top of her head with several chopsticks. At the memorial service, she wore it tightly braided and it already felt wrong.

The Honda wagon was packed mostly with winter clothing, her own bedding, and Bob's pillow. For all of their years as foster pet owners, they had only one full-time pet and that was Gremlin, the cat. This had allowed them to provide temporary shelter to many animals that Bob brought home, all desperate, all injured. Gremlin had helped nurse those animals that could tolerate his rasping lick; his nursing skills were famous at the clinic. After Bob died, Gremlin, who was a stout twelve years old, grew restless and spent longer and longer periods of time outdoors. Finally, in mid-August, he did not return. Rocky suspected that the marauding coyotes had finally nabbed Gremlin, waiting him out, sensing the slimmest change in his ability to run away. Other neighbors on their road put up computer-generated signs about their missing tabbies as well. The coyotes had come in and made a clean sweep. She wanted the coyotes to know that Gremlin went willingly; that they had not been so masterfully cunning. Gremlin was looking for Bob. Animals do that; predators and prey walk mercifully together through life. When deer or cats lose their strength and nimbleness, predators will oblige and give them a swift death. Rocky wondered who would oblige her. She envied Gremlin. As soon as she thought this, she wondered if this is what it felt like to step off the shores of reality—and would there be a way out for her as perfect as Gremlin's exit?

Rocky wanted a ceremony of her own to mark Bob's death. She turned on the light in the bathroom and peered at her reflection. The memorial had been a ceremony, the eulogy by Bob's business partner had been a ceremony; she wanted a ceremony. Some Native American cultures cut their hair whenever there is a death, a year's worth of hair, about six inches. She decided that Bob's death deserved more than one year's worth of grief. She looked in the mirror and pulled the dark, tightly curled hair with one hand and cut it at jaw level.

She held the detached hair in her hand and saw the equivalent of four-years' worth of grief hanging from her hand. The act of cutting her hair did not alter the metallic taste in her mouth that lingered since Bob's death, nor the way her senses were changed, as if they belonged to someone else.

Bob once said that she had African hair. "No, really," he said. "The Italian part of your family probably has ancestors from across the Mediterranean. It just makes sense."

She had to agree, and pictured old sailors in her family tree living on the northern shores of Africa, mingling sweat, sperm, ripe eggs, and genetic coding for hair that would never be straight. Her father had been mildly outraged by the suggestion and unnerved by Bob's clinical observations of ethnic groups crossing boundaries.

She cut it all off at jaw length and her dark hair stuck out expectantly, so she cut more, making the top shorter. She did not exactly recognize herself. "I don't know who you are," she whispered into the mirror, speaking close enough to leave a circle of fog on the glass.

She swept up the hair, put it in a paper bag, and released it over her September garden. The weeds in the garden did not tempt her as they had before. She saw them differently this year.

"I want them to grow from beginning to end, uninterrupted," she said when her brother had come by for the key.

The deal was that Rocky would call her brother, Caleb, when she got a place. They were only two years apart and he had hovered since Bob died.

"Let me drive you out there and you can pack some more stuff," he offered as he watched Rocky tossing her hair into the garden.

"No. Everything I need fits in my car. Rent the house if you can, send me half the rent money. I'll write," she said, rubbing her newly shorn hair, feeling naked without the weight of it.

Caleb bent down and yanked a clump of crabgrass that threatened to choke out a thin group of chrysanthemums. "Look, I promised Mom that I'd drive out with you. She's worried about you. You know how she was after Dad died, and she thinks you're one step from the loony bin."

Caleb sounded uncomfortable with the switch in roles with his sister. She had been the one to comfort him and urged him on through the special-ed classes where all kids got tossed who had learning disorders. She had defended him when schoolyard bullies tried to tease him about the resource room. But in more ways than one, he had inspired her to learn about the brain, how memory works, why trauma takes some people by the throat and other people churn through it like a slow, steady tugboat.

Caleb had the same thick hair as Rocky, only his was lighter, nearly golden when he had been a child. His lack of facility with arranging numbers and abysmal spelling turned out to be overshadowed by his genius with color and art and a willingness to work hard. In the warm months, he painted houses; in the winter he worked in his pottery studio making clay musicians who wailed on saxophones and trumpets. Rocky took her favorite with her, a woman leaning impossibly far back, hair struck by an invisible wind, fingers spread out on the pads of a saxophone, eyes squeezed shut with ecstasy. Rocky rolled the sculpture in her comforter and put it on the passenger seat.

"You want me to feel better and I may never be better. This is the way I am now," she said.

She put her hand on his sleeve and squeezed his arm. They were too close to hug all the time and besides Rocky had long sensed a discomfort in Caleb when she tried to hug him. Bob had explained it to her.

"It's because he probably peeked at you in the shower when he was fourteen and he couldn't help but fantasize about you in the only way that addled fourteen-year-old boys do. He's still a little embarrassed. He'll get over it by the time he's sixty."

Rocky let go of his arm. "I'll call you when I get a place. I'm staying at a motel until Columbus Day, when the season is over. I promise."

She avoided the big roads like the Mass Pike and instead took side roads, ambling east and north to Portland. She had called ahead and made a reservation on the Casco Bay ferry. Taking a car on the ferry was an entirely different matter than just walking on. Reservations were required. She was now one of the purposeful people who drove a car on the ferry, clearly not a tourist, a day-tripper. She knew she appeared to have a reason for being, and the absurdity of her appearance felt hollow. In reality she had no reason to stay, no reason to go and felt so untethered that if she had not held tight to the railing, the breeze could have picked her up.

She had only been to the island once, long before she met Bob, and the memory stayed with her like a beacon. Her family had driven to Nova Scotia for a vacation. While Rocky remembered little of Nova Scotia at age ten, she vividly recalled an afternoon stop in Portland and an impulsive side trip on the ferry to Peak's Island. They stayed long enough for Rocky and Caleb to climb on the rocks along the shore and eat hot dogs before heading back, but long enough for Rocky to hear her mother say, "Do you think people on an island ever worry?"

Her father answered. "They fish a lot. How much can you worry if you fish?"

The family never returned, and Rocky didn't know if anyone else even remembered the day the way she did, the way it stood bathed in sunlight, full of hope. It was not much to hang on to, but Rocky drove straight off the ferry and into the flicker of memory.

The few weeks in the motel overlooking the ferry dock disappeared into mist. Rocky walked the beaches and the inner trails and noticed as the days went by that the crowds of tourists thinned, one by one until after Columbus Day, and a quiet settled on the island. The air, as if on command, turned cool and the mornings required a jacket. She read the local paper at Stan's Seafood Diner. She noticed the job announcement after she heard a waitress point it out. "Animal Control Warden," said the waitress. "We haven't had one of those all year. Budgets must be looking up."

Rocky folded the paper in half and asked the waitress what she knew about it. She had on a shirt that said *University of Southern Maine*.

"You need to talk to Isaiah Wilson, everybody knows him. Tell him you heard about it from me. He and my father are old friends." Her name was Jill and she looked like the shirt belonged to one of her kids.

Isaiah was the director of public works on the island, a

former Methodist minister, and currently a substitute shop teacher over in Portland, when they were desperate. Jill had supplied the essential background on him. Rocky went directly to his office and filled out an application. She wasn't sure what she was doing, but she felt like she was peeling off her old self and stepping out of her skin.

To apply for the municipality on the island, Rocky had to give a reference and a job history. She paused after writing in her name, Roxanne Pelligrino, and held the pen still in the air, and finally wrote the truth . . . psychologist, and gave Ray as a reference. Isaiah looked at the application and his forehead wrinkled.

Rocky explained. "Before you say anything, I want you to know that my husband was a veterinarian. When he was starting his practice, I helped him in the evenings with the animals that had to stay overnight in the clinic. I learned how to handle sick animals and I can tell which ones will bite and which ones won't. But if you hire me, I want my personal life to be private. I don't want to be a psychologist here. I need to start over."

Isaiah had a full head of gray hair and his eyebrows had the wild look of men his age. Long strands of hair stuck straight up from his brows and a few flipped up and pointed to the top of his head. His reading glasses sat low on his nose. His skin was dark, and from the slight cadence in his voice, Rocky thought he might be from Haiti.

"Divorce?" he asked looking up at her over his glasses.

"Dead. My husband is dead. Heart attack. He was young and we didn't know anything was wrong." Rocky had practiced these facts and this was her trial run.

Isaiah took off his glasses. "I'm sorry." Rocky saw the minister settle in and the public works director receded. "When did he pass away?"

"This spring, the end of the spring." She suddenly felt like she was in the chaplain's office and she shifted in the chair.

"'After the first death there is no other.' Do you know who wrote that? Elizabeth Barrett Browning? I'm not sure. I remember the first time I heard it and I knew it was true. The first death changes everything, and all deaths afterward bring us back to the first death. I'm sorry; I lost both my parents last year and even at my ripe age, I feel like an orphan. Death changes everything doesn't it?"

Rocky brushed an escaping tear from one eye. "If you hire me, I'll do a good job. If I don't know how to do something, I'll ask. Just keep all this private, okay? I'm not ready to be a widow yet. I don't want people to treat me like a psychologist. I need time to work hard and do physical work. I have a year's leave of absence from my job. I can give you one year, right through next year's tourist season."

"I'm a professional secret-keeper. I was a minister for fifteen years and that's part of what I did. I held secrets. The same as you. Prying secrets out of us takes an act of Congress."

He stood up and held out his large paw of a hand to Rocky. "Let me show you about your new job and all the fancy extras that go along with it." She let him take her hand. She knew he wanted to make physical contact with her; that's what ministers do, they take your hand. "Don't be overwhelmed by our advanced technology here on the island. You get a truck that can't pass emission control standards on the mainland and the key to the storage shed. When can you start?"

"Now. I can start right now," she said.

He nodded. "Are you settled in for the winter? Do you need a place to live?"

"I was waiting for the off-season rates to start before I looked around," she said.

"I can help you with that. I have a rental house, nothing fancy. In fact, very far from fancy. And the off-season rates just started this minute."

Chapter 3

Isaiah opened the door and a terrible whiff of dead fish hit them. His nostrils flared and his eyes squeezed shut, the opposite of what was needed. "Damn! The last renters left their garbage under the sink. Whatever's there has been building steam for a week." It was the smell of death, rotting flesh, and Rocky reeled backward, lost her footing, and fell down the three steps of the deck stairway. She dusted herself off while Isaiah flew to her assistance. "This is no way for my new dog warden to start. Don't take this as an omen. Just look at it as the best introduction you could have to summer people."

The cottage was the last on the dirt road. Beach grass, stiff and breeze worthy, surrounded it. "Most people don't winter here; you'll see that for yourself. You're not that far from some of the year-round people. But the back of the house is up against wetlands, so it can't be built up. That's the good news. The bad news is that in June and on days when the wind drops off, the mosquitoes will drain every ounce of pleasure along with most of your blood. Stay here while I go grab that maggot-filled garbage and open the window."

Rocky gratefully stood on the small deck, bleached silver by the salt and sun. The front of the house faced south and east and stared directly out to the expanse of the Atlantic Ocean. Between the house and the ocean was a quarter mile of thick vegetation, held together by a cross-hatching of vines that looked like honeysuckle. A hobbit-sized path wound through it to the rock-covered coast.

Isaiah cursed and Rocky said that the last renters of the season left more than fish garbage. Rocky pulled her eyes from the ocean and headed into the house to give him a hand. She prepared for a disaster within the cottage. She was relieved that disasters were not the sole domain of her life; even good men like Isaiah had unexpected calamities. "Did you bring garbage bags? Let's just haul all this stuff outside," she said.

He stood in the midst of a kitchen covered with crumpled papers, cups half filled with butter that had once been melted for lobster, bowls with the hard unpopped kernels of corn on the bottom, paper bags filled with slightly crushed beer cans. "At times like this, I think the whole human race is going to hell," said Isaiah. The refrigerator revealed bowls filled with chili and sticks of butter left on crumb-coated saucers, an open juice container, and a Tupperware container filled with contents that neither of them chose to investigate. The couch pillows were on the floor and every dish in the house was in the sink, covered with food gone stiff. It was a mess, all right. Rocky hadn't seen a mess this big in long time.

"I hope you got a huge deposit from these people. Who were they anyhow, small-time drug lords?"

"You wouldn't believe it. They drove a new Volvo and said they were teachers. That was either not true or our education system is being sabotaged. And the deposit was not worth the stink that they left. But they won't ever rent on this island again."

Rocky and Isaiah opened all the remaining windows, hauled out the trash, and set the dishes to soak. Rocky ran an ancient vacuum cleaner over the floor. She shook the few scatter rugs outside and made a mental note to take them to the Laundromat. The place began to look like someplace where she might be able to take off her shoes. Isaiah left with his truck brimming with black plastic bags of garbage, mumbling about the world ending because of people who can't wipe their behinds.

Rocky scrubbed the countertops in the kitchen and the bathroom. Isaiah's wife Charlotte delivered a box of cleaning supplies complete with rubber gloves. She said her husband was so mad that he might never rent again after Rocky. Charlotte was darker than Isaiah, with a sprinkling of white hairs on her temples. She wore sweatpants and a jacket. "Sorry about my scruffy appearance, but I was in the middle of putting some of my gardens to bed when my husband came home sputtering about low-life trash who drive Volvos. Can you handle the rest of this? We won't charge you for the full month of October."

After Charlotte left, Rocky examined every inch of the cottage. The living room/dining room had the best view over the top of the dense shrubbery, out to the ocean. Every house on an island faces out like a sentinel looking for ships or whales, storms creeping across the sky. The two bedrooms were small, room enough for a bed, dresser, and chair. Rocky picked the bedroom that had two windows instead of one, which made up for it facing north.

When the cottage was as clean as she could get it and all the signs of the former tenants were removed, including a tied-off condom draped over an ashtray on a dresser, she began to unload her car. By dusk, her sheets were on the bed. They were queen-sized and hung to the floor on either side of the small bed. Her winter clothes were folded in the dresser drawers. She'd brought two electrical appliances from her old life: a boom box and a hair dryer. She arranged her brother's sculpture on the end table by the couch.

Dusk changed too quickly into night and the completion of her unpacking left her with the sudden despair that comes with darkness when no other footsteps are expected. This was the worst part of the day and getting through it was an exercise of endurance, of sandbags strapped to her arms and legs while foot soldiers pointed bayonets at her dry throat. She prepared for what she knew would be a full night of altered time, thick with grief and self-accusations while she replayed the morning of Bob's death. The gray wire mesh that fit tightly over her brain began to descend until it squeezed a tight band over her eyes.

How many times had she helped clients with the lightning bolt arrival of grief that kidnapped people from their daily life? Hundreds. Each time, she offered the space to talk about reactions that sounded too bizarre even for the survivor to tell their best of friends. "I saw my father this morning; he walked across the classroom and looked at me. How can that be?" "I can't help wondering what is happening to her body, what she must look now. Is that grotesque or what? But I think of it every day." "I want to die to be with her; nothing else matters here."

But what her clients had not told her was that her own

sweat would smell different, the chemistry of her body would alter until she would no longer know who she was when she looked in the mirror, that food would taste like cardboard, and she would wake up with a full-blown panic attack at three A.M. and drive herself to the emergency room two months after her husband was dead. She had been oddly convinced that her heart was exploding and had been embarrassed to learn that she was having her first-ever panic attack. Or had her clients told her, and she listened only with part of her brain, thinking that this is temporary, this is part of grieving, and looked for the first sign of return without fully grasping the horrible landscape of the present? There was something essential and awful that she had missed, and here was one more thing to blame herself for: she failed to save her husband, and she had failed to see the true terror of the land where mourners traveled.

She heard a clear penetrating peal, like a light that pierces the fog. She looked at the sliding glass door and a striped feline face stared in at her from the base of the door. A tabby, eyes wide and insistent, white chest and calico body, had come calling. Rocky slid the door open and the cat dashed past her and leapt on the couch, purring with urgency. The creature paced the couch with familiarity then bounced to the floor and headed for the exact place on the kitchen floor where two saucers had been sitting hours before.

"Oh no, they left you behind," said Rocky, crouching beside the cat before she knew what she doing. The cat pushed her spine hard into Rocky's palm, offering her a generous view of her back end. A female, although she had already guessed that by her head size. Bob had always said, "Male cats generally have a bigger skull. But there is no correlation between head size and intelligence. The brain of a tom is located in his cajones."

The cat moved in with a shocking level of confidence that Rocky wished she could have patented and injected into several of her old clients, people who were tentative, fearful, and anxious about the invisible audience that judged them from morning through night. The cat lived in a world without audience and expected attention without hesitation or explanation. Rocky immediately saw the irony of the situation; both of them had been left behind and both were pitiful. The cat did not appear to know its pitifulness, did not know the fate that awaited it if she was returned to her negligent owners or to the abyss of an animal shelter.

She did not want the world to treat her like this abandoned cat, in need of food and sympathy. She pictured the owners of the cat driving away in their Volvo, having decided at some point that the rent they had paid entitled them to not touch their own garbage. Being filthy and irresponsible with a rental was one thing, but she could not fathom the decision to leave the cat and hated them for it. Thus she began her career as animal control warden by not looking for the owners of the cat. She judged them harshly and, she believed, correctly. The cat slept on the couch the first night, but Rocky imagined that she heard her purring all night and breathing and padding around the small house. For the first time in months, she awoke not at three but at four A.M. and she thought that the hour was reason enough to keep the cat.

Chapter 4

The first two weeks of the job offered a sampling of island life in the post-tourist season. The island slumped, partly in relief, partly in the crash after an exhausting summer when the island exploded with people ten times the winter population. The dilemma of the love/hate relationship with tourists was temporarily relieved but exacerbated financially for those who had not budgeted well. The sprinkling of conversation that Rocky heard at a local breakfast spot sounded like a family where the obnoxious, cigar smoking, yet wildly wealthy uncle had just left after the annual visit during which your mother made you be polite all summer.

Several places closed immediately: the yogurt hut, the kite shop, the T-shirt businesses, and the fudge shop. The kayak company put up most of the sleek kayaks for the season, leaving just two on the porch for the owner to use on days when the ocean was quiet.

Rocky found a small gang of dogs that were left behind by tourists that had to be taken to the mainland animal shelter. Isaiah and Charlotte invited her to lunch one Sunday and they commiserated on the low-life nature that creeps into a certain segment of humanity. "What gets me is the elevated way that some people can carry on and then act like such jackasses with creatures that depend on them," said Isaiah, in reference to the abandoned cat. Charlotte had fixed them huevos rancheros with a robust salsa made from the last of her tomatoes.

Rocky wondered if Isaiah's promise to not say anything about her past had extended to his wife. She pictured someone telling Bob a secret and asking him not to tell Rocky. What would he have done? He was the gold standard for every circumstance. But Isaiah was a minister, or he had been. And ministers, priests, and the lot of them were bound by confidentiality. Rocky was lost in thought about the bounds of confidentiality when Charlotte brought out a fresh pot of coffee. "Isaiah tells me that your husband died this past year. I'm sorry. This must be a terrible time for you."

Rocky threw an accusatory stare at Isaiah.

He grimaced. "I apologize. It's not Charlotte's fault. She caught me talking to myself when I hauled off the garbage from those idiot renters. I didn't even know I was doing it. I'll have to watch myself as I get older and start blathering everybody's business. Won't that be the worst-case scenario for an Alzheimer's patient? I'll be telling the world all the secrets that people have told me about affairs, scandals, incest and petty jealousies. They'll have to put me in the solitary confinement zone of the Alzheimer's home. I could be a national security risk." Clearly, he was horrified that he had spilled the beans with a person who knew the absolute importance of maintaining secrets. Tiny beads of sweat popped out on his forehead.

Charlotte ignored him and sipped her coffee. "You're not

ready to say the words yet are you? I was a small girl when my grandfather died. Not long after his funeral, I was with my grandmother at the beauty parlor and she had a new girl working on her hair who kept asking her questions to be polite, and because African-American hair takes longer to work on than the last ice age, we were there for a long time. She asked my grandmother where she lived, did she know so and so, and finally the girl asked her some questions about her husband. My grandmother said, "I'm a widow." And she hadn't been ready to say it. Her face collapsed and she looked sadder than the day of the funeral. You don't have to say the words until you're ready. And I'll try and keep my husband from talking to himself in public."

Rocky felt the outrage melt down her tight neck muscles. She trusted Charlotte never to say a word about this again. Charlotte understood. "Thank you," she said.

Rocky called her brother as she promised she would.

"I'm fine. I got a job, a very part-time job, probably not more than ten hours per week. It's on an as-needed basis. And I've rented a little cottage," she said in what she hoped was her most convincing voice.

"Yeah, you sound like shit to me. Where are you again?"

She heard water running on his end of the line, which meant he was washing his dishes and that it had been his wife's turn to cook. She pictured the thick curling hairs on his hands that grew in patches along his fingers. Her brother Caleb was an anomaly among men: he liked gadgets with extreme selectivity; a cordless phone was as advanced as he went in the department of communications. If gadgets did not have to do with house painting or sculpture, he saw no reason to bother with them. She glanced over at the sculpture that she brought with her.

"I told you. I'm on Peak's Island and I'm going to stay for a while. I want to be where nobody knows me, nobody wants to talk to me about the saddest, most horrible parts of their life. It's an island; people fish and they sell stuff to tourists. Oh, I'm the new dog warden. Except they call it Animal Control Warden."

"What the hell do you know about being a dog warden?"

"Probably nothing. Ever hear of on-the-job training? How hard can it be?" she asked.

"Oh, this is brilliant. Because Bob was a vet, do you think you picked up special dog-warden skills? You hardly stepped foot in the clinic the last few years. Or do you think that working at the college makes you smart enough to do anyone's job?"

Rocky was jolted by the mention of Bob. This was going to be the place where no one said his name and she didn't have to say his name. She felt like she had suddenly swallowed wood chips and now they were going to churn through her body.

"We're talking lost cats and dogs," she said.

"Just get a tetanus shot right now, Rocky, and if you see a raccoon that's foaming at the mouth and walking in circles, shoot it."

"Shoot it? I'm not supposed to be that kind of dog warden. They didn't give me a gun." Sparring usually felt good with Caleb, but she had not been able to spar with him since Bob died. She had tried, but she couldn't find the right equipment.

"Is everything working out with the renters?" While

Rocky was still at the motel, Caleb had found people to rent her house.

"They're harmless. And useless. He's an English professor, he told me. He asked me about the oil burner like it was a rocket or something. I'm going over there again to give him another lesson in how to run it. Guess they don't have those in Indiana."

"Thanks. If Mom calls you to check up on me, tell her that you talked to me and I'm okay. Will you do that? I know she's going to call you."

"I should tell her that you sound like shit and you took a job that you know nothing about. Would you at least go get a book that tells you how to recover animals?" said Caleb before he signed off.

Rocky met Tess in the only bookstore on the island, in the nonfiction section, when Tess turned to her and said, "During the winter people on the island either drink too much or read too much. Which are you?"

Rocky wasn't sure she'd do either and wondered if those were her only choices. She had come to the bookstore to get a book on wildlife of the eastern shores, and ended up getting Peterson Field Guides' *Mammals of North America*, a broader selection.

She wondered why this woman would ask such a strange thing. Had she let slip her secret somehow, had she worn it on her face that she might need to drink? Could this woman know that she couldn't save her own husband when she had the chance, that she couldn't make him breathe again as he lay on the bathroom floor with shaving cream still thick on his neck?

"Oh, you're the new one. Maybe you've thought of some-thing else to do over the winter." She put her hand on Rocky's arm and squeezed it for a second. No one had touched her since she had arrived, other than Isaiah who had shook her hand. Rocky pulled her arm away.

"Welcome to the island. People mostly come here for the summer and leave for the winter. Guess that makes you an opposite. I'm a caretaker for some of the houses over the win-ter and manage a couple of rental properties in the summer. Let me know if I can help you get acquainted," she said. She wrote her name and number on a sales receipt.

Rocky took her book home and began to study about the only animal that she had thus far encountered, a cat. *Felis catus*. The coat is shed and regrown every spring and fall, gestation is fifty-eight days (that part she had known because Bob lamented the reproductive capability of cats) and that cats will refuse to learn something that is not to their advan-tage. Her own adopted cat demonstrated this by refusing to stay indoors during the day. She arrived at the sliding glass door each evening demanding to be let in and campaigned as heavily each morning to be let out. Rocky obliged.

The first official call that she got was from Tess. "Some fool from the summer left a cat on the north side of the is-land. It won't come to me and it looks like it's starving or sick. Can you come get it?"

Rocky called Isaiah, just to check on Tess, to see if she might be some weird old woman who was left here by her family to haunt the islanders. Isaiah laughed when she asked him.

"You mean Tess? Good God, they don't come more solid than her, once you get to know her. She's been out here for

years, since she retired. Or she's mostly retired. If she tells
you that a cat has been abandoned, then that's the truth."

Isaiah told her the best way to get the cat. "Start with the
Havahart trap. Save the snare as back up. Cats are not as easy
as dogs."

The snare was an ugly contraption that frightened her. She
was afraid that if she started using it, she might get too comfortable with it, and start to act like a prison guard gone bad,
the kind who starts out good but who ultimately gives in to
the uniform. She couldn't quite stomach the idea of snaring
a cat.

Rocky thought it was best to wait until early morning. She
didn't want to keep the cat overnight. If she caught it early,
she'd still have time to get it over to Portland to the pound. As
she lay in bed with her newly found cat purring on the dresser, she considered her options. She would generously bait the
trap with wet cat food and hope for the best.

The next morning she pulled up to the house, several miles
north of the dock. She hoped the cat wasn't peeking from the
bushes so she could set the trap unobserved. She pulled the
tab on the can and the rich smell of fish byproducts reached
her nose. She hoped that this wouldn't draw every cat in the
neighborhood. A black Saab pulled up as Rocky finished her
job. Tess stepped out of the car.

"Let's go for a walk while the cat meets its destiny. I'll
show you some of my favorites spots along the shore."

They walked on the dirt road that ran along the north
coast, both of them slapped by the wind, and then they headed for the beach. It was surprisingly easy for Rocky and Tess
to fall in step with each other. When they returned several
hours later, a tattered cat sat howling in the trap.

"There's your first customer," said Tess.

Rocky delivered the cat to the Portland animal shelter right in the trap, not wanting to tangle with the very sick looking creature. Tess went along for the ride because she said she needed to buy some fish at the docks.

Tess was about thirty years older than Rocky, a trim woman whose movements were swift and light, as unattached to earth as a bird. They agreed to meet for walks; Tess claimed to know every trail and Rocky felt less of the bottomless pull when she was walking. Tess reminded Rocky of the image of a wood sprite, a nymph who blended in easily among a pine needle forest floor or the firm grasses that grew on sand. "I'm no wood nymph," said Tess. "I'm just a retired physical therapist. There's a difference."

Tess had painted a Buddha on her blue bathroom door, and had a Christmas tree of dried deciduous branches festooned with seashells and dried seaweed, which stayed up twelve months of the year. "Well this certainly looks more like the house of a wood sprite than a former physical therapist," said Rocky.

Rocky was surprised that Tess so suddenly entered her life. They walked several times a week and before long, she had accompanied Tess on her job of house-sitting for the summer people. The people who didn't want the hassle of draining their pipes for the winter hired Tess. Tess made periodic checks during the winter, wandering through their houses, opening doors, letting in fresh air, and checking for invasions of mice and chipmunks.

"Come with me, we have to freshen up one of the houses, blow out the ghosts who think they can take over. We'll save the big house for last. They have a hot tub big enough for a football team," said Tess after they had hiked on one of the inner trails for the morning.

Tess brought her favorite CDs and urged Rocky to dance with her. Rocky awkwardly declined, surprised that movement was so natural to Tess and so alien to her. Tess flitted through the house, running with an assortment of scarves flying with reggae music, chasing out the idle spirits that she swore invaded opportunistically. She had turned on the hot tub in the master bedroom and when she was done shooing unseen things away, they both dropped their clothes and settled into the multi-jetted pool. Rocky thought the older woman's body looked more like a prepubescent girl, or a fish. Even her breasts, as she approached her 70s, did not hang or point south; they sat like poached eggs on her chest.

"I read one poem per day," said Tess. She reached for her canvas bag over the edge of the tub. "I'll read you the one I picked up today. It's by Mary Oliver." And she read a poem about following a river with rapids lurking in the distance. Rocky leaned her head back on the edge and saw herself tumbling over the edge of a watery precipice and shattering as she hit the bottom.

Rocky's second call was a skunk emergency. She looked up skunks in the Peterson guide. *Mephitis mephitis.* Skunks were trash hounds and when tourists left behind their abundance of overflowing trash bins, the skunks became particularly brash until the cold weather set in, which would slow them into a drowsy trance. Mrs. Todd called to say that a skunk was in her garage and that she was unable to leave her house.

Skunks will spray only as a last resort. They will first stomp their feet, growl, spit, or clack their impressively sharp teeth. This should be warning enough for anyone, except dogs who blunder through and misread all those warnings. Rocky thought her chances were good of remaining scent free while relocating the skunk with the same Havahart trap and a hamburger patty.

"Mrs. Todd, don't go out to the garage and absolutely don't let your dog out of the house. What kind of dog do you have? Oh, a terrier. Don't even open the door when you see me drive up because your little terrier thinks the skunk is a big rat and he wants to grab it by the neck. You don't want that to happen. I'll be there shortly."

Rocky took her time loading the tarp and the trap into the truck. She dawdled in the grocery store after picking up the cheapest grade beef available. Her preference was to give the skunk a good head start and not deal with it at all. She sat in the truck and read in the Peterson guidebook about the skunk. If it was a female, it would be likely to burrow with another female for the winter. Males were more solitary. But they don't hibernate. Their eyeshine was deep amber. That's the reflected color of their eyes at night, when they peer at you from the darkness. With nothing left to do, Rocky drove out to Mrs. Todd's house.

There was no sight of a skunk, but evidence of trash that was not tightly sealed. Rocky offered suggestions for a new garbage can and offered to pick one up the next time she was in Portland. Solutions in this job were easy.

For the remainder of October, she rounded up the discarded cats and took them to the shelter on the mainland. They had seven days to be located or rescued before they were euthanized. She pitied the person who had to kill the cats. Bob used to rage about people not neutering their animals.

He called his neutering clinics Nip and Tuck Day, neutering as many cats and dogs as he could from early morning until seven P.M. He'd said that for every pair of male and female cats that go unaltered, who lived uneventful lives, and if all their descendents lived for six years also unaltered, that would amount to 420,000 cats.

Rocky had at first scoffed at him. She suspected an urban myth. She wasn't against neutering, but she saw no sense in exaggerating. Then one day he took her with him to the veterinary school where the cats and dogs were being euthanized in staggering numbers.

"Nobody wants these animals and they can't all survive. And some dumb fuck was too stupid and too cheap to get them neutered. Even if two cats couldn't produce a lineage of 420,000 babies, every one that gets set loose to fend for itself will either be killed by a car, a dog, a coyote, by illness like feline leukemia, or they get the terminator injection. It's not right."

Nip and Tuck Day was twice a year, when it was off with testicles and tucking at the bellies of the females, making them all the last of their line. Bob would call up all his vet school buddies weeks before to see if any of them had fourth-year students who could be trusted with scalpels. If he was lucky, he got at least one who was eager and capable. Bob charged everybody the same fee, $10, which also entitled them to one can of food as a treat for the recuperating patient.

By the time he'd get home, it would be around eight o'clock. Rocky catered to him on those nights. The rest of the time they both might forget to buy groceries or quarrel about who should cook. But on these nights, she'd forget all about that and order Chinese for them, serve warm sake. His eyes would get bloodshot and his shoulders would sag, and she'd know he wasn't really noticing anything that she did and wouldn't really remember details. After eating, she'd coax him out of his clothes and lead him to the bathroom, the one downstairs with the old claw-footed tub. She'd take off her clothes and slide in behind him, making the water go perilously close to the top, gurgling the release valve into action. She'd start at his head and rub and massage him. She knew he wanted to be held, to be the one who had things done to him, not to be the deciding one. She'd wash him from top to bottom, rolling him on his side when she needed to slip her hand under his winter white bottom.

"Let go, I'll do everything," she'd whisper.

She thought that this was how people loved in war camps, or when ocean liners sank and a few survivors clung to lifeboats; all daily defenses fell away. She knew that he needed to be filled up again with hope and tenderness because all of that had been drained out of him on Nip and Tuck Day. Neither of them would speak much, only bits. "Here, roll over, there, I'll do that," was all Rocky would need to say before she'd mount him in the water gone cool.

Rocky met Tess for breakfast the next morning before she was due to meet Isaiah to talk about additional duties. "He wants me to start documenting any change in erosion along the south beach. I'm not sure how I'm supposed to do that. I mean erosion is change, and that is probably best done over a number of years."

"You sound like a scientist. What did you say that you did before?"

"I worked with kids, young kids, in a day care center," Rocky said. The lie felt partial and thus tolerable.

Tess sipped tea. Rocky had gotten her coffee from the self-serve part of the counter where she pumped out something called Morning Ethiopian. It was too early for her to eat. When Rocky bent over to pick up a dropped napkin, she whacked her elbow on the metal strip along the edge of the table. She grimaced, closed her eyes, and let out one prairie dog yelp.

"That must be pure orange. I can feel that from here," said Tess.

"What?" said Rocky, cradling her elbow.

"When I hit a nerve like that I see orange for as long as it throbs."

"What do you mean?"

"I have synesthesia. Two places in my brain go off at once. When I stub my toe, I holler orange, because that's what I see and feel at the same time."

Rocky paused, recalling only vaguely having read about this in a neuropsych journal.

"I didn't know the name for it until about ten years ago when I heard a guy on NPR who wrote a book about us. I broke down and cried. I didn't know I was a member of a club."

"Do you see colors only when you hurt yourself?"

"No. Everything has a color. Like letters, *B* is light green with a dark base. *T* is gray and shiny. The days of the week each have their color and shape. Tuesday is a blue cube and Wednesday is muted red globe. Sunday is light yellow and sort of floppy."

"You are a multi-media event," said Rocky as she sipped her coffee.

"That's just the half of it. Now that I've learned more about synesthesia, I know just how plain and unfortunate your poor world is, I'm sorry to say."

"I've never thought of my world as plain."

"That's because you don't know any better. Your name is green because *R* is green. How old are you?"

"I'm thirty-eight."

"OK. Numbers one through ten go up a gradual slope, then eleven through twenty are on a plateau, twenty-one through thirty turn right and the thirties zigzag back the other way. So now when I think of you, I'll see a green *R* zigzagging backwards. "

"Jesus," said Rocky.

"Exactly. Now, doesn't that make your number system seem a little plain? I'm sorry; I don't mean to say that your world is plain. It's just that I'm a synesthete out of the closet. There's nothing as annoying as the newly converted."

Chapter 5

Tess did not regret for one minute the uniqueness of synesthesia, only that it took her so long to know its name and
that she was not alone, that there were others. There were a
few kindred spirits out in the world who were touched by the
cross-firing of senses, touched by the same tweak in genetics
as Tess, and finding them had changed her life. As a child,
she was driven to silence when she discovered that none of
the other children saw numbers as colors. She would say,
"The answer is number four, right next to the red three."
The second-grade teacher tilted her head as if to hear her
better and squinted her eyes trying to see her better. "No,
Tess. We're only doing the numbers now, not the colors." In
one horrible moment, built up from a few months of clues,
Tess understood that her teacher and her classmates lived in
a monochrome world where numbers were only black lines,
sad lonely things. Piano notes did not brush against their
cheeks and smell like cinnamon, and most odd of all, when
they fell and scraped their knees, they did not shout, "It's too
orange, now red!" They cried of course, as she did, but they

could not see the pulse of the pain in great orange splats with a deep red core.

Tess was a freak and she knew it, hid it from everyone except her mother who said, "You can say it to me, but don't let anyone else hear you. They'll say you're crazy." Tess did not know until much later that synesthesia is an inherited trait, and that her mother probably struggled with and then hid her own multisensory world. But her mother's appendix burst when Tess was eight and things got bungled up at the hospital and before Tess knew it, she was staring straight at the colorless body of her mother laid out in the coffin. She had never seen her mother without color before. She had always loved the apricot glow of her mother's laugh and her warm, smooth touch. A body without color was the most terrifying sight of her life and she had nightmares for years of a monochrome body. Synesthesia didn't stop for Tess when she buried her mother, but she didn't speak of it again for over fifty years.

When she graduated from high school, the war in Europe and Japan had ended, and she begged her father to send her to college. Tess had a huge capacity for memorizing anything and she graduated at the top of her small Nebraska high school. When teachers marveled at her academic abilities, she failed to mention to them that she had a different way of remembering facts and ideas. When numbers and letters each have their own color, shape, and size, subjects like history and math fit into neat packets that Tess could pull out at will; she had constant access to a color-coded file system in her brain. Math was particularly easy for her. She was most fond of the number five, which was a metallic shade of turquoise and had a commanding sound.

Her father sent her to a teacher's college, where, in the midst of taking as many math classes as seemed logical for an aspiring teacher, she moved on to biology. When she took a class in anatomy, she was in heaven, at last picturing the heart, the blood vessels, the hard-working liver, all the interiors of the body opened up to her in a splendor that she had not known existed. Other students agonized over the nervous system, forcing their monochrome brains to memorize an unseen world. For Tess, optics nerves were bright yellow and looked exactly like clothesline rope. The nerves that ran down the arms and spread out across the hands were sky blue and smelled like lilacs. Who could not remember them or what they did? Her anatomy professor said, "If you were a young man, I'd say you had all the makings of a fine doctor. But you'll be married before graduation."

Tess, for all her fine multi-sensed brainwork, had not noticed what her professor had seen from the first day of class; a sandy-haired boy in the back of the room who stared at Tess everyday. By finals, they were spending evenings in nearby cornfields, sipping beer, and gazing at the stars from their entwined position on a sturdy wool blanket that Len had stashed in his return luggage from the war. By their final semester of college, Tess was pregnant and uncomfortable in her simple wedding dress. Len had promised the most exciting thing of her life; they would marry and go to Boston where he would start medical school in the fall.

Tess often told people that alcoholism is a thief of the worst sort, and it is the camouflage of the monster that throws even the most observant person off guard. By the time Len's drinking had resulted in the despair of vomit, broken glass, one fractured wrist, two car accidents, and a serious threat to his job security at the hospital, Tess took the two children, by then in junior high, and divorced the man who no longer resembled the sandy-haired boy she met in college. After some urging by a friend of Len's, she applied to a school to study physical therapy and excelled as if she had never paused from her years at college.

She had been almost sixty years old when she heard a program on National Public Radio about synesthesia. That was ten years ago and she counted most of her time before that as painful and ill spent. She made friends with her ex-husband again and let him get to know her. He had remarried in an alcoholic whirlwind and when he finally sobered up, discovered he had married someone far more addicted to alcohol than even he had been. After losing his medical license Len attended AA five times a week. When Len sobered up, his second wife left him. He summed up his life.

"My first wife left me because I was a drunk. The second one left me because I got sober."

Tess came out to her grown children. Her two little grandchildren were born knowing that their Grannie heard motorcycles as jagged brown, streaked with battleship gray. If they spotted motorcycles, they cried, "Grannie cover your ears, the brown and silver are coming by!"

She knew that synesthesia had skipped her own children, but her grandchildren had a filtered down version and Tess gloried in it.

And now the new woman on the island, the animal control warden, was keeping Tess busier than she had been in years. Tess was drawn to things that didn't fit; shoulders that had popped out of their sockets, vertebrae that had squiggled to one side, muscles that had tightened so much that they were unrecognizable, and people who didn't fit, either in their own skin or because they were in the wrong place at the wrong time. She didn't know if synesthesia accounted for it; she'd seen no evidence of that in on-line chatter from the synesthetes. But she was sure that Rocky did not fit.

Chapter 6

Lift with your knees, not your back. Rocky heard the old tape running through her head. She wondered why some tapes automatically turn on. Other well-worn messages too: be careful of eating fish, you could choke on a bone. She never ate fish without hearing her father's voice, "Check for bones, this is bony fish." Her father hadn't eaten fish unless forced to and sat nervously glancing at his two children and his wife who flirted recklessly with death as they ate. He was Italian and without fear of Italian stereotype, preferred to eat pasta seven days a week. When things went well between Rocky's parents, her mother gave him ziti when they ate fish. When they were in their bad spells, she slid a bony piece of fish onto his plate and turned her back.

Now Rocky wondered how she could lift with her knees and not her back. Someone had called in a complaint about a black lab sort of dog who had been scrounging the south beach for several days and was acting strange; drooling and limping, bobbing his head. Rocky dreaded the thought that he might have rabies. When she got the call, the dog was last seen by the Dumpster in back of Stan's Seafood Diner.

"He could be sick. Eighty percent of all raccoons have ra-bies and he could have been bitten by a raccoon," said Phil, who washed dishes at the diner.

How did people come up with these statistics? If eighty percent of all raccoons were rabid, then why weren't they dead? This was the kind of question that she would have asked Bob, as if he were the encyclopedia of wildlife. She made a mental note to go back to the bookstore.

Rocky watched one large raccoon visit her garbage can nightly, wrestling with it, standing on its back legs, tipping the green plastic garbage can on its side. That raccoon had looked healthy enough. After cleaning up too much sticky, aromatic garbage from her walkway, she bought a bungee cord that finally raccoon-proofed the can. Her raccoon visitor didn't have rabies; she was just hungry. Most of what hu-mans do is not so different from what animals do; much of what we do is based on hunger, or the fear of being hungry, selecting a mate, and protecting our young. The guidebook of mammals said that raccoons, *Procyon lotor*, did not mate until late winter or early spring, so this gal was just beefing up for courtship.

Rocky stopped at the grocery store and bought a small package of low-grade ground beef. She drove the old truck up to the diner, hoping that the dog had not left already. As a dogcatcher, she learned how to make animal-catching easier. Bring food, squat on the ground, talk sweet, say "Good dog, what a good dog," letting her voice rise slightly, moving slow-ly. And try not to appear vicious. In dog language, she wanted to show first the offering of food, then firmness and calm.

She pierced the plastic wrap around the meat with her truck keys and walked around the back of the building. She felt a sharp tingle in the early November air. Tonight would be hard on a sick dog outdoors.

She saw him scrunched next to a pile of wood covered by a bright blue tarp. She announced her arrival.

"There you are, good dog." He lifted his head with a cloudy-eyed weariness. She crouched down about eight feet away.

"Come get some breakfast, buddy." She held out the meat. His deep brown eyes focused on her and she thought for a moment that this was the look of great despair that she saw on people who were deep in mourning or in the throes of a major depression. She shook her head to unscramble her brain.

The dog tried to stand, and yelped when he put his weight on his front legs.

"OK, big boy. I'll come to you. I'll deliver breakfast."

He lowered himself back down and accepted the meat that she placed right in front of his nose. For a moment his eyes softened. He sniffed the meat and gave it one lick. He looked too sick to eat. She rubbed his head after letting him smell her hand.

She reached over to the front leg that he was protecting and gingerly felt around.

"Oh, no." Her hand stopped on something jutting out of his shoulder. She leaned over cautiously. He had a shaft sticking out of the front of his chest and she could feel the heat of the infection.

"Bend with your knees and not your back." She couldn't possibly pick up this dog without hurting him. She untied the blue tarp from a woodpile and went inside to get Phil. The two of them slid the dog onto the folded tarp and then they lifted him to the back of the truck. Rocky closed the camper shell and headed straight for the ferry landing. The first ferry of the day was getting ready to go to Portland and she knew Sam Reynolds would be on it. He was a vet with a practice in South Portland.

She reached the ferry as the crew was starting to latch the closing chain across the landing.

"Wait!" yelled Rocky as she jumped out of her truck. "You've got to let me on. I've got a dog that's been hurt." Then she scanned the deck for Sam and saw him, hugging a plastic coffee mug. She waved her arms at him. He lowered his mug and headed down the metal staircase. The ferry opened up and waited for Rocky. There was room for her truck and she pulled in beside the other pickup trucks, mostly carpenters going off island for the day. Sam opened up the back of the truck as Rocky described the injury.

"Let's just wait until we get to my office. There's not much I can do here," he said. Sam felt the shoulder and the chest area. He unzipped his green jacket. "This is an arrow. He probably broke it off trying to get it out." He got in the truck when they landed in Portland and she drove to Sam's office. They backed the truck up to the front door. Within thirty minutes, Sam and his vet tech had the dog inside and hooked up to an IV.

"He's being prepped for surgery. Nothing left for you to do here, Rocky. I can get a ride to my car in Portland. Why don't you go back home and I'll give you a call tonight."

Sam and his wife kept one car parked at a friend's house off island and one car exclusively for the island. Rocky knew that he would save the dog if he could. She had already taken a series of sick cats to him on his one morning per week that he had office hours on the island.

But instead of taking the next ferry back, she drove to Portland and parked the truck in a parking garage to get it off the street. She had breakfast, went to the library, read the newspaper, and used the library's Internet to check email, none of which she answered.

She returned to Sam's office in the middle of the afternoon. He rubbed his head as if searching for hair that he used to have, now only a memory of dark fuzz on the top of his head that he clipped short. Sam handed her the tag that had hung around the dog's neck. It was a piece of octagonal aluminum, painted with yellow reflective paint.

"This would have been a lot more helpful if it had all the rabies information, and the local vet. But it probably helped the owner to see this guy at night. We went ahead and gave the dog a rabies shot along with enough antibiotics to clean out Boston Bay."

Rocky tossed the dog tag in her hand. "How's he doing?"

"Thought you'd never ask. Come on back. Be careful. He probably won't remember you."

Rocky knew if she were a dog she would run like crazy to get out of a vet's office. The smells were awful. Even her inadequate human nose could smell fear and pain, loneliness. Sam pushed open the new metal door to the recovery room where postoperative animals stayed. And it smelled like Bob.

The Lab was in the largest cage that they had and he was on his left side. The white bandage around his right front leg made Rocky wince. They had shaved off his fur right up past his shoulder. He lifted his head when Rocky knelt down. Sam opened the door wide. The dog thumped his tail once when Rocky put her hand near his nose.

"He's well enough to sniff out a good-smelling woman."

"Sam, you're too young to be saying stuff like that and get away with it. Old-geezer vets can say things about how women smell and we excuse them and call them cute, old men. Even your lack of hair doesn't put you into the geezer category."

"That's unfair."

"You've been hanging around dogs and cats too long. Don't start telling your clients how they smell."

Sam was in his late thirties and had worked long enough so that all his student loans were paid off and he and his wife, Michelle, were finally feeling expansive. Business in the winter was slower with all the summer people gone, but this gave Sam time to flirt with the dog warden.

The dog gave a heave and tried to stand up. When his right leg hit the floor he yelped, but he stood up anyhow, dizzy from the anesthetic, keeping most of his weight on three legs. She remembered Bob telling her how Labs and golden retrievers will overcompensate; if they feel pain, they will grit their teeth and plow on, especially if it meant running or being with their people. She winced at his pain.

"You know they heal faster than we do. He's a young, strong dog, probably four or five. In a couple of days, we'll start looking for a foster home for him until we can locate the owner." The dog turned his head and looked straight at Rocky.

"Be careful, he has just given you the look. When Labs give people the look, it is a powerful, mind-altering drug that makes you think you have been personally locked into a soul contract."

"I'm not an easy mark. I just don't like to see a good dog

suffering. If you haven't contacted the owners by the time he's ready to be released, I can be the foster home until we find them."

She stood up and wiped her hands on her thighs. This is what she and Bob would have done. "Or maybe I shouldn't. I just remembered, he'll be alone while I'm working . . ."

"That's right. And while you're out, he'll be sleeping. Dogs would hate for this secret to get out, but they're a lot like cats. They look for a good place to curl up and sleep."

Rocky took a breath and shook the memory of past foster dogs away. "Yeah, yeah. Show me his meds. Or will he be done with meds by then?"

The conversation was making Rocky's head go woozy. In the early days of their marriage, Rocky had assisted Bob in checking on animals that had to stay overnight. This was the longest time that she had spent in the back room of a vet clinic since Bob died. She walked over to a cool steel table, put her hands on the edge and leaned into it.

"Are you feeling okay? This dog is going to be fine, I'm not trying to stick you with a dying dog." Sam sounded like he was trying to reassure her.

"You really are new at this, aren't you?" Sam asked.

For a moment Rocky wanted to tell him that nothing was new, everything was new, that he should be careful because he and Michelle could have their world pulled out from under them by a drunk driver, a predestined heart attack, or lightning could strike and everything that he loved would be taken from him.

She pushed off from the table. "You're right. I'm new at this."

* * *

In two days, Rocky got the call that the dog was ready to be released.

"I've been out of town for a day. When you come get your dog, I want you to come and take a look at the arrow that I pulled out of him," said Sam.

"He's not my dog. I'm just sort of a canine rehab center for this guy. He belongs to somebody. He misses somebody."

"Whatever you say. We close at noon today. Stop over then. You'll need to bring your truck."

Reserving a place for vehicles on the ferry was difficult for visitors to the island, especially during the season; full-time residents had a year-round pass. But Rocky discovered she had the additional power to make last-minute requests if she was on emergency business, as she had been with the Lab. And this time of year, there was a pleasing absence of vehicles loaded down with deck chairs, bikes, and beer.

Dr. Reynold's clinic had a cat door and a dog door. The two sides of the clinic were delineated by the neutral zone of the receptionist's island. Rocky paused a moment and went in the dog door.

Sam opened the door behind the examining room where all the supplies were kept. On the counter was the shaft and point of the arrow that he removed from the black dog.

"Did you notice anything about this arrow?" he asked her.

"I didn't see it. I only saw the shaft of the arrow and I was honestly thinking a lot more about the dog. But you want to tell me something, so let's jump to that part."

He rolled the shaft around in his palm. "This entire arrow is handmade. Look at this," he said, pointing his finger at the string around the arrowhead.

"This stuff that looks like string? This is made from ten-dons of a deer, wrapped around the shaft to attach the point. Probably used hide glue. Do you know how long it takes to make one of these? From start to finish? If you include the time it took to cut and dry the wood, and I'm told this is prob-ably Osage, about three months. I know that if you go to the trouble of making one of these, you don't shoot it at a dog. You go for the whole, pure experience. You want to shoot a deer, a turkey, a pheasant. Something is very wrong here." He dropped the arrow into her hands.

"Does anyone on the island have this as a winter hobby, like rug braiding or bookbinding? You must know everyone," said Rocky.

"I have never heard anyone brag or do a show and tell about making a bow and arrow the good old-fashioned way. And that's the kind of thing someone would have to brag about."

Rocky leapt through the obvious possibilities in her brain. "So this probably wasn't the work of a child. This was an adult hobby. Have you ever seen a dog shot by an arrow be-fore?"

"Not on the island, but it happens. That's why I got on the Web when I took a good look at this thing. I found several places that specialize in this type of arrow; one in Minnesota and one in Nebraska." He shrugged his shoulders. "The good news is that this is a strong animal, and he will heal without too much damage to the quality of his life. The surgery was messy. Had to remove some necrotic tissue, which was unfor-tunately muscle. I'd say he walked around with that arrow sticking out of him for maybe three days. No matter how bad he's feeling now, he's feeling better than he was."

"Can I keep this?" she asked, holding up the remains of the arrow.

"It's yours."

Sam had already called the Portland police to let them know about the dog. He said they sounded unimpressed. They sent over an officer a few hours after Sam made the call and asked a few questions. They said it was probably the last of the tourists who thought the island was a good place to shoot, and the dog was in the wrong place. One of the Portland cops came over every morning, drove his car around the island and left on the next ferry.

Sam rode in the back with the dog while Rocky drove. The ferry was not crowded; late afternoon in November resulted in only a third of the ferry passengers. As they approached Rocky's rental house, she suddenly saw it as Sam might see it. He and Michelle had just remodeled their house on the south side of the island. She wondered how she looked in Sam's eyes, a woman in her thirties, living on the part-time salary of animal control warden, single, and living in one of the cottages that will only marginally make it through the winter. Sam's khaki pants picked up dirt from the back of her truck as he slid out.

She hesitated to have Sam enter the little rental. She was suddenly jealous of his life, the completeness of it, of his wife and kids. He and Michelle had two young children and the addition on their house, although delayed, was due to be done by December. Rocky had turned down several invitations for dinner with them.

"Let's lift him down and see if he can make it in the house," said Sam.

Sam wrapped his arms around the dog's rib cage and

Rocky lent support to the rear end. When they set him on the ground, he limped five feet away and squatted slightly as he let loose with a stream of urine.

"He's not ready to stand on three legs yet," Sam said.

The three of them made it up the wooden steps that led to her deck. She unlocked the door and urged the dog in. Sam looked around with the quick eye of a medical assessment. "I used to live in a place like this in college, except there were four of us and one guy never washed his own dishes and finally the rest of us wouldn't wash his dishes either, so we all used paper plates. It looks like you're a lot neater."

No one else had been in the house, not even Tess. Just the cat, and she only stayed part of the time. Rocky had started to call her Peterson, after the guidebook.

Rocky listened to Sam's voice, and although she didn't hear his words as such, she was measuring the level of her rapid breathing, and noted that since her breathing was not increasing in pace, a panic attack was less likely and she would not have to face the consequences of gasping for air in front of Sam. She was a four on a ten-point scale of anxiety and she could ride this out. She hadn't had another panic attack after the first one, two months after Bob died. And although the sound of another person breathing in her house was now reaching tolerable levels, the thought of Sam and Michelle seeing inside her house made her want to throw up. Her blood noticed the threat and picked up the pace and her heart rate quickened. There was always flight; she could run away into the tangle of vines and rhododendrons that formed a thick boundary between her and the beach road. There was fight; she could rage, make a scene, wait for the hapless man to make a wrong move and seize on the moment to hurl him out. Or freeze, like the rabbit, the deer, or the lizard and keep Sam in her sight as he left damp trails on her linoleum floor. Her ancient brain came forward like a crocodile, eyes bulging, peeking over the surface of the water.

"Do you have a water dish for the dog? If you are going to be the nursemaid for this guy, you might consider a way to feed him."

Sam looked too large in the house, too scruffy with his dark stubble blossoming from his face. The front part of her brain got up and bumped the old animal brain away. Taking a breath, she said, "There's a pan under the stove, I'll use that. Did you bring in the amoxicillin? Seven more days with the meds, right?"

The dog, limping and exhausted from his ordeal at the clinic, the ferry ride, and the bumpy ride in the back of the truck, now slid to the floor and panted.

Sam picked up Rocky's phone and called his wife. "Yeah, it's Isaiah's rental, off Bracken Road. OK. See ya." Sam leaned his backside against the chipped Formica of the counter. "She'll be here in about twenty minutes, then we have to pick up the kids at day care."

Rocky uncovered the rectangular pan from beneath the stove. She tore open the top of the Science Diet bag of kibbles and scooped out a handful and let them chink into place. The dog picked up his head, looked at Rocky, and she thought he smiled. She knew Labs and retrievers always looked like they were smiling, putting them in the same category as panda bears and koalas, disarming all humans. She just couldn't believe anyone could smile that much. Bob had disagreed with her. "No, Rocks, these dogs really are smiling. They are in a state of contentment," Bob had said.

By the time Michelle pulled up, Rocky had put the cap back on the adrenaline, but her armpits were drenched from the experience. She had not had a panic attack, but the effort of averting one had drained her. When the couple left, she was exhausted. Sam had been her first visitor. Isaiah and Charlotte didn't count because they owned the place.

She looked at the dog. "I'm no bargain, but I'm all you've got until we can find your owner. I'll try to be a good host."

The cat had kicked up a royal fuss when Rocky let her inside, hissing and pushing her spine into a curve of hysteria, then fleeing for the dresser in Rocky's bedroom. Both Rocky and the dog ignored the behavior and viewed the tabby as far down on the list of critically important dilemmas.

Rocky was struck by how quickly the black dog had recovered from his injury. The gaping wound left by the broken shaft of the arrow drew together faster than she thought possible. In the first years of Bob's vet practice, she sometimes helped him with late-night emergencies. She saw dogs and cats with legs pointing in the wrong direction, jagged skin flaps peeled off necks and shoulders, and crushed hindquarters. She learned that animals could survive the worst horrors, that skin grew back together and bones mended, and that dogs always acted with a sort of immortal grace.

The dog looked at Rocky. She took the throw rug from the bedroom and bunched it up near him. He was her first save and she didn't want this to go wrong. He slept in the kitchen on the first night, near the front door, like a shy houseguest not wanting to intrude.

He had all the signs of depression: listlessness, lack of enjoyment in the things normally enjoyed, he even turned his black nose up at food. And his sleep was fitful, waking several times during the night. Being a dog, he couldn't say things like, "It wouldn't matter if I was gone, no one would notice." But Rocky wondered if that was exactly what the Lab would say if he could. She did what she could for him in the first days of his foster care, postoperative life. She was assured that his recovery would not be a complicated one. Infection would be annihilated by the broad-spectrum antibiotic, he would be stiff and sore from the surgery, shocked by what-ever happened to cause an arrow to be shot into his shoulder, but dogs were made of powerful stuff, especially his breed. Their drive to be with a pack, to be with another creature, either canine or human, was impossibly strong. Perhaps just being with him was the medicine that Rocky could offer.

She let him figure her out slowly, smell her as much as he needed to, always offering her open hand slowly, letting him sniff. When he stood, she understood that he needed to make the compulsory crotch sniff. "Hope your memory is good; you only get one full, unfettered snoot there." He raised his head and breathed in the scent glands that traveled easily to him through her jeans. She crouched to stroke his head, to find out what he liked. Was it under the chin, behind the ears?

The dog was polite, he let her touch him, but he couldn't tell her much because his heart wasn't in it. "Take your time, big guy," she said to him as she refreshed his water for the second time of the day, made sure that the few kibbles he had taken were replaced.

Fussing over him would only wear him out. She settled into a chair to read one of the mainland newspapers that she had mostly avoided for months. She was instantly distracted by the thought of a person shooting a dog with a bow and arrow. She knew little about this sort of weaponry. To her it was an obscure art. Once while on vacation in San Francisco, she and Bob had seen an archery range in the Golden Gate Park. They stopped to watch an Asian woman preparing to shoot by going through tai chi motions, slowing herself to a point of stillness, then picking up the bow with exquisite grace, placing the arrow, and joining in a moment of perfection before she released the entire arrangement by simply letting go. Bob had turned to her and said, "Is it just me, an East Coast guy, or does everything out here look like sex?"

She could not imagine the graceful woman ever doing anything as cruel as shooting a dog. She couldn't picture any person who would.

"Who in the world would do this to a dog?" asked Tess. She had come to stay with the dog while Rocky went to work. Sam had burst the membrane on her compound of isolation; letting Tess in had been easier. When Rocky came home, she found the older woman and the dog sitting together on the floor, Tess with her back against the wall, her legs stuck out like a young girl. The dog, like all good dogs, kept himself between Tess and the door. When Rocky opened the door, he stood and she cringed to see him rise to a seated position.

"Did you give him the antibiotics?"

"Of course, an hour ago. He gets one more before you go to bed. I can stay the night you know."

"We'll be all right. Well, maybe you should stay until I take him outside to pee. If he falls or something, it's easier for two people to carry him." Rocky knew the dog wouldn't fall, but she did want Tess to stay a little longer. Something about her felt good.

Rocky and Tess put on their coats and coaxed the big dog outside. The wind came in surges, just like the surf of the ocean. The dog gratefully peed, wisely not trying to lift a hind leg, but squatting like a puppy. She was called into service to help with the black dog when Rocky brought him home. The sight of the wound on his shoulder made Tess wince and imagine the blasts of red and orange that the dog had endured before Rocky had found him.

"You can't keep calling him Black Dog. That's like calling someone Furrowed Brow or Capped Tooth," said Tess as she and Rocky sat once again in the dog warden's kitchen.

Rocky reached over and patted the dog. "Somewhere that dog has an owner and he has a name. I just can't change his name. That's horrible to think about, being hurt and lost and no one knows your name and suddenly you are called Roberta or Ethel," said Rocky.

"No one is called Ethel anymore. I suspect there is no danger there." The wind swooped down on the house, seeming to come straight down in a vertical stab from the sky rather than across the ocean.

"I want to wait. I've got calls in to the animal shelters and dog wardens on the mainland. I called in an ad to the newspaper. I already know that he doesn't belong to anyone on the island. And this dog had no computer chip on the back of his neck."

"Good for you," said Tess to the dog. "I don't plan on getting a chip either. He needs a strong name, one with deep, mellow tones to match his voice. And a name with an eccentric sense of dignity. He is one of the most dignified dogs I have ever seen. He looks like an ambassador. Who knows, we might come up with his real name." Tess squatted down by the dog and looked into his dark eyes. "Lloyd. Lloyd!" she said. The dog lifted one ear up.

"That could make him seem like a criminal. Don't people named Lloyd end up robbing banks?"

"No, that's Wayne and only when it's the middle name," said Tess.

As a temporary name, they decided it would do.

It was bad enough that the dog was injured and was now recovering from surgery, but something else was really wrong with him, something that Rocky had seen in his eyes on the day she found him. He had lost someone and it was horrible for the dog. Rocky knew that food, a warm bed, lots of water, and encouraging words would not be enough. He longed for someone.

She tried to picture what might have happened, how a big dog like this would have gotten separated from his owner and then shot with an arrow. Maybe it was the owner who hurt him, a deranged, despicable person, the kind of person one reads about in the grocery store tabloids. But no, this dog would be different if that was the case, he'd be shy, passive, hide his tail between his legs. Or he would be aggressive and in a state of constant vigilance. That wasn't it. Maybe someone stole him from his really loving owner who was grievously worried and had put up lost-dog posters in the hometown of someplace like Oklahoma.

After Tess reluctantly left, Rocky squatted by the Lab. "I'd sure like to hear your story."

Chapter 7

No one on the island, except for Isaiah, knew she was a psychologist. Not that being a psychologist was so extraordinary, but it was what she had been and now she was nothing that she had been before. Here, the work was cleaner. Relocate the raccoons, the skunks. Capture dogs abandoned by the summer people, the new litters of kittens destined to become feral. Pick up the dead seagulls. Report on beach erosion. The beach erosion part was extra, not a part of her original job description, and the first time that she gave Isaiah a report on changes along the beach after a storm, he told her that the animal warden's job had obviously expanded.

"Don't go writing yourself a new job description. All we're paying you for is animal control," said Isaiah as he leafed through a three-page document.

"You're the one who suggested it. I'm just trying to systematize things, to help the next person on the job. I've put some beach markers along the shore, and measured the distance to water at high tide and low tide. Nothing fancy," she said as she leaned back in one of his straight-back chairs.

On her own accord, she added other duties to her job. Walk

on the cliffs, look official. Clean up litter that she couldn't stand to look at any longer. Here the work had a beginning and an end, like house painting or carpentry, and if she didn't want to talk to anyone, she didn't have to. She filed weekly reports for Isaiah and left them in his mailbox if he wasn't around.

She had been slow to get to know people other than her boss and Tess. But she had a neighbor, Elaine, a teacher at the island grade school. They had passed each other on the dirt road for months, their cars kicking up spirals of dust. When she saw Elaine at the grocery store, her arms filled with white plastic bags, struggling to get out the door, Rocky had an impulse to turn her head and pretend she didn't recognize the woman, but it was too late.

"Hello, neighbor. Can you get the door for me? I feel like a pack mule with all this stuff," Elaine said with a broad smile.

Rocky accepted the invitation to dinner because she was out of practice at declining. How had she and Bob said no before? "Let me get back to you after I check at home." That's right, that's what it had been like. Having a partner was a buffer, an excuse to contemplate, and a reason to say no. Without him, she didn't know what to say. Later she realized she could have used the dog as an excuse; he was perfect.

Elaine had one of the houses on the island that was not quaint or dripping with gingerbread bric a brac. It was a 1950's ranch-style house and someone had attached a second story to it. Rocky arrived with a bottle of wine and seltzer water, even after Elaine had said, "No, this is my welcome to you. I'm already guilty of bad manners for letting you be here for months before I invited you in. Maybe I'm that way because of all the summer people; there's too many of them to get to know."

Fresh tomato sauce filled the house with an abundant smell that drenched Rocky with sharp images of Bob eating more pasta than humanly possible and suffering with burps that smelled like compost. Rocky suddenly remembered that she liked pasta and bread and butter, but she couldn't remember the last time that she prepared it. She handed over her offerings to Elaine.

Elaine turned her head to the door leading into the living room and Rocky remembered what her college roommate said about the fundamental difference in facial features. Some faces were destined to be finely chiseled in marble; others were best described in soft clay. Elaine was in the clay category, soft round cheeks, the start of a furrow between her eyebrows.

"Honey, it's dinner," said Elaine to the open doorway. Rocky had not seen anyone else with Elaine when they passed each other on the dirt road. She waited to see who honey was.

A young girl appeared, with her hair pulled back tight, her ears sticking out like a mouse. She wore bulky sweatpants, running shoes, and a T-shirt with a partially zipped-up sweatshirt.

"Melissa, this is our neighbor, Rocky. This is my daughter."

Rocky felt the hit first in her solar plexus, where she always felt it. She put her hand out to Melissa and got back not a solid athlete's grasp but a cold, dry reluctant hand. Even as the two hands touched, Melissa offered a profound determination to pull away. The skin on Melissa's face was tight, but because she was young, no one was yet alarmed. Before

Rocky could stop herself, she said, "Track or cross-country? Let me guess, you do both."

Elaine, who was taking the cork out of the wine bottle, stopped in mid pull. "How did you know?"

Rocky flicked a glance at the girl. "I've known a few cross-country people. Really, it was the shoes. You wear them only if you really mean business."

Elaine asked her the sort of questions that she dreaded: where did she come from, what did she do before being an animal control warden. She had settled on a stock answer. "No children, used to work in child care, not married, just coming out of a relationship, and trying out the island." She was surprised at how well her answers worked, how easy it was to change who she was. Rocky was more comfortable asking the questions and quickly turned it to Melissa.

"I haven't seen you with your mother before," said Rocky.

"I stay at my Dad's in Portland some of the time. Every other weekend. Sometimes more if I have school stuff."

Elaine's mouth tightened up as if she had set her teeth together. "We've done it for so long, I sort of forget that it must sound strange. We've been divorced since Melissa was eight."

Rocky didn't have to watch long to see what Melissa was doing with her dinner. The girl patted her stomach and said, "I'm so full from eating after I ran, I don't know how much I can eat." She put lettuce, sprouts, and cucumber slices on her plate. She went to the fridge and got a lemon, and squeezed it on her salad. Then she put a golfball-sized portion of spaghetti on her plate with a tablespoon of sauce. She elaborately sliced the cucumber into eight pieces like a pie. The spaghetti was pushed around and rearranged without one strand going into her mouth. She ate a mushroom from the sauce and suddenly stopped.

"Did you put oil in the sauce, Mom?"

"Oil? No. Well, I had to use a tiny bit of oil when I sautéed the mushrooms." Elaine shrugged her shoulders. She looked down and tucked her highlighted hair behind her ears. Rocky knew this was not the first time that the girl had questioned her mother about ingredients.

Melissa was the kind of kid that Rocky had not wanted to work with at the counseling center. Not at first, but after awhile she had begged her director, "Don't give me one more starving girl!"

Rocky's mantra as a therapist had been, "I don't specialize in eating disorders," and because another therapist at the clinic did, she had sent all the determined starving young women to her. Ellen was the perfect therapist for girls with disordered eating. She was round, unembarrassed by her own girth, and no threat to girls who were in competition for deprivation. The unhappy army of girls, defined by skin, bones, and grit, found solace with Ellen. Rocky had watched them arrive for their weekly meetings, hardly allowing their sit bones to touch the chair and pulling their osteoporotic spines straight. From her office, she could spot their skin, desperate with goose flesh and extra hair, trying to warm the bodies that insisted on living without fat.

None of her training had truly prepared her for the tenacity of anorexia or the pure malevolence of the voice of an eating disorder that wrapped around the girls like a smirking python. With Ellen as resident specialist, she was off the hook. Ellen went to all the eating-disorder conferences, talked about eating disorders during lunch (which Rocky found

particularly distressing), and became absorbed by the world
of restricting. All of this meant that Rocky passed on the big-
eyed skinny girls with their hair pulled back tight and their
baggy pants and big sweatshirts worn to hide the clatter of
their bones.

And then Ellen left. She married a dentist and moved to
Albany last winter. The director of the clinic said to Rocky,
"We have to talk about our clients with eating disorders now
that Ellen is gone." She knew what this meant, and a solid
sense of dread had lodged in the back of her throat. She tried
everything to escape them.

"It's not ethical to offer services that are beyond our scope
of expertise. We can refer out. Let's put this in the job description, 'must have experience in eating disorders,'" said
Rocky.

She said anything except the truth, which was that the
tiny young women who refused to eat, but who thought of
nothing else all day except food, terrified her, outwitted her,
showed that all of her training was for naught. She finally
settled on seeing the clients with bulimia. She understood
gulping down life in vast quantities, and even had a therapeu-
tic understanding of a sudden change in heart and throwing
up. And most importantly, she never wanted to reach out and
grab them by the ears and shake them into eating the way
she did with the army of anorexic girls.

On the island, no one expected cures from Rocky. They
expected that she would catch, remove, and relocate animals.
Her job was confined to the battered yellow truck, finding
abandoned animals, picking up roadkill if the town truck
missed it.

At her neighbor Elaine's house, she watched the girl rearrange the lettuce without salad dressing and the yolkless, hardboiled egg. She wondered if Elaine knew. As the mother, she will be blamed no matter what she does, the way mothers of autistic children used to be blamed because they were thought to be too cold; this was offered as the sole cause for what turned out to be a neurological disorder. If Elaine doesn't know, she'll be blamed for being in denial. If she does know, she will still be the culprit for colluding with her daughter who refused the egg yolk.

Rocky shifted her attention to the girl and a suddenly liberated mean streak ran through her. "Hey, can I have a slice of that egg white? It looks delicious." She reached across the table with her fork as if to stab the egg white. The mother and daughter drew in tight. Rocky had broken through the perimeter of their rules. She put her fork back on her plate and scooped up more pasta. Rocky reveled in the freedom of being non-therapeutic.

When all the food was mercifully taken off the table, Melissa slid her chair back and said she had too much chemistry to do. Rocky tried to salvage the rest of the evening by talking about Lloyd, but the tone of the earlier welcome had cooled, and she made an early nine P.M. departure. She knew that the evening had gone badly.

Sleep had always been a comfort to her, but since Bob had died, sleep was an unpredictable landscape. As she rose and fell through stages of sleep, the dark mask of grief momentarily lifted and cool air rushed beneath and freshened her cheeks, under her eyelids, and up and down the slope of her nose. When was life ever like this? When had she walked so weightlessly?

She woke hard, the sting of morning raked across her skin.

The first hint of panic took hold: Had Bob been dead so long that even the ghastly comfort of grief had loosened and he'd moved farther away?

In the first few months after his death, she had dreamt endless versions of the cardiac resuscitation she had attempted with Bob. In one dream she tried to plug his heart into the hair dryer to shock him back to life. He sat up and said, "Stop it! You're burning us."

But now, try as she might, her dreams flitted away before she could grab them and she awoke each morning blinded by the complete darkness of sleep. If she couldn't remember her dreams, would she forget Bob?

She tested herself. What did his face look like? She closed her eyes and the image of him was distressingly impressionistic. Her breath caught and then quickened. Adrenaline fed in a fury throughout her body, quickening her heart. Could she still smell him? She pulled Bob's pillow into her face and she tried to curve her entire body around it, one leg pulled around the bottom edge as if it were Bob's leg. She'd been sleeping with his pillow for six months, judiciously at first, only sniffing it lightly, skimming over the polyester-filled sack with her eyes closed, conjuring up visions of him as if she were a witch commanding his spirit back. She flared her nostrils to catch his scent. But the pillow, after months of such work, was giving up the last memory of Bob, his oily skin and heavy aroma, which used to make Rocky put her face on his chest and close her eyes.

Her heart beat too fast and she noticed that her hands were trembling. Is this what a heart attack is like? Should she pray for a secret heart ailment so that she could die too? In the first months after his death, she had tried to find the paths of either impulsivity or resolve that would lead her to suicide, but the connections to Caleb and her mother were too strong and the cords of family would not release her. If she died of a respectable early heart attack, would she find him? She couldn't stay in the house with the pillow that bore such little scent of Bob, with the dreams that foretold of surfacing farther away from him.

The well-meaning say that the dead are not really gone, they live on in our hearts. Rocky wondered if she ever said that to anyone. She remembered a client, a tough-skinned woman whose brother died of AIDS. "I can't stop crying in my dreams, I can't stop wanting him back," she said to Rocky. Had Rocky said that her brother would live in her heart forever?

She wanted to find the client, go back to her and look her up, call her and say, "I was full of shit, I'm so sorry. The dead are gone. I can't find my husband in my heart. The dead leave us. Death is unbearable."

The wind shook the tightly woven nest of vines and trees outside. These trees, shrubs, and vines had adapted to the savage winds off the ocean. Their roots were deep and determined.

If Bob were here, she would have wanted to make love. He was always ready; an easy sell job. "All I have to do is touch you with my pinky finger and you have already decided on sex. How do you do that?" she had asked him on a windy morning like this one. He would have already pulled her to him, letting her straddle his body. He would have put his warm hands on her hips.

"This is nothing. You should see horses mate. The stud has no other inclination. Every force within him is concentrated on the focal point of mating. He doesn't care, I'm sorry to say, that the mare would sooner be eating hay, prancing about the pasture practicing her high jumps. No, he mounts her, sometimes bites hard into her and then has at it," said Bob.

Rocky always had the same reaction to Bob's nature lessons; she balanced between arousal and revulsion. "If you bite me, Mr. Horse, I'm sending you out to be gelded."

No, he was gone; the pillow had even given up his scent. The memory of him had slowed her heart again, numbed it back into sadness, and the dog, who had been in the room the entire time, began to pace as if even he had had enough of this reverie. It was Saturday and she was out of tampons, a realization that announced itself with a dark red splotch on the sheets. She walked the dog briefly and drove down to the small grocery store.

Rocky was in the aisle of feminine hygiene products deliberating over Playtex Multipack nondeodorant tampons or Playtex regular when Rocky spotted Melissa before the girl could duck around the corner.

"Hey!" said Rocky as she put the two boxes behind her back. "Do me a favor and pick left or right. I can't make up my mind." This was an effort to be more neighborly with the girl, perhaps redeem her poor behavior from last night.

Melissa looked mortified. "Go on, pick one, I can't stand the indecision. Come on, left or right?" said Rocky, hoping that her voice was light, that this was perhaps funny, inviting.

Melissa froze, and Rocky knew she was once again going down the wrong path with the girl, but she was unable to stop. Melissa pointed a bluish hand to the right.

"Ah, the variety pack, a tampon for all occasions. Thanks, track star," said Rocky.

Melissa remained in a state of frozen stupor, and Rocky stared hard at her, first at the blue tint of her hands, then at her face. Rocky pulled in her bottom lip and pressed down with her teeth. She saw the evil sneer of the child's eating disorder peering at her behind Melissa's thin shoulders.

"Oh. Your periods have stopped, haven't they? How long?"

Melissa jolted out of her shocked state. Her eyes opened wide in savage exposure.

"You're nuts! There's something wrong with you. You don't belong here," said Melissa and she ran out of the store, abandoning what she had come for.

Rocky felt guilt descending on her for coming down so hard on the girl, for slamming her with the weapons that the food-deprived child was not prepared to deflect. She had a big, blossoming eating disorder and Rocky knew it. And the kid thought she was fooling everyone in the drunken state of restricting and hiding and measuring. But it was unfair of Rocky to take a swipe at her if the kid couldn't fight back.

Still, Rocky was not her therapist, she did not, would not, be so god-awful careful and strategic and firm and fucking nurturing. She was an animal control warden. No one here expected her to be able to fix this kid. No concerned parent or high school teacher or kinesiology professor would call to say, "You've got to do something. She won't eat." She didn't have to take the call.

But she did not have to persecute her. Rocky had to do something to even the score on her bad behavior in the store. She called Melissa when she got home and said, "Hey, I think I was kind of too blunt with you the other day. And I'm sorry about today at the store. I can be that way. People tell me that all the time. I was wondering if you could take care of a dog that I'm fostering for a few days when I'm on the mainland. Yeah? I'll bring him over with his mountain of food. Could you stop by and bring in my mail? Oh, and put some cat food out for the cat, Peterson. How long? I'm leaving on Friday and I'll be back on Sunday. Yeah, I'll give you the key."

Rocky felt slightly better, as if the cruel stab at the child had been partially erased. She wrote a couple of paragraphs in her journal about how she didn't wish every day that she'd die in an accident, or in her sleep, or like Bob did, suddenly, brutally and without a moment's thought to those left behind. She had told clients who were grieving that doing anything sometimes helped: writing in journals, talking, walking, or painting their house. Make some announcement to the universe that you are going to continue and will not give in to the pull of grief. Or become a dog warden. Was everything that she told her clients worthless? When her father had died, he gave them lots of warning. He developed cancer of the pancreas, and although everyone said that he died so quickly, both Rocky and her brother said that it was oddly one of the best times of their lives; they had never felt closer to him.

She gave up on writing in her journal and forgot after a few days, and left it sitting on her small dresser. If Bob had been alive, she would have slipped it into a drawer, as a courtesy to both of them. Without knowing it, she had made an adaptation to living alone.

The visit to her brother's house was compulsory. Both her mother and Caleb had said that if she didn't come, they were coming out to the island to see her and she didn't want that.

She didn't want this ascetic life disturbed by their caring, by their distress.

Her mother had flown in from California where she had moved several years after Rocky's father died. "Why California?" she had asked when her mother announced her decision. Her mother, who had been a junior high science teacher all of her adult life, went back to college to study horticulture at UC Davis. She had recently gotten a job at a vineyard in the Sonoma valley.

When Rocky brought the dog to Melissa's house, she had explained again about the food, about the mail. "Here you go, kid, front-door key. Most of the mail is addressed to Resident and they're ads for Wal-Mart." She had handed the key over to Melissa, who had been in the midst of doing homework.

"You do homework on Friday morning?" asked Rocky. It was 6:30.

"I can't finish it all at night." She had her game face on, indecipherable, the good-girl look that probably worked so well with her coach. She was ready for Rocky if she said something nasty.

"OK, well Lloyd will park himself somewhere between you and the door. He's still gimpy in the leg so don't take him running with you no matter how much he tries to convince you. Dogs will force themselves to keep up with you even if they can't. Know what I mean?"

"I know how to take care of a dog."

"Right, sorry. You'll do fine. Here is Tess's number in case you need anything. Do you know Tess?"

"I guess so. The old lady with the hair?"

Rocky paused. She hadn't really thought of Tess in that way, but yes, Melissa apparently did know her.

"That's the one." Rocky left after bidding goodbye to Elaine, who stepped into the kitchen, with coffee cup in hand, dressed for work and with a softer look in her eyes than the last time Rocky had blundered into their lives.

Chapter 8

The first place Melissa went when she got home from school and the club was Rocky's house. Lloyd came with her, happy to pee on everything that required his urine-soaked messages to other dogs. He could now balance on his two front legs well enough to once again raise his rear leg. The cat greeted them at the door and instead of wanting food, she dashed out, between Melissa's legs. Rocky had told her she didn't know if she should leave the cat in or out. The answer was clearly out.

She took in the mail on Saturday. The animal warden had been right. Everything was addressed to Resident.

It was thrilling to be in someone else's house alone. She opened the cabinets over the sink; two coffee cups and a couple of glasses. This woman traveled light. All the cabinets revealed the same hollow sparseness. Two pots, one fry pan, nothing matched.

Melissa opened the refrigerator. "Let's see what she eats." One quart of milk, a loaf of bread, peanut butter, grape jelly, margarine, a jar of salad dressing, Newman's Own Vinaigrette.

"Well, she's one to talk," said Melissa to the dog, who raised a questioning ear at her.

She closed the refrigerator and moved on to the bathroom. She thought immediately of the girls she knew at high school who threw up. Everybody knew who they were. You can't throw up after lunch in high school without everybody knowing about it. She hadn't tried it. She didn't have to, because she ran. The girls who threw up didn't get that part, that if you ran and did 300 sit-ups at night in your room, quietly so no one heard you, who needs to throw up? She opened the mirrored cabinet above the sink and inspected each item: ibuprofen, peroxide, rubbing alcohol, boring stuff, no makeup.

Then she went into the bedroom and caught Rocky's scent on a fleece scarf tossed on the back of a chair. She went straight to the dresser, as if it was meant to be, as if she should find it, and she put her hands on the black journal and opened it.

"Oh, this is good, this is very good," she said to the dog, reading the first page.

It was a black book, the kind with blank pages. She had received a blank journal for her last birthday and had not used it once. Her grandmother had sent it to her, a pastel blue and yellow book with delicate flowers on the cover. It was so wrong to write in something that her grandmother thought was good. If she lost more weight, she might be able to write in it, but not before.

She ran her fingers along the lightly embossed cover as she read the entries that started last spring. She saw the labored handwriting, erratic spiking and pages that had been scratched, destroyed by a pen dragged fiercely across the page in a tantrum. "I'm sorry . . . I hate you . . . I want to die," was the message in jagged lines. She began to thumb her way through the pages, slowly, hungrily, savoring each entry and noting the date.

July 16. There is no one here to give me caution and I am glad of that. I do not need to close the cover of this book to protect someone else's sensibilities. I leave it open at night and in the morning, no hand has disturbed it, no eyes have scanned my thoughts. What would it take to join you, my love? Is the human organism difficult to extinguish? You were not. Of all the ways, carbon monoxide seems the best and the surest, the least likely to alert the outside world. You would be furious, shocked, disgusted if you saw me plotting my death. But I am not worried about your disapproval, I am terrified about the unknown, about not finding you if I kill myself.

Melissa closed the book. She had been sitting on Rocky's bed and stood up startled, and dropped the book to the floor. She hurriedly smoothed the blankets on the bed, grabbing the book from the scratched floorboards. Where exactly had the journal been? Which direction had it faced? She would be more careful when she came back tomorrow to read more. She would know everything about Rocky.

On the way out of the bedroom, her eye caught on a silky thing in a green laundry basket, a camisole. Yes, she thought, that's what it was called. It was red, bordered by lace along the top. She ran her fingers along it and without knowing why, she folded it tight and slipped it into her jacket pocket. The dog looked at her from the doorway.

She knelt by Lloyd. Melissa had one hand on the slickness of the camisole as she ran her other hand over the ridge of

Lloyd's neck. She felt him press his head into her hand and a tremor ran from her tight and empty belly down the length of her thighs. Her cheeks flared with heat, and even though she was alone with the dog, she turned around to see if anyone had seen this thing that had moved into her.

"Come on, Lloyd," she said with a sense of alarm.

At home, Lloyd stayed between Melissa and the door, any door, at all times. If she moved to the kitchen he gathered himself up from what looked like a deep sleep and repositioned himself. If she went to her bedroom for another round of science notes, he rose up and took his post between Melissa and the bedroom door. Once, when she walked into her bedroom, she looked at the cross-country jacket that still had the red camisole in the pocket and she ran her thumb and index finger over the fabric, pausing at the lace, letting it imprint on her skin. If she was really, really good, she wouldn't touch it again and she would bring it back before Rocky returned on Sunday morning.

"I will, I'll bring it back," she whispered to the black dog.

But her hand dove into the pocket and pulled out the bit of red and in one moment she draped it across her face and a smell that was complicated and warm and demanding filled her senses. Tonight she would put it next to her when she slept and then she would have to move it to a safer place. Nobody could find this. Lloyd opened his eyes.

"Don't look at me," she suddenly growled. He shrank to a sadder size and put his head between his large paws.

This would require more sit-ups than usual. She was permitted to eat if she did the full crunches, which had risen to 400; this trouble with touching the red silky piece of cloth could mean 500. She might be able to eat then. She folded a towel into thirds the long way to protect her backbone and began the trance of motion, hands behind her head, knees bent for rapid, unrelenting crunches. When she was done, she felt worthy of logging on to her special website. This was something that no one knew about, not even Rocky.

Rocky could spoil everything for Melissa. No one had said a word to her about not eating enough until Rocky came to dinner and blew her cover. That wasn't entirely true; her mother had begun to make everything that Melissa had ever said she loved to eat, and even took to bringing home Chicken McNuggets from the mainland.

Melissa logged onto the websites for girls with eating disorders. She knew her mother would never think to track where she had been on the Web and this gave her the freedom of a world traveler, disguised as a high school girl, an honor student, track star, but really she was a terrorist. Her camo gear included sweatpants, pristine running shoes, two layers of shirts, and sometimes two layers of pants. When she heard her mother go to sleep, the click of the bedroom light, the outer gear came off and bone girl appeared, skin stretched smooth over bone, enough toned flesh to keep her running. On to the websites. Her favorite was www.annierexia.com. The sites of resistance, the guerrilla fighters of world food. How to do without, to exist on defiance with an apple for lunch, to live on the razor's edge between perfect brevity of body and the hospital. At all cost, said the Web-page star, do not let them put you in the hospital. As a prisoner of war, they can do anything to you, restrain you, and take away privileges. At the very worst, they will slide a feeding tube down your throat and defile you with a disgusting mixture of blended drinks that no one should have to endure.

Melissa shuddered with pleasure. Her nipples tightened at the heroic Web-page girl. She was ashamed for not being as brave, as strong, as perfectly beyond her body as Annie was. She couldn't possibly be called Annie, could she? Melissa's friend Krystal had been her starving partner last year, but now Krystal had a boyfriend and she had lost her edge and lost her time to be with Melissa.

As if by magic, Lissa spotted a new flag on the site that said, *Going Solo*. She clicked on it and the text sprang up.

"If everyone has left you, and gone back to food it's because you have something that they don't. You are ready to cross over. I'm not stopping. Are you?"

Her breath stopped, and then she clicked off, suddenly fearful. She had a cooked egg white waiting for her downstairs that she would have to eat by tomorrow morning, but the whole day could stay under 700 calories. She could easily move down to 600.

Was she just average, soft, not special in any way? She had to remember to put tampons on the shopping list on the fridge. She couldn't let her mother know that her period had stopped. This was the third month and she had nearly forgotten to keep up the pretense. She padded silently down the stairs and into the kitchen.

She pushed the hardboiled egg across the plate, separating the yoke from the whites, and with deliberate strokes, cut the egg white into tiny cubes.

She stood at the kitchen table, refusing to sit. She burned more calories standing. Already, her body was chilled, her skin springing into goose flesh. She looked down at her hands and noted the strange bluish color. This was something new. Just like the lightheaded feeling when she stood up quickly.

She wrote her schedule in small letters, numbering each task, listing the amount of time for each one. The cubes of egg white looked like granite blocks on her plate. She lined them up in grids, a small pile for each direction, north, south, east, and west. After she finished her calculus, she could eat the northern pile. After finishing the calc, she let one pile of cubes plunk dangerously into her belly. She waited an hour before eating the next pile and by then she was done with her chemistry and well into rewriting her history notes. She loved the way her schoolwork looked in the late hours of the night, each pile of work lined up perfectly straight. When she wrote, she used a precisely sharpened pencil, so that errors could be erased, and rubbed clean. By the time she was done with her homework, the books were lined up on the Formica counter, ready to be stuffed in her book bag early Monday morning. Two piles of egg cubes were left, and because her belly did not feel expanded, she pierced the rest with one tine of the fork, careful not to touch her teeth. This last group of creamy cubes had to wait on her tongue, pressing them to the roof of her mouth. The cubes had to compress into flat compliance, then of their own will, they dissolved, traveling the long journey over the rough backside of the tongue, down where throat muscles must squeeze and push and escort the flecks of egg to the unwelcome cavern of the stomach. She knew she had to wait, uneasy, and that she had to count to one hundred several times because she promised to eat, to let the cubes stay in her body. The dog, who labored in determination to come down the stairs to be with her, positioned his black body at her feet. His body glowed with warmth and she placed her feet under the blanket of his belly.

Chapter 9

"Dear, do you want to kill something?" asked Tess.

"No. I want to learn archery, feel the Zen of centering, pulling the bow, then the release," said Rocky.

The dog stood up and with the barest limp, repositioned between the women and the door. Tess winced, as she always did when she saw the dog limp. She squeezed her shoulders up to her ears, then released them with a shuddering sigh and shook herself.

"There is something oddly perverse about you wanting to learn about bows and arrows after this dog was nearly killed by a fool shooting him."

"I know, but I can't stop thinking about it," said Rocky. "You would think I would be repulsed by the idea of archery, but I'm not. I don't want the dog to know. I mean I won't do it around him. I won't even keep the stuff here. I'll go over to the mainland. I looked up some places."

"Why don't you take up Tai Chi or Qi Gong. Why must you allow yourself to be pulled to something so hard and straight, and without mercy?"

Tess was helping Rocky winterize her cottage. They hung

plastic on the windows in the living room and her bedroom. Rocky plugged in her hair dryer and aimed it at the plastic that was attached to the window frame with double-stick tape. All the fold marks from the packaging remained. She aimed the hair dryer slowly up and down, making a path from top to bottom following the directions on the cardboard insert.

"Oh, that noise!" said Tess, putting her hands over her ears. "It's bright green and disagreeable. That hair dryer must be as old as I am. I'll be outside until you finish."

Rocky kept shrink wrapping her windows and paused for a moment wondering what it would be like to be Tess and have sharp noises be green, see the days of the week as big cubes that each hold their own niche in space. When Tess learned that Rocky was interested, she let her know more and more of her synesthete world. Tess didn't hide it from people, but she didn't elaborate unless she knew someone was truly interested. Tess told her that a Ford Taurus on her road hums like an air conditioner from the 1970s, with a tinge of blue. When Tess whacks her elbow or stubs her toe, that part of her body glows bright orange and sends sharp orange lines along her nerves all the way to her brain.

Rocky turned off the hair dryer. She saw the strong wave of Tess's white hair as she walked past the deck, inspecting something along the ground. The dog sat sentinel at the door, knowing that his pack was divided, one out and one inside. His look of distress suddenly lodged in Rocky. She had seen dogs do this before, when she and Bob had taken in foster dogs. Before they knew it, the dog had become part of their pack and took a role that was either protector or protected, either the alpha or the puppy. This was now her world, a dog who could not tell her his secret and a woman who held her ears to keep out the bright green noise of a hair dryer. And she had a palpable yearning to put her hands on a bow and pull back the string.

Despite Tess's warning about archery, she looked in the Yellow Pages for sporting goods stores in Portland and called while Tess was outside. She phoned the very first one listed, Sporting Equipment Store, and asked if they had archery supplies. Ron Wilcox, the owner, said, "We got all the compound bows. What we ain't go, you can order."

When Tess returned to the little house, and the dog visibly relaxed with a sigh, Rocky explained that she had found the store that she was looking for.

"But I didn't understand something that he told me," Rocky said. "What's a compound bow?"

Tess shrugged. "How should I know? I'm a retired physical therapist gone Buddhist, not a sports woman."

Rocky drove her own car, ever doubtful of the yellow truck's legal standing off island. Lloyd seemed well enough for a car trip, so she brought him for the ride. He was the perfect passenger.

The mainland seemed suddenly foreign to Rocky. The smell of the ocean was still present along the streets of Portland, but less dense. She had a growing sense of what living on an island meant. She was keenly aware that she was living on the tip of a mountain surrounded by ocean. But more often she felt like the entire island was a loosely anchored raft. She woke in the middle of the night and worried that the island was unsubstantially connected. What would it take for it to break free? On the mainland, the land felt suddenly still, and the 3,000-mile stretch from coast to coast bore down on her as she turned the knob on the Sports Equipment Store. A bell clattered overhead as the door jarred it.

A large-bellied man held open the pages of a magazine. He looked up from behind the desk. Behind him was an arsenal of guns, riflescopes in glass cases, pistols resting like reptiles under the glass countertops. She smelled oil and metal.

"I called yesterday about archery equipment?"

Rocky was suspect of other women who ended statements as if they were questions and now she wondered if women did this when they were afraid. This store felt like the suburban Pentagon and she was an unwelcome delegate from the UN.

"Yeah, over here," Ron said as if he were a hunter leaving his blind. "Is this for you or someone else?"

"For me."

"What draw weight are you looking for?"

Rocky was amazed at how quickly she could be stripped naked in places like car garages, lumberyards, or now, sporting supply stores.

"I've never used a bow before. I don't know anything about it. What do you mean, how much weight?"

She followed Ron past the camouflage vests and pants, hip waders, hats with flaps over the ears, folding camp chairs, all the way to the back of the store where archery supplies were lined up.

"I'm gonna expand this section next year. We've got more people looking into archery. There's more houses smack in the middle of the woods, less room to hunt with a gun. With these, you only need a good twenty yards, the closer the better. What do you plan to hunt?"

"Nothing. A target, I guess. I just want to learn how to do it."

Rocky looked at the bows, complicated devices with pulleys that looked like a combination of technology and medieval utility. This was not what she was expecting. He explained how the pulley system on the compound bow did some of the work and that the archer did not have to exert as much power consistently.

"Are these the only kind you have?"

"These are the only kind I have in stock," he said.

"When did bows start to look like this?"

"Back in the seventies. These compound bows are all anyone ever asks for," he said.

Rocky remembered she had the remains of the arrow that had nearly killed Lloyd. She pulled it out of her bag.

"I mean this sort of arrow, a bow for this."

She held up the broken arrow.

"Oh, now that's a different thing altogether. You're looking for someone who's into traditional archery. I don't do that here." He folded his arms across his chest to close the conversation.

"Who does?" asked Rocky, crossing her arms over her chest.

She followed him back to the counter. The wall behind the counter was covered with business cards. He pulled the tack out of one of them and handed a card to Rocky. "This guy hunts with traditional bows. Hill Johnson. He used to give lessons. I don't know if he still does. He's up in Brunswick. You can't have the card; it's the only one I got. You need a pencil to write down his number?"

She thanked him and left. While she drove, Lloyd sat in

the passenger seat. Rocky had cracked the passenger window several inches to clear the car of dog breath. As they drove, Lloyd turned his snout to a tendril of scent going by a restaurant. And then he leaned his upper body toward the window and tilted his nose skyward as he savored the breeze filled with smells unnoticed by humans. Lloyd closed his eyes and his soft lips fell into a Lab smile.

She pulled into a Dairy Mart to a get a Coke, full sugar variety. She hoped that the man who taught lessons and who used traditional bows was not a weird survivalist. She imagined he would be older, a lot like the man who ran the sporting goods store.

As she got out of the car, Lloyd assumed a more proprietary posture and looked like a regal walrus, staring casually ahead. Even though it was early December, she opened her window a crack also and opened the roof vent. She looked back with encouragement at the dog.

"I'll be right back."

A green-and-black SUV pulled in right next to her, too close, and she said under her breath, "Big asshole." She would have to get in on Lloyd's side of the car.

She went to the front door and with studied sarcasm, held the door open for the tight-jawed man who leapt from the vehicle. Rocky wanted him to say something, she wanted to let loose with a tirade about guzzling eighty percent of the world's resources so that he could drive his Behemoth to the Dairy Mart. But both of them stopped dead as the black Lab went off like a bomb in the car. The hair on Lloyd's back stood up straight and the car rocked as he thrashed his body.

"Jesus, Lloyd. Cut it out. What's gotten into you?" The

man did a double take when he saw Lloyd and then looked hard at Rocky.

"Is that your dog?" he said.

"Yeah, I don't think he likes you," said Rocky.

He offered her a contemptuous look, but since Lloyd did not let up his show of force, the look was brief. Rocky noticed that his brown hair was short, but just long enough to be meticulously combed to one side. He stumbled backward to his vehicle and seemed to forget whatever he had needed at the store. He made a tire squealing exit.

Rocky went back to her car. The dog stopped as quickly as he had begun, yet the fur on his back was still raised in ominous warning. Rocky ran her hand over his head to settle him and she imagined the danger button in his body switching back to the off position. "So you're not mister nice guy all the time," she said.

The entire encounter took about one minute and Rocky wondered if she should have paid more attention. She wondered if Lloyd knew that guy and if he did, why did Lloyd want to rip off his head? Bob had said that some people give dogs the creeps and there was no explanation.

Later that evening she called Hill Johnson to set up an initial lesson in two days. Rocky stumbled when she told him that she wanted to learn archery and he let her. That was the first thing she noticed about him. He listened and she imagined him watching her over the phone.

"Are you still there?" she asked him.

"I'm here. I was waiting for you to finish. The best thing to do is to come out and try it once, then decide if you want lessons," he said.

Later that week, they stood in Hill's backyard in Brunswick.

Rocky asked him about his name. "Hill? You mean Hillary? That must have been a tough one in junior high."

"Nothing tough about it. It's a family name and Hill is what I've always been called. Only my grandmother called me Hillary and she's no longer with us," he said.

His archery shop took up half of his garage, right on the apex of a cul-de-sac street. Hill looked younger than she was by more than a few years and taller than she had expected. She was startled by his features, the combination of dark, rich eyebrows highlighting his face in contrast to an adolescent rosiness in his cheeks. And his eyes did not exactly match; one eye was blue-green and the other was green-blue. An unexpected nudge from her lungs forced her to take in more air and her torso shifted forward toward Hill's slightly oversized chest men can get, offering a preview of future expansion. She pulled back instantly.

If Rocky had seen him in Stop n Shop, she was pretty sure he'd be cruising the meat department, followed by the bread aisle. They hadn't gone into his house, instead they had skirted around his garage to his backyard.

Rocky assumed the lessons would begin immediately. His backyard extended at least an acre and bumped up against a railroad track. Two paper targets were tacked to hay bails. He handed Rocky a bow. "My wife started on this one," he said. "This is a good size for you."

She was relieved there was a wife. Now they could be all business without an undercurrent of sexual tension. She hefted the bow in her hands and attempted to look knowledgeable but quickly decided to drop the pretense. "I don't even know where to start and I'm not sure what I'll do with this."

Anyone who had watched her miniature performance, the relief when he said wife, the defensive posture when he handed her the bow, the decision to drop her defenses, and the admission of her novice standing, would have thought that she was a complicated woman. Hill chose to attend to archery.

"Today, you'll start with breathing and flexing your knees. If you can become still enough, you'll move up to pulling the bowstring."

"I notice you didn't include arrows. No arrows?"

"No. Too breezy anyhow." There had not been one hint of breeze until that moment and suddenly the treetops began to dance.

"Good call," she said.

Rocky discovered that she had become gradually inaccurate at judging ages, but as she watched him more closely, she guessed that he was late twenties, early thirties, even though his dark hair sprouted an early scattering of white near his temples. Something about him said military. Way too young for the Gulf War. Maybe just ROTC and a tour of duty. Maybe back from Iraq. National Guard. What was it that looked so military about him? No, not military. He was a hunter.

"I just watched the weather channel," he said and let her have a loose, slightly crooked smile. "I'm one eighth Lakota, but I don't think one eighth of anything counts for much. I'm half Irish, and then some Austrians got into the mix. Then there's the English part. That's where Hillary came from. I bet the Indians even watch the weather channel." Rocky noticed that the only people who said "Indian" anymore usually were Native Americans.

"OK, stand sideways with your left side closest to the target. Turn your head to face the target. No, just your head, not your shoulders; they're like the arrow. Your arms and shoulders are going to become part of the whole arrow. You're holding a lot of energy between your shoulder blades, let it drop down until you can feel your feet touching the earth."

The wind picked up, carrying messages from the south. Rocky's tightly curled hair flipped up, exposing her forehead, making her feel naked. She shook her head around to get the hair to come back down. They practiced soft knees, turning heads, shoulders going still. They practiced finding her center, dropping energy down, pulling energy up, breathing from the belly, letting all the breath out, and then the deeper stillness.

"Everyone wants to pull the arrow back and let her rip. That's like saying to a mathematician, 'What's the final answer?' The arrow is the least of it. What did you eat before you came here? Your energy is too high up in your body."

"I can't remember. Let's see, I had a juice and coffee. I haven't had lunch yet."

"That's part of it," he said getting into the stance himself. "Watch me. Tell me what you see."

He closed his eyes for a few seconds and turned to the side. His thick eyelashes rested on his cheeks. His chest and belly filled up with air. He opened his eyes. On the release of breath, he turned his head with hydraulic fluidity. His shoulders were back and down. He looked like a tree trunk swaying with imperceptible movement. And then he entered stillness. He pantomimed pulling back an arrow with his right hand, which glided smoothly from a spot an arm's length in front of his back to his ear. Finally he released the imaginary arrow. Rocky thought she could hear the thwack of it hitting the target. Her eyes darted to the target despite what her brain knew. She looked back at Hill, who remained in his still posture. She knew he had noticed that she looked at the target. Tiny muscles around his lips struggled to keep from smiling.

"In this posture, nothing should be able to knock me over. It's like being anchored to the ground, but the upper body can stay flexible. Push me," he said. "Hard."

"This demonstration is not going to be very effective, if you're trying to show how powerful you are against equal strength. I don't have a lot of brute strength these days. I must have left it somewhere else," said Rocky, feeling strangely hypnotized by his movements.

"Well, give a really big push, then."

What was the point of this, that a woman would ricochet off him in an attempt to tackle him? She was suddenly irritated at the predictability of the exercise. There was something about the hint of childhood taunting that motivated her in the moment. She impulsively put her head down and dove into him with her shoulder, the way she had seen football players do. She imagined the man as firmly planted as a tree, so the point of this demonstration was to show what little impact she could have on him, and she simply did not care. She wanted to hit someone hard. She plowed into him with a force that welled up from dank, unused places. She knocked him over. Or more exactly, he seemed to collapse like a bridge that had rusted out.

"Damn," he said from the ground. "I never know when

that knee will go out. Football is a surgeon's favorite sport, a real moneymaker. All this from playing football at a state college, division-three ball." He rubbed his knee from his flat-back position. "You sure you want to learn archery? You have potential in the more aggressive sports, like hockey."

Hill stood up, rubbed his knee some more and said, "Practice breathing, practice everything you did today, except the part where you tackled me. I've got space for one more student. I lost a student a few months ago. Oh wait, I'm assuming you want the lessons. Do you?"

Rocky had not tackled anyone with such satisfaction since sixth grade when she could still overpower Caleb. And she had not touched another man, other than griever's hugs, since Bob had died.

"Are you sure you're not hurt? Yeah, I want to sign up for lessons. I'm not a hunter. But there's something about archery. I want to learn how to do this."

Hill grabbed his jacket from the picnic table and put it on. "Lots of people will start something like archery, but when it gets hard, they quit. How about you, what do you do when things get hard?"

What did she do? She shoved her hands into her pants pockets. "I don't quit," she said.

They scheduled lesson two for the following Wednesday afternoon at three. Hill offered to give her some of his paper targets, complete with his special stamp in the lower right corner, but Rocky declined; she had bought her own at the Sports Equipment Store. Hill taught English at Brunswick High School and Wednesday was the only day he didn't stay late. Rocky tried to picture an English teacher grading papers after a day of shooting deer.

Chapter 10

Lesson two was harder.

"The first thing we have to do is test for eye dominance. That will tell us which hand will hold the bow and which will pull the bowstring," said Hill.

"I'm right-handed," said Rocky.

"That may be, but we don't know if you're right-eyed or left-eyed. Hold both hands out at arm's length, put your hands loosely together like this so there's a hole to look through. Keep both eyes open and look at the center of the target. Keep it in focus and slowly move your hands toward your face. Keep going, slow and steady."

This was already more personal than she imagined, she just wanted to shoot the arrow. Aim and shoot. This felt like going to the doctor. She pulled her hands toward her slowly.

"Your hands are pulling over to the left eye. Center the hole over your left eye and focus on the target. Now do the same thing over the right eye. Which one is it?"

Hill stood with his legs spread wide, his arms rested lightly at his sides. He waited for Rocky to figure out what he already saw.

"It's my left eye. How can that be?"

Hill shrugged. "Happens all the time. People think that their eyes work the same way on each side. We are not symmetrical. Let's see how strong your left arm is. That's where the trouble lies; we have to balance out strength with accuracy."

He put a bow in Rocky's hands. "This is the long bow, the only kind of traditional bow that I use. It's not fancy like the recurve bow, but I prefer it. Take a wide stance, right side to the target. Hold the bow with your right hand and pull the bowstring with your left. Point your elbow higher, pull your hand right up near your jawline. We'll work on finesse later."

Rocky struggled to pull back the bowstring. Her arm shook with the effort. Soon the entire bow was wobbling as she grimaced and finally pulled back the string. Then she did the same on the opposite side; left side facing the target, left hand holding the bow, right arm pulling the bowstring. Her arm pulled the string back in a nearly steady effort. Rocky felt her face pull into a smile.

"There's our answer. Your right-handed dominance is going to be more important than your left-eyed dominance. You pulled the bowstring back in a smooth line with your right hand. That's the good news. The bad news for you is, that's a child's bow. You've got a lot of work to do."

Rocky's shoulders slumped. "That's a kid's bow? What the hell does a real one feel like?"

"You're about to find out." Hill flipped a tarp off the wood picnic table and an array of bows appeared.

When it seemed to Rocky that Hill had found her lacking in the archery department, the competitive spirit in her flamed to life. When had she last really wanted something, wanted to get better at something? She was horrified when Hill gave her a child's bow after her quivering inability to pull back a bowstring with even a thirty-pound draw weight. And then the final insult still left her reeling.

"You don't have enough mass, and what you have is not muscle mass. Let me say this in another way; you don't have enough weight in the right places in the right density. Your ability to knock me over had to do with a combination of my bad knee and lucky physics, and I think you were also pissed off at something, but that's your business. I'm trying to say this with some degree of sensitivity because I've heard of men being murdered for even mentioning weight in refer-ence to a woman. But plainly speaking, you just don't have enough mass."

Rocky pondered this on the drive back to the ferry. She put her hand to her thigh and wondered if this leg was hers. Wasn't hers bigger, ready to spring? Standing at the dock, waiting for the ferry, she opened her coat and put her hand on her waist, inched upward and connected with a set of newly exposed ribs that had not been there six months ago. She put her thumbs into her waistband and pulled out. Pants that had once been snug now gapped by inches. Rocky carried the child's bow under her arm, zippered in its canvas case. Like everyone else, Rocky headed for the enclosed room on the ferry. The wind was too cold for even the hardiest passenger.

What worried her most was not that she had lost weight, but that she had not noticed it happening. Were other things happening as well?

Bob would have noticed right away if she had lost this much weight. First, his hands would have noticed, a hand on her breasts or her hips. His hands would have paused, retracted from passion to medical analysis. He would have said, "Don't go skinny on me. I need something to hang on to." Then later, his eyes would have followed her, tracing her face, and with economical accuracy, her glutes. As she walked by his chair, he would have grabbed her, wrestled her into a playful struggle.

"Rocky, we need healthy mares in this pasture, the kind that eat and whose ribs don't show from across the road and their rumps are firm and happy, winking at all the studs." And she would have punched him hard on the arm and said, "You're starting to worry me with all your horse talk." But that's what would have happened if Bob were there. Bob was dead.

The next day was shrill with sunshine and cold wind. She had no place that she had to be; no animal calls had come in, and even Isaiah was gone today so that an impromptu visit at his office was not possible. Then she remembered her body. This was the first day that Rocky truly remembered she had a body. "If I was not in my body, where have I been?" she wondered.

Bob was seven months dead. Her dreams were laden with the exhaustion of searching for him, but as much as she longed to see him again, she feared recrimination for not saving him. When she did find a wisp of him, an echo, or feather touch, she could not bear to wake with the renewed grief of knowing him only in her dreams. Since banishing Bob from her dreams, she could recall no dreams at all.

The winter sun had come in hard and low and touched her arms. The thin hairs on her forearms, invisible at other times, were now backlit and harsh. The winter air was cold and deep. Angry cells from her skin stood up and caught the rake of the sun's light. "I'm falling apart, I want to be back in my body again. How did I fall out of my body?"

If she were back home, she could get a massage, or cranial-sacral something, Reiki, acupressure, deep Swedish massage, anything to put herself back together again before her bones flew apart, before her ears fell off and her skin unzipped. But on the island, there was no one who did any of those things. Well, Tess could but Rocky feared coming undone under her expertise and she wasn't ready to fall apart in front of Tess. She would have to do the putting together herself.

She stepped out of her clothes and they fell around her like petals. The rental house had a long mirror, but she had taken it down when she first moved in and slid it behind the couch. She pulled it out again, pounded a nail into the living room wall and hung it. She stared a long time at her face, at her torso, her legs, at the uneven trouble of hair in the middle of her body. The first place she could bear to touch was her knees, and she ran her thumb over and around her knee-caps, owning first one and then the other, wondering how to reconstruct herself. The cat and dog watched her from a pool of sunlit floor. Peterson the cat had recently agreed to sit in the same room with Lloyd.

Maybe she had lost weight, so what? It's not unusual after a death. A spouse might lose weight, gain weight, come down with an autoimmune disease or crash their car in a late-night one-car accident. What truly astounded Rocky was that she had not noticed. Hadn't she always had broad shoulders? Now they just looked angular. The swimmer's build, Bob had called it. When they first married, he introduced her as the one with the shoulders. Somehow, he had made her more real, gave her definition, without her ever noticing how it happened.

She thought she had been real enough before they met, before she had seen him swimming laboriously in the town pool, his dense bones dragging him down, paddling like a large poodle, straining to keep his head above water. Surely she had been the one to be in the physical realm, to know her body. She had been the one with the whistle around her neck, the SPF 30 on her nose, pausing to ask him, "Do you need assistance?" And he, barely able to ask one more thing of his body such as turning his head, had eyed her with one eye, the way a whale might, and with the same effect. If a whale ever looks right at you, with its one-sided watery vision, you are never the same.

With much sputtering, Bob had dog-paddled his ultra dense bones to the side of the pool and said, "I've been working on this all summer. If you think this is bad, you should have seen me in June."

She didn't know where he'd been practicing his tortuous swimming program, but it had not been here at the town pool because she had been life guarding all summer each afternoon.

He had pulled himself out of the pool with all the grace of an unfortunate elk that had fallen in, and he grappled and slipped and finally pulled himself to a seated position. Rocky was fascinated by his determination. She squatted down and extended a muscled arm and said, "That was a most extraordinary pool exit."

Maybe that was it, that first touch, culminating in the combination of her well-defined body and his determined body, undefined but denser than a black hole, coming together in a way she had not imagined.

"I can show you how to make more efficient use of your strokes," she said.

He later told her that was the best line he had ever heard. He had just graduated from veterinary school. She had one more year of grad school before completing her doctoral degree in psychology.

She lifeguarded right through graduate school at Iowa State University and had been the target of no little teasing among her psychology classmates. "Complexes about saving people should be more subtle. Don't you think lifeguarding at the town pool is too dramatic?" asked Glen, her study partner in statistical research. "I only want to save myself."

They started swimming lessons and dating simultaneously; a one-hour lesson after Rocky was off duty followed by sandwiches at the bagel place across from the university. Each lesson was more fascinating to Rocky than the one before. Bob's body was unlike anyone else's she had ever encountered. He was a stone, filled with granite instead of blood and bone marrow. She had always been able to teach even the most water-phobic person to swim, teaching them about their breath, relaxing their spine to float, eventually rejoicing at seeing the newly found freedom when a first-time swimmer skimmed across the pool like a water spider.

"What happens if you just try to float, or even lightly tread water?" she asked him on the third swimming lesson.

"I'll show you," he said as he stopped his vigorous stroking and kicking. He became horizontal in the water for a moment, languidly moving his arms, and as if his feet were extra dense, he began to sink feet first, straight down. Rocky watched him slowly sink to the bottom of the twelve-foot depth, landing lightly on his toes. She expected him to spring back up, push off with his knees bent. But instead, he sank even more and sat cross-legged on the bottom of the pool and placed his palms on his legs.

Rocky waited a moment, treading water above him, and then waved at him to come up. Another moment passed. Then she jack knifed straight down to him, her head coming even with his, her feet kicking about her. She looked at him sternly and gave him a thumbs-up sign for him to get going. His cheeks were puffed up and he stared directly into her eyes and slowly began releasing the air out of his lungs.

Rocky's body went into the automatic training that had been ingrained into her brain and into every cell since she had first been trained as a lifeguard in high school. Here was a victim, and everything else about him was irrelevant. She gave a huge kick that brought her body down until her feet touched the slick bottom of the pool and she wrapped one arm around his neck and torso, and at the same time that she kicked off, she heaved him up and got her hip under him. She had never pulled anyone off the bottom except in practice and never anyone filled with granite. She aimed up and diagonally for the side of the pool. As they broke the surface, her fury gave an extra bolt of strength and she nearly threw him on the edge.

"What the hell is wrong with you?" she spit out.

Bob had swallowed a bit of water and coughed it out of his lungs. The lifeguard on duty came over and said, "Do you need help over here, Rocky?"

"I was just giving lessons to an idiot who decided to sit on the bottom of the pool and exhale." She waved off the life-guard. She glared at Bob, checked to see that he was pulling himself up on the ladder, then strong-armed herself on the side of the pool. "Don't ever pull that stunt again," she said.

"Look, I wanted to see what it would be like to be saved, to be really saved by an incredibly beautiful woman." He reached for her hand. "I was an asshole. I'm sorry."

As soon as he touched her she felt the jolt of energy going through her all over again. He smiled his big-toothed smile. "But if you had to, would you do it again, would you save me again?"

His penance was to be the official victim for the water-safety class. After they made love for the first time, he whispered to her, "I'm in love with a woman who won't let me drown. What an incredible extra."

She was ten years out of graduate school, and swimming took less and less time in her life. But she had still used it as a meditative cleansing, swimming laps, feeling her body blur with the watery sounds. Lunch hour offered her just enough time to swim thirty laps, shower, and dry her hair. Had she stopped when Bob died? She had to think back. Yes, there was the world before Bob died and the world after. It occurred to her that her swimsuit and towel waited for her back in a locker in a Massachusetts university along with shower gel, deodorant, and skin lotion.

She was going back to another archery lesson in seven days. She would pull back the damn child's bow and move up five pounds. She set up a practice target in back of Tess's house. She had already decided that Lloyd shouldn't see her in the act of archery. She didn't know what kind of post-traumatic stress disorder dogs could muster up, but it seemed cruel to expose him to a reminder of his nearly fatal encounter. And she was going to have to build her body back up again.

She spent the next day in Portland searching for an athletic club, signed up at the YMCA and got a trainer to work with her for an hour. The trainer was young and eager. He admonished her to go for a full-body, free-weights regime, and not just upper bodywork as she had requested.

"It doesn't matter if you used to be fit, you're starting from scratch," he said as he wrote down the number of the free weight that Rocky pushed over her head. Rocky stopped, and the two plastic coated, six-pound weights paused overhead like heavy birds. She slowly lowered them.

"You're right, I'm starting from scratch, aren't I?" She knew that this happened sometimes, that strangers could speak as sages, pulling truths from the air so deep that it seemed like they were momentarily inhabited by wisdom completely beyond them. Sometimes people get the offer of free advice from the gods, spoken by innocents, and there is always the choice of whether to listen or not, whether to act or not.

"That's what I'll do, then. Start from the beginning."

Chapter II

The track coach was surprisingly easy to fool. He was old, maybe as old as fifty. Melissa knew he was from pre-anorexia times; he just didn't get it and acted impressed about her well-defined calf and thigh muscles. He even held her up as an example in September when they started training for cross-country.

"Look at Melissa," he intoned to the team. "She doesn't have to huff and puff carrying around an extra ten pounds. Remember, picture yourself with a five-pound bag of sugar strapped to each shoulder. That's what extra weight does to you. Good job, Melissa. I can see you kept training this summer."

She figured at least four of the other girls went home that day and said they were too full to eat dinner. She could tell by the angry, frightened look in their eyes when the coach spoke. "Let them try," she thought, "they still won't catch me. I'm way ahead of them."

If she could have felt guilty, she would have done so about the depth of the deception with her mother, who was not easily fooled. Her mother asked, just the other day, "Is this going to be a problem? Is food going to be the enemy?" Melissa had put on her most shocked and exasperated look and rolled her eyes. "I've seen the after-school specials and heard the lectures in health class. You just don't know what it's like to take running to the limit. All the runners look like this." For added emphasis, Melissa put a hunk of cheese, an apple, and a PBJ sandwich in her book bag. On the ferry ride to the mainland school, she threw tiny bits of the sandwich to the seagulls that followed alongside, looking at Melissa with conspiratorial glances. She could hardly wait to throw the cheese into the trash barrel at school. She ate half the apple in history class and half at lunch, so that it appeared to everyone that she was constantly eating.

Chris was in her last class, Chemistry. She had known her since freshman year. Chris was gone for the last month of the freshman year. Everyone knew it was a suicide attempt. Then last year Chris was all GSA; Gay Straight Alliance Club. Melissa said to her, "Of course that doesn't matter to me. Everybody's the same to me." But she worried that if she hung out with Chris, people would think she was gay, too. She just wanted to make sure that people knew she wasn't gay.

Chris had talked the principal into announcing the GSA meetings over the morning radio station. It was like Chris had decided to become the most out lesbian on earth. Chris had changed in other ways, too. Melissa noticed that she had gained weight. Actually, she could tell exactly how much she had gained with perfect accuracy. Eight pounds. She knew what eight pounds looked like; hips, maybe as big as a size ten. Melissa knew she would never let that happen. Looking at Chris, she planned the 400 crunches she would do silently in her room that night with the lights out, with a towel folded in half beneath her so that she wouldn't bruise her vertebrae into a line of vertical dots.

But here was the first big lie. The mere deceptions didn't count. They were like playacting. But not telling her mother that she was going to the athletic club to work out was a lie. She had told her mother she was visiting a friend after school on Tuesday and Thursday, just for a while, walking around the Food Court in downtown Portland, a safe enough place. She knew her mother, and she knew that if she said she was working out any more that the careful balance she had constructed would collapse and questions would be asked in a more desperate way. Her mother was no fool and Melissa had the tiniest hint of regret about playing her for one.

She had her routine; go right to the Y after school on the days she didn't have cross-country practice, reserve forty-five minutes on the elliptical, and thirty minutes on the Stair-Master. That's all. Well, maybe a little run on the treadmill to shake it all out before working on the weights. Thirty minutes on the treadmill if there was no one else waiting. The time of day was right; no neighbors from the island came here, she had already checked for their names. Her mother's teacher friends all rushed home to take care of their kids, so they weren't even a possibility.

She walked into the women's locker room. She had asked for her favorite locker, 266, which was unfortunately taken. She hated it when someone else had it; so she asked for the one that was next to it, number 267. She dropped her bag on the wood-plank seat between two rows of lockers and headed for the toilets. She wanted an empty bladder, to feel as light as possible. She heard one of the showers shut off and the shower curtain shoosh open.

When Melissa came out of the stall and headed back to the

lockers, she stopped short. Seated on the bench was a woman with her back to Melissa, a towel hung loosely around her. What she saw was the perfect asymmetry of a moment, one shoulder blade poking out, the other in, as the woman twisted, paused in her moment of dressing. Her shoulders were wide and the muscles that ran down her back produced long gullies on either side of her spine. A blinding flush started in the recesses of Melissa's hard, flat abdomen and spread out like a kerosene-fed fire across her breasts, straight up the highway of her neck and pooled in her cheeks. Something had skipped her brain entirely and she felt, for the first time in her young life, a full out blast of lust.

The woman turned her head to the right, so that Melissa could see the profile. Melissa felt another competing rush, this time of loathing and fear. It was Rocky.

Why is she everywhere that's mine, why does she have to follow me around? Melissa ducked back around the corner, back to the stalls where she stayed with her pounding heart until she heard locker 266 slam shut.

Would anyone be able to tell what she was thinking, that she had been overwhelmed, caught in midair, breathless? The image of what she had to do came immediately and unbidden. No matter what, she was not eating anything tonight when she got home. She would simply tell her mother that she was sick. That would eliminate any dinnertime petitions to eat, or have soup, or please have something.

The thought of food, even not having food, had started the surge of her digestive juices, and she felt the cleansing burn of hunger, which she hoped would last all night and like the self-cleaning oven that worked by extreme temperatures would, with surgical exactness, cleanse her of such terrifying emotions.

She wanted something really awful to happen to Rocky. Maybe she would get bit by a rabid animal, lightning would strike her, or maybe her propane stove would blow up. No, not that. Melissa didn't want anything bad to happen to Lloyd. She had moments of relief when she was with the dog.

She felt her world begin to split open with Rocky's dead-aim stare, the way she looked through Melissa's sweatpants and jacket and hooded sweatshirt. Everything was fine until Rocky got here.

Now Rocky had invaded her secret place. If she could figure out when Rocky was going to come to the club, she could avoid her. But Melissa had a schedule that was perfect. Everything had been perfect, even the way that she showered, grabbed a Diet Coke and an apple on the way out, carried the apple while she was exiting and took two big bites, one while she opened the door from the women's locker room, chew and swallow, and one bite while she passed the front desk. When she got outside, she could spit the second bite out. Save the rest of the apple for the ferry ride home. Make sure to bring both the Diet Coke bottle and the apple core home, drop them both noticeably on the counter in a way that her mother couldn't miss. The Diet Coke made the charade believable; her mother never would have believed a non-diet drink.

She was going to make sure that she went to her father's house this weekend. She needed to become invisible and there was no better place to do that. When she was at her father's house on the mainland, every other weekend for sure and every weekend if she wanted, he simply didn't notice. She didn't have to work as hard with him to keep up the pretense of eating.

Her father had his own body-fat ratio measured and asked her if she wanted to also. "Runners don't need to carry extra fat around," he said. Of course he meant his body, not hers, or so he said, but Melissa had already swallowed it like a fish swallowing a hook.

Her father ran every Saturday with his buddy from law school, Alex. She declined their offers to run with them. They were in their forties and she couldn't understand why they wore such tiny running shorts. She was embarrassed for them and embarrassed to be with them. They looked so old and sinewy.

While her father and Alex ran on Saturday mornings, she prepared her lunch. She woke up thinking about food, went to sleep thinking about food and this worried her. Was she losing her grip, her control? She didn't want to think of food, but since she still did, she planned to whip it into obedience. One rice cake and cucumber for lunch. The cucumber was peeled, then cut in half the long way, then in half the other way, then she held all the long spears together and chopped those into chunks. She filled a cereal bowl with the cucumbers and threw in one-half cup of nonfat yogurt. By 11:30, her father and Alex were generally in the home stretch. By the time he came in the door, she was seated at the table with the bowl in front of her, a rice cake in hand.

"Eating again, honey? I don't know where you put it."

Chapter 12

Rocky expected to see improvement; this was the third lesson. She had worked out a deal with Tess to use the old clunker car that Tess kept on the mainland. Often, if people could find a spot in Portland to leave another car they did, rather than paying for the more expensive car ferry. Rocky knew she was ready to move up to a heavier bow and part of her was eager to hear Hill say, "Good pull and release. This is the day to move up to a twenty-five-pound bow."

She had practiced for two hours each day behind Tess's house. She stood with her left side facing the target, set the arrow, pulled out and up, right arm pulled back, elbow up, right thumb even with her jaw, sighted the target, took a breath, steadied the body, released the breath, then in the empty space between breaths, released the arrow. When she had first started, the arrows had flown wildly over, under, and to the side of a target, which was the size of a garbage can lid. The first time that the arrow actually hit the target, she was amazed at the thrill she felt.

Tess, who knew nothing about archery but a lot about Qi

Gong, said it was the repetition, through repetition comes freedom.

"Repetition gives the body a chance to expand and be creative. Look anywhere in nature, in concentric rings in sunflowers. Look down from an airplane the next time you fly and look at cornfields in the Midwest in all their wonderfully repeated rows. That lets us see the exception in the change. Your body is getting the hang of this Rocky, even if your brain can't believe it," said Tess.

She was anxious for Hill to see the improvement. She had eaten breakfast and lunch and the last time she checked, her energy was right where it was supposed to be, dropped down low in her body. She parked Tess's car on the street in front of his house. She walked to the backyard after not finding him in his shop garage. He was already pulling back on his sixty-five-pound bow as if it were no harder than the rubber band that secured the Sunday paper. Thwack! He hit as close to the center as an arrow could get.

There was no question of startling him, she knew that. He was a hunter and he listened to sounds like any wild animal. Rocky pictured him noting the sound of her car door closing, the knock on the shop door, and the way she had let the gate slap shut when she came into the backyard. For the first time, she noted that Hill moved his body in a way that was graceful. She had always liked that in a man, whether he was a dancer or a roofer; some men moved with grace and Rocky had an appreciative eye. His shoulders swiveled in perfect opposition to his hips. She had forgotten that she appreciated anything.

She greeted him with sudden shyness, and tried to pull back hard into a sisterly approach with him, as if he was Caleb, and she was commenting on one of his sculptures. Hill tipped his head slightly as if he was scanning her for important information. After the general greetings, she unzipped her bow from the canvas bag. She took her stance, and began to slow her breathing. She prepared to pull back.

"Are you married?" asked Hill from his perch on the picnic table.

She crumbled minutely in her core, let her arms drop, and she paused to figure out her answer. She was baffled. Why did people have to ask this? Wasn't she enough as she was? But as soon as he asked, she was thrown into a whirlwind of decisions. Was she married? Surely she felt the same attachment as someone who was married; every single night she missed her husband's body next to hers. She had not divorced, she had neither asked for or been asked by another to divorce. But no, of course this was different. Finally, she said, "Not anymore, I'm not married anymore."

He picked up his bow again and walked toward Rocky. "Tough answer. Simple question," he said. "I've thrown you off. Sorry. Let me take a couple of shots while you recuperate."

He turned his left side to the target. "Here's where archery is like fencing. Remember, these are weapons of battle and in battle you want to expose the least amount of body surface to the enemy. No full frontal attacks. Your side can take an arrow, and it's better if you're a lefty so your right side faces the enemy. Keeps your heart farthest away and protected."

"I'm right-handed and left-eyed," said Rocky.

"I know. You'll have to watch your heart."

She wondered if she heard everything as a double entendre, was everything a sign? Why would she have to watch her heart? All she had wanted this morning was to hear the validating words from Hill that she had gotten stronger, that he could tell she had been practicing. She suddenly hated that she cared what he thought.

The wind started to pick up from the east and tossed Rocky's hair forward. She still wasn't used to hair that needed so much training. Long hair had been easier; braid it, tie it up, clip it. But this was different. She armed herself with a pocketful of clips to pull her chin length hair out of her eyes. On the island, she took to wearing a baseball cap for just that reason.

"What did you say you did out on the island?"

"Animal Control Warden."

He leaned his upper body slightly forward and with one motion he pulled the bowstring back with his right arm and extended the bow with his left.

"I'm sighting the target with one eye. The thing that takes awhile to get is to stop your breath. But you've been practicing, right? Your footsteps sounded eager when you came in, not dragging reluctantly like the kid who hasn't done her piano lessons. Right there, that's the stillness. Now the winds will want to carry it to the left. Account for that, use it, use all the information that you have, and release."

His arrow went true to the center of the target. Rocky saw the flawlessness of his movements, the sparseness of motion that comes with practice, where every muscle knows its job perfectly and springs to service. She had a feeling that even if his brain was absent for the moment, his body would remember the pull and release, the pause between breaths.

"What do you hunt?"

"Do you mean what do I kill? Deer mostly. I had a friend who taught me to take down pheasants. I liked that." He pantomimed by pivoting on his heel, pulled back the arrowless bow, aiming first at a point near the ground then moving with amazing speed to a point forty-five degrees higher, and finally let go. Rocky could almost hear the thud of a pheasant hitting the ground, wings spread wide.

"Have you ever heard of a dog being shot by an arrow?" she asked.

He turned around and faced her. "A dog? Most people don't take dogs bow hunting because they keep the game away. But I have seen them hit, mostly by accident when a dog is in the wrong place. Why do you ask?"

She unpacked the borrowed bow and notched the arrow. "Because I found a dog a few weeks ago, four weeks now, who had been shot. That's how I found you, indirectly, asking about traditional bows. Then I got curious about shooting. So here I am." She took her stand and although she wished that she could erase his presence so that she could concentrate better, she could not. But she did pull smoothly. And the arrow did hit a good mid-zone on the target.

"Do it again," he said without further comment about the shot. "There's no bow season on your island. There was a special deer season declared a few years back to bring down the deer population, but it wasn't a bow season. So who shot the dog?"

"Nobody knows, or nobody is saying. Isaiah thinks it might have been a tourist."

"Who's Isaiah?"

"My boss, longtime resident, public works director, minister. Older Black man. There's probably more that he does but I don't know everything. He's a little sour on tourists these days. The last renters trashed his house."

Hill's jaw muscles tightened and his eyes narrowed slightly. "Anyone who is a skilled archer is not going to mistake a dog for a deer. There's no excuse for idiots like that who forget that they are working with a major weapon. Or worse yet, someone doing it on purpose. If someone was trying to shoot a dog on purpose and the dog lived, then they were a lousy archer to begin with."

"The dog is recovering. I've taken him in until his owners can be found, but that is looking less likely all the time. Usually, owners are either frantically searching for a dog or they don't want to be bothered. There's not much in between." Rocky paused, suddenly noticing the lack of something at Hill's house. No dog sounds, no dog barking inside. Wouldn't a guy like Hill have a dog? And his wife was never here, or if she was here, she was the quietest woman on earth.

"Do you have a dog?" asked Rocky.

Hill picked up the next weight bow with the twenty-five-pound draw, and handed it to Rocky without comment. "Used to. My wife and I are separated and the dog went with her. We had that dog for five years. She was a good strong mutt, smart as anything. Julie said I'm not home enough to have a dog. Let's see you try that bow," he said.

She was less accurate with the next size bow, but not bad, and she knew she'd be better by the next lesson. She knew she'd do even better if she could get more sleep, which still eluded her.

The dog's recovery was remarkable, flesh grew back with flesh, muscle accommodated, bones meshed. He had a limp that grew less noticeable, his large black body tweaking less to the left. But Rocky noted that his early-morning restlessness continued. She woke everyday by 4:30, pulling herself reluctantly from her dreams where she searched for Bob, scoured the land where souls of the dead live to catch a glimpse of him turning a corner, catch a scent of him. When she woke, exhausted from her journey into the land of death, the dog was always there, standing near her bed, his ears up in alarm, and with a whine coming from his throat.

As soon as she peeled back the covers, the dog appeared to relax, his ears settled down, and he put his nose into her hand.

"You too, big guy? Looks like neither of us can sleep."

She made coffee and they went outside to walk the beach. Walking brought her back into her body and she knew the dog needed to keep moving to get stronger. Tess had told her that physical therapy for the dog was important and Rocky added in a few more minutes of his walk every day.

In mid-December she left the island for one night, meeting with her brother about details of her house that had been rented out for the year. The temperamental furnace needed to be repaired or replaced. She knew Melissa would be at her father's house so she asked Tess to keep Lloyd for the night.

"Tess, will you keep Lloyd with you while I'm gone? It's easier if he stays on the island." She forgot to warn Tess about the dog's restlessness. When Rocky came back she said, "You're probably never going to take him again, are you? He's a restless guy at 4:30 in the morning. Sorry."

"What do you mean?" said Tess. "This guy didn't budge until I got up at seven. I'm not one of those old farts who gets up at dawn."

"No way. This dog is wide awake every morning at 4:30 when I get up," said Rocky.

Tess handed the bag of dog food to Rocky. "That's the hour of the distressed. Why are you waking up then?"

The truth of the situation hit Rocky. The dog woke up because she did. She was the one disturbing his sleep.

When she had been on the mainland, she read a newspaper article about dogs trained to alert people of impending seizures two hours prior to the event. It was speculated that they smelled the chemical change happening in the human. Maybe Lloyd smelled her sadness in a way that others couldn't sense. Bob used to tell her about the neurotic behavior of dogs who belonged to anxious people. Or of dogs who were overly protective of people who were afraid of everything, who were sure that criminals lurked in every corner. "There's not much about us that they don't know," he had said.

Rocky set the dog food back on Tess's counter. She knelt by the black Lab. She gave him her hand to sniff. "Lloyd, I think I'm keeping you awake at night. Sorry buddy."

Chapter 13

The dog still caught old wisps of her scent, once at the food store, again on a beach chair stacked near a restaurant, and when he did, the pain of first loss rose up in him. He knew, in the place where scent traveled through neuron, leaping over synapse to the perfect place in his brain, that she was dead. The smell of death was given to all dogs and it was carried back throughout time from the very first death when dogs came in from the bush to join humans.

It was a primordial scent that announced the end of one human, a different smell than the death of another dog. Once dogs joined the packs of humans, this smell was unlike all others. He knew she was dead, the one he had joined with, slept near, awaited, greeted, licked, cajoled into play, soothed through bad times, lowered her heart rate, her breath, sighed deeply to her to signal that it was time to go to sleep. And she in turn had loved him, remembered him, delighted him with food, thrilled him with car trips where he hung his great black head out the car window, and together they had been majestic.

She was gone. He had failed her, failed to protect her, and

save her. An unspeakable tear had ripped through them. His powerful nose tortured him in moments when a thread of her scent caught him off guard and made him halt in his tracks.

The new human who had saved him, and he knew that without her he would have perished, needed extra watching at night. By day he kept a leisurely vigil between her and the door, between her and unknown people. Her thin substance blew in and out of rooms, houses and cars as if she was the alpha one, and he let her. When she slept, her attempt at alpha nature evaporated and her terror began. He smelled it the first night, even groggy from his own surgery, his own disaster. He sensed the alarm, the hunt. Her body restless in sleep, carried traces of an ancient hunter, tracking senselessly, flailing about, sending off waves of scented pain to him.

He had tried to follow humans before into their dreamscapes and the road was treacherous. Following them meant abandoning his watch here, leaving the house unattended, and it was not wise to do so for long. Humans heard nearly nothing while they slept. And they smelled even less. He had experimented many times, walking right up to them in their slumber, holding his nose right up to theirs and still they slept.

To join them in dreaming was a drastic measure, but he feared for this human. He did not want to lose another. He waited until her breathing deepened, then grew quiet. He smelled her sleeping. He crept on her bed, careful to adjust his bulk to not wake her, although any dog would have roused long ago. He lowered his weight and pushed one paw toward her, touching lightly at her back and closed his eyes, chancing that he could find her in their dreams.

He fell through the waking and let himself wash away, perilously so. There, there she was, rushing through houses, opening any door, searching. A wave of acrid smoke caught him, with a flavor of desperation. She would be willing to do anything to find the one she hunted. Here is what he needed to know, she tracked a dead one. Now he understood. This was where she spent her nights. Only sickness will result from this journey of hers. He followed her all night, not needing to hide himself because she had eyes for nothing but her precious dead one. He left her weeping in the dust and could finally stay no more. He pulled himself out of the dream, back to his furred body, next to her in bed. He rose from the bed, walked to her side and whined in alarm until she opened her eyes.

Once she was awake, he urged her outside. The fresh air was a relief to him, blowing all her dream horrors away. They made their way to the beach, and each day, he urged her along a bit more, going farther every day.

Chapter 14

She could not afford to trust Rocky. The woman was rude and chaotic and she seemed to peer directly through Melissa's skin, into the abandoned quarry of her stomach. Yet when Rocky had asked if Melissa wanted a job walking Lloyd after school, she thought only of the chance to be with the black dog. Cross-country season was over. She could skip some of her workouts at the Y until Lloyd was fully recovered or until Rocky located his real owner. Right now, he needed Melissa. They had agreed that Melissa could take Lloyd for a walk every day if Rocky was not home by five. Once she had agreed and it looked like Rocky really had not seen her at the club, she was relieved that her efforts at extinguishing a momentary flaw had been successful. Let Rocky work out at the club, Melissa didn't care.

After school she hopped the ferry back to the island and walked the mile from the ferry to Rocky's house. She knocked to make sure that Rocky was out, even though the truck was gone. She found the key under the mat and let herself in, calling to Lloyd as she entered.

"Hey, Lloyd, it's me, just me." He greeted her with the unabashed joy that only a full-sized black Lab can offer. Direct, caressing, embarrassing, nose, lips, teeth, tail, and the snap of black claws on the linoleum. "Touch me, touch me!" signaled the dog as he offered his head, the scruff of his neck, and the favorite spot above his tail. "I have missed you more than anything, and now you have returned and I adore you," his body and dark brown eyes intoned to her.

Melissa let him out for the quick pee. She stood in the doorway, her thin hands rubbing the painted edges of the frame. He bounded back into the house, knowing that Melissa was, on this day, the bearer of food. She closed the door and it was just the two of them, which is how Melissa liked it. She sighed and for the first time that day, relaxed the barest fraction.

She opened the closet where a full-sized plastic garbage can held his fifty-pound bag of dog food. Rocky must have brought this from the mainland. Melissa scooped out three cups. Rocky had insisted that dry food was enough, but several times a week Melissa brought a can of wet food and Lloyd was guaranteed to do an appreciative dance at those times, bounding from one side to another for a few steps.

"Not tonight, sorry," she said.

He was a lay-down eater. That's what Rocky called him. He lay down with the dish between his front paws and dipped his head into the dish, eating his food in a surprisingly delicate manner, one kibble at a time. Melissa liked this part the best. She scooted near him, pressing her back against the wall, exhaling stale air of her restricted day as he ate with sureness and innocence. She marveled at this.

Melissa had eaten an apple at school, half for breakfast and half for lunch. She was so hungry that part of her thought of nothing else. By afternoon her head hurt and her thinking was jagged and filled with holes.

"You are so good, Lloyd. Everything about you is good."

He paused and lifted his ears as he listened to her, thumping his black tail twice at the sound of one of his favorite words.

Watching Lloyd eat was fascinating, as if there was nothing more amazing than seeing his sharp teeth crack open the fat kibbles, his long tongue guiding each one in, and finally delivering it to his throat. In between kibbles, the dog looked over at Melissa, and she thought she saw his eyebrows knit together.

He stopped eating; a few kibbles remained. He looked at the girl, and she saw her image reflected in the light of his eyes, a strange glint from the kitchen light giving her the opportunity to see her hair pulled tight, her eyes looked larger and not unlike a puppy. Lloyd stood, wagged his tail with encouragement, burped as best he could to welcome her and sat back on his haunches.

Her brain was rumpled, but her body read all the messages from Lloyd and slowly she reached forward, moving to her hands and knees until the dish was within reach. With her butt pushed up and her head down to the floor, she peered into the dog dish, and saw three kibbles amid the slick of saliva and Lloyd's oily scent. She looked back at the dog. She took his soft-mouthed smile as a sign. She put her face into the dish and opened her lips around one kibble, and tasted the sweet grain and meats. She scraped her teeth against it and she remembered a hundred flavors that had been lost for months. She softened each kibble in her mouth and swallowed.

Chapter 15

Rocky brought a weekly report into Isaiah's office. It was an accounting of dead animals removed from roadways, animals taken to the mainland, calls about lost cats, and calls requesting her help with troublesome animals. She also added, although Isaiah had said her level of detail was not necessary, an accounting of her walks on the shore, of sea gull carcasses, and of unusual high tides that ate a new inch out of the cove.

"You're not responsible for the work of the ocean," he said when he read one of her reports for the first time. "I know I mentioned that you could keep track of beach erosion, but I forgot that you would be such a scientist."

"I think there should be an accounting of it, of the changes. Someone should know that a gull died."

He put the report on his oil-stained desk, then he reached into a box beneath his desk and extracted a folder and put the report in it. He wrote on the manila folder with a ballpoint pen, "Life as recorded by the Animal Control Warden."

"Agreed. Write down everything happening on our fair island," he said.

And she did. After the dog came along, she added in his recovery and his speedy rehabilitation. She added in brief notes about her archery practice. One week she wrote, "Five hours archery, no change." The next week she recorded, "Moved up to the twenty-five-pound bow. Now it is hard all over again."

Rocky had just stopped by with the latest report. Isaiah read the report, nodded with approval and said, "I haven't asked you because you told me not to back in October. But is this helping you in any way, pretending to be who you are not? Is this all constructed so you don't have to talk about your husband? People handle death in all sorts of ways. I've seen some whoppers; people will try the never talking about it method, and on a rare occasion, it works. I can't say why, but it's not the way for most."

He had both of his hands wrapped around a blue coffee mug that said, "Mutual Life." Rocky still had her coat on and her nose stung from the cold wind that pummeled the island. She weighed her choices. There was something about the hiss of the woodstove and the way a jet of steam rose out of the dented aluminum pot of water on the stove and the way the black dog suddenly gave one deep-throated bark from her truck.

"Let me get the dog if we're going to talk awhile. He gets worried that I'll get into trouble if I'm gone too long."

Since the dog had come into her life, Rocky had been thinking more about bodies, about how everyone might live in bodies but only like a prom dress or a tuxedo, a costume for the play. She had watched Lloyd struggle with his injury, fight to survive, endure the worst loneliness and despair, just to keep living in his black-furred body that had miraculously healed. But his body had changed. His limp was integrated into a slightly altered body. Lloyd had a new life and a modified body.

Her body had changed also. First, after Bob's death, she had stopped caring about her body; exactly the opposite reaction of the dog. She'd lost interest in sustaining her lonely shell of a body. But somewhere between the dog and archery she had slid back into her arms and legs, wrapped her torso around her heart and lungs, and started making, and eating, grilled cheese sandwiches.

Rocky and Isaiah talked for hours, until his wife called and said where in the world are you at this hour, and he told her. Then they talked more and Rocky told Isaiah everything about Bob, about the way he could put his hand on the small of her back and warm her entire spine, and how he had two free spay-and-neuter clinics every year that just about killed him, and how they talked about having kids and had not ruled out the idea but they both knew it was starting to get late. She told him about tossing Bob's ashes in the deep fryer at the local restaurant. She stopped and asked him if he had ever in all his years as a minister ever heard of anyone doing that and didn't he think that she was crazy for doing that.

He rubbed his knuckles with his thumb. "Yes, you were crazy to do that. We often go crazy with death. I hope you didn't keep throwing things into that poor man's deep fryer, did you?"

"No, just that once. Nothing else," she said.

"Go on, then. Tell me what happened next," he said.

And she did. Lloyd was asleep by her feet. Sometimes his feet danced in dream, running, and she saw his muscles contract in his haunches.

"So now you're here and you've just about worn out the usefulness of pretending that you're someone else, someone who you must have thought would be less touched by life. Someone who should have been able to save her husband. How's it working?"

"You sound like the talk show therapists," she said, pulling her head back in surprise.

"Maybe I should try that career. Me by the woodstove, or better yet, on the porch in my rocker, giving out advice. Let's make it a call-in show. So how is it working, Rocky?"

They were in the hours of early morning where most pretenses fall away. Dawn was still several hours down the road. The wind had picked up and rattled ill-fitting windows in Isaiah's office.

"I liked being someone else, or thinking I was someone else. But I never was anyone else. I was still essentially me in a different costume. Do you think that's what being dead is like? Do you think we shed the body and the essential us continues?"

She prayed that he would say yes, that in fact Bob might just be sitting there with them, listening in on the whole discussion, that he would always be with her. And she would believe anything that Isaiah would say, because this moment was filled with truth and they both knew it. If he told her that Bob was an angel, she would buy it. Anything, just say it.

"I think you've gone a long way into the land of the dead. Let the dead ones answer some of their own questions. What is it like to be alive? That's the question," he said.

Chapter 16

The throb had started prematurely, because grieving was supposed to take a year, at the very least a year, and she wanted to believe that. Where had she first read that it was a year? She had read it so long ago that it had become accepted and unquestioned.

What about Queen Victoria? She made the entire country mourn with her, wear black, slide their feet along the floor noiselessly, and speak in whispers. She let almost all of Ireland starve and die, horses go unfed, colonies rise up, and all because she held on to her grief like it was sewn into her skin.

Rocky was not prepared for the flutter that she felt when Hill brushed her forearm at their last archery lesson. Her body had arced and sputtered, her battery started up as if AAA had sent out the big-deal charger. Bob hadn't been dead but eight months and she still searched for him in her dreams.

Hill had said, "Pull your hand back even with your jaw, make it one line," and he lightly grazed her skin. They had started holding their lessons twice a week in the old Grange building. He had set up two targets on hay bales. It had been just the two of them in the large cavern of a room. And ever since he had touched her the last time, she felt her inner circuitry begin to power up.

This can't be right, she argued with herself. She endured all the signs, the quickened pulse, the sudden fit of energy, and the three A.M. wide-awake restlessness that felt remarkably unlike despair. She even walked the dog at that hour, although she discovered that it is hard to keep track of a black dog at that blackest of hours. He kept disappearing every time the moon dipped behind a cloud. One night they walked until dawn, came back and went to bed and when she finally did sleep, she dreamt of Bob. She had found him quite by accident; he was dressed in a crisp white uniform, selling ice cream bars along an ocean boardwalk in a wood shack.

"Eat it before it melts," he said, handing Rocky a Creamsicle that had already begun to ooze over her fingers. That was all she remembered.

She sat up in bed and said to Lloyd, "He's selling ice cream, big guy. I think he's going to be okay."

She had found him, and it had not been as she had imagined. She did not try to pull him from the land of death and he did not yearn to come back with her. And she had not pleaded to stay with him.

Rocky and Hill had agreed to skip a few weeks of archery lessons over the Christmas weeks. He had family to go see. Rocky was going to tough it out on the island no matter how much her brother threatened to haul her butt out of there.

She fed Lloyd and waited until a respectable time to go

to Tess's house where she could practice archery. Lloyd had never seen her with the bow and arrow in hand; she thought that might be too much for him to bear. She left him at home to sleep undisturbed.

She practiced with the twenty-five-pound bow for two hours until she started getting negative returns, as Hill would call them. She started hitting only the outer ring. Her muscles were fatigued and needed recovery time. She wanted to strengthen her arm muscles so that when Hill got back, she would no longer have quivering arm muscles or a spasmodic trapezius.

Tess was a retired physical therapist and only took a few patients privately for the oddest ailments. When Rocky tumbled into Tess house, Tess put her hands on her hips and said, "At least let me do a little acupressure to keep you from seizing up like an engine without oil."

Rocky gratefully climbed on her treatment table with her nose and mouth peering through the open slot at the top of the table. Tess talked as she pressed her thumbs and knuckles into key places on Rocky's back.

"It was a sheer waste of time for me not to come clean with my synesthesia when I was working full-time. I would have had a different shingle like, 'Synesthesia assisted techniques.' People are more accepting now; ten years ago it was harder. Do you want to know how I see your body?"

"Sure, what do you see?" said Rocky.

Rocky was relieved to hear Tess talk. It kept her from thinking about the next archery lesson and Hill.

"Most bodyworkers see through their hands. There are the mechanical ones who see the body in an architectural way, bones attached by joints and ligaments and tendons and nerves. Their hands see which muscle is pulled tight, which tendon has sprung. And their hands send them a picture of what's out of place and they figure out how to get it back in place."

Tess's hands paused over the area between Rocky's shoulder blades, then jumped to a place at the back of her neck, and with surprising gentleness, she placed a knuckle above her tailbone. Rocky felt a clear buzz run up her spine.

"Now others see or feel a certain tick, a rhythm that each person has. It's not a pulse from blood pumping, they say it's something else, and by tuning into it, they can tell if it's too erratic, too fast. The PT sort of joins with it and changes the beat. I don't know how to do that. Not my style. When I close my eyes, I see a picture of your body, color and texture."

She placed one hand on the front of Rocky's left shoulder and one on the backside and guided the shoulder in a small circular motion.

"I see some burnt umber here. Not screaming orange, but tiny muscles that have been overtaxed and need time to repair. The body is amazing; you let these muscles rest for two days and they'll be ready to go again. You might consider using some moderation."

"I've never been good with moderation," said Rocky through the hole in the table.

Tess placed a shockingly hot palm on the small of Rocky's back.

"Oh. Now this is interesting. I feel a swarm of pollen-filled bumblebees. Not really, but that's the sort of buzz I get. This area is about sex and creativity. Generativity."

Rocky abruptly pushed her body up with both hands.

"Thanks, Tess. That's all the healthy intervention my body can stand." She swung her legs around and leapt off the table. She grabbed her parka and left. When she got into the yellow truck, she felt the gushing drone of honeybees, drunk with nectar, between her hipbones.

Chapter 17

It was deep into December when Isaiah called Rocky and told her to meet him for coffee. "I think I've got some news about the dog."

Rocky was well into her second cup when Isaiah came to the diner. At this time of year, the counter seats were filled with carpenters and men who had retired but still headed out of the house every morning. Isaiah gave them all a nod and ordered a cup of decaf.

"Charlotte says I'm too old for anything but decaf. Fortunately, I can't tell the difference. It's not often when you have to give something up and it goes down so painlessly." He slid an Orono newspaper, several days old, toward Rocky. It was folded to a second page article. "Take a look," he said, tapping the specific article with his pointer finger.

Rocky read the article. A woman's body had been found in a house in Orono. Although the body was badly decomposed, and thought to have been there for a month or more, the police did not suspect foul play. The body had been identified as Elizabeth Townsend, age twenty-eight. An autopsy was being conducted. The mother, who lived in Providence, said that her daughter had a history of mental instability and she had not been in contact with Elizabeth for over a year.

Rocky pushed the newspaper away. She shrugged her shoulders. "I don't get it. You think this woman was the dog's owner? That's quite a leap."

"She had just bought a house here. The old Hamilton place. It was a rental for years; fifteen years easy. The original owners were island people, came here every summer. But when they died, the kids couldn't be bothered with it and rented it through a management company in Portland. The sale was done by a realtor off island, which is not all that unusual these days. We never even saw a for-sale sign on the island. This Elizabeth purchased the house in October, just about the time you got here."

"Did you ever see her?"

"No. She probably only owned the place for a few weeks before she died. Unofficially the cops are saying it's a suicide. They said she left a note, most of which was incomprehensible, but clearly the intent was suicide. She had owned the house in Orono, sold it, and was just renting from the new owners until the end of the year."

Rocky switched back to diagnostic thinking. Her first stopping place was manic depression; a blast of manic purchasing induced Elizabeth to buy a house on an island, followed by a bottomless depression. It sounded like she had burned bridges with her family, which meant that she might have had severe episodes without medication, severe enough for her mother, or Elizabeth, to rupture their relationship. First diagnostic impression.

"I can't say I recall seeing her. The only person who can say for sure is one of the kids working the ferry in October. He says he remembers her because of the dog."

Rocky had seen people bring dogs on the ferry. If they had their cars, they usually kept the dog in the car. But if they were out, she noticed a variety of dogs, some overindulged, overfed, some surprisingly calm in the presence of all the un-yielding metal on the ferry. But almost all the dogs balked at the grated walkway from ferry to dock. More than a few dogs held up the line when they feared putting their paws on what must have looked like a plummet into the sea.

"So what did he recall about the dog?" asked Rocky.

"The kid was waiting for the dog to dig in his heels. You almost always have some kind of hitch with dogs. But this dog never looked down. He just walked across. He thought at first he might be a guide dog. That's when he noticed the woman, expecting her to be blind. Fits the description of her. Young, dark hair, short with lots of blond streaks. Nose stud. He said she looked like a tourist, not the kind who really wants to live here. And he said the dog was a big black Lab."

The Portland police, who came once a day to the island, told Isaiah more of the details that the newspapers didn't have. The woman had been found dead on the mainland af-ter a mail carrier contacted the police, after the unmistakable odor found a crack in the house and reached the nose of the only person who came close enough to notice. The cops said that it had all the earmarks of a suicide, even without the note. The doors were both dead-bolted from the inside. This had been a very determined, don't-try-to-save-me suicide. Empty prescription bottles were found near the body. Autop-sy results were pending, but the police unofficially called the death an overdose.

The police had taken a look in the old Hamilton place and

found only a sleeping bag, plastic bowls on the floor with dog food remains, and some canned soda. They speculated that she had only been there a day or two at the most.

"The place was going to need a lot of work before someone could move in. She might have just come over for a day or so to look it over, see what needed fixing. Nothing has been done to that place for years, and you know what a place can look like after fifteen years of renters," said Isaiah, still smarting from his previous renters.

Both of their cups were empty. "Rocky, it could be that your dog, I mean Lloyd, might be her dog."

Rocky felt an ill wind blow past her. She had images of the people in the Midwest who, in good faith, adopt a baby and suddenly the birth mother, or father, come on the scene two years later and want the baby back.

"There's one more thing. Charlotte looked up the obituary on the Web from a Providence newspaper. They said Elizabeth was an accomplished archer. A competitive archer."

"She shot her own dog? Is that what you're thinking? Most people with mental illness hurt themselves, not others. And surely she wouldn't kill a creature that provided her with the relentless adoration that only a dog can generate." But Rocky knew it could happen, if delusions were severe enough, demanding enough.

"It won't be hard to figure out if the dog belonged to her. Contact the vet clinics in Orono for starters. You could contact the mother."

Rocky recoiled. She didn't want to call a mother who was wrestling with the death of a daughter after they had been estranged for over a year. And she particularly didn't want to call about a dog, as if the death of her daughter wasn't the most horrible thing that had ever happened to this woman.

"You'd be better at it than I would. You must have been called on hundreds of times to talk with people after a death. We count on you guys for this. We want you at hospitals and funerals. This is what you used to do, right?"

"If the dog did belong to Elizabeth, then the mother needs to know. By rights the dog was property and should be handed over to the family of the deceased."

Was Lloyd property? He seemed more like a co-pilot, at least while she was driving. Or a companion.

"Let me check into the Orono clinics. I'll ask Sam if he can do this. He must have some swift way to e-mail particular areas. There's no reason to bother this woman's mother yet, not until we find out."

Rocky rushed home, driving the yellow truck as fast as she dared. If Isaiah was right, his owner, Elizabeth Townsend, had shot him. Labs are a loyal dog, loyal beyond all reason and they are the sort who attach primarily to one person. They might be fond of other people, even have a host of friends, like the most popular kid in class, even look forward to some people visiting, but they have one main human who is theirs and they would lay down their life for that one. She fought down an image of Lloyd looking unflinchingly at a woman as she raised her bow. What kind of woman would shoot her own dog?

She pulled up to her rental house and Tess was there, just opening her car door. Tess waved. She had on a knit cap and her white hair stuck our beneath it.

"I wanted to give Lloyd a walk. He needs to keep that shoulder moving. . . ." She stopped in midsentence when she saw Rocky's face. "What's wrong with you?"

Rocky didn't pause; she jumped on the deck and pushed open the green front door. Lloyd was waiting, had heard the truck and was ready to greet her. She dropped to one knee and wrapped both arms around him and then she started to cry with one hand over her face. Lloyd squirmed, backed up and sat down.

Rocky eased back into a squat. "Isaiah told me he thinks he found Lloyd's owner. A woman who killed herself. Probably killed herself," Rocky said in a thin voice. "She was an archer. I think she shot Lloyd."

"Oh, no. Now you don't know that. Tell me what you really do know," said Tess as she reached an arm down to pull Rocky up. She brushed the hair out of Rocky's face. "You either need a hair clip or a good haircut."

Rocky repeated what Isaiah told her at the diner. Tess had her repeat the part about the house on the island. "I wondered what had happened to the Hamilton place. It had a different look to it this fall. Sort of broken, cracked, and it smelled like metal, like aluminum. Should have known the place was sold. But I think you're wrong about this woman shooting Lloyd, and I can't even tell you why."

As soon as Tess said that, Rocky remembered the man at the convenience store in Portland and the way Lloyd nearly blew the top off her car when he saw this guy. And how right after that she had called Hill and set up archery lessons and hadn't thought of it again.

"There was this guy in Portland who Lloyd recognized, and the dog went nuts in the truck. At least I think Lloyd recognized him; he definitely didn't like him. And the guy looked startled to see Lloyd."

"What was the guy doing?"

"He had just gotten out of his truck, and he was walking toward the front door of the convenience store. I was at the door going in."

"So Lloyd saw him coming toward you, and Lloyd was stuck in your truck." Tess looked down at the dog, who actively lapped his testicles, no longer interested in the two women. "Sounds like he was trying to protect you. Has he done this again?"

"No. The most aggressive thing Lloyd has done was to nose me awake a couple of times when he had to go out. This guy is like a big koala bear. Hang on a minute, Tess. I'm calling Sam's office to see if he can get me a list of all the vets over in Orono. I'm going to start calling them to see if they know the dog. At least we can find out what his real name is and stop calling him Lloyd."

"His name should be Lloyd. It suits him," said Tess.

After Tess left, Rocky went down the list that Sam's assistant had faxed to the island library. Each time she called, she said the same thing. "This is the Animal Control Warden on Peak's Island. I think I have a dog that may have been one of your patients. Was Elizabeth Townsend the owner of a black lab?"

She called six offices before she got the direct hit. She knew it right away when the receptionist said, "Hold on please, I'm going to have you speak with Dr. Harris." Two minutes of local radio music followed. Rocky stood next to the kitchen counter and drew jagged lightning bolts on an envelope addressed to Resident.

"This is Ann Harris. You called about a black Lab."

"Yeah, I have an injured Lab that I've been fostering for about a month while he's been healing. I'm trying to locate the owner. We just learned that Elizabeth Townsend was found dead in Orono. She bought a summerhouse here in October. Did she use your services?"

"I read the obituary. Liz had a dog that we took care of since he was a puppy. She'd been coming here for about five years. We were hoping that nothing bad had happened to the dog. Didn't he have his tags on?"

"No, just a reflector tag, nothing else. He's a big guy, probably around ninety pounds, although he was thin and dehydrated when I found him. Easy temperament. A few white hairs on his chest."

"That could be him but it could also be a lot of black Labs. I offered to install a locator chip in Cooper, but Liz didn't like that idea."

"Cooper? The dog's name is Cooper? Lloyd will be very pleased to know that we've finally figured out his name."

The dog had been lying on his side in the afternoon sunshine on the kitchen linoleum. At the sound of his name, his head came up and his legs contracted, bringing his body to standing, as if he had heard a bugle call.

The vet continued. "We had heard nothing about the dog being found in her house. She would have been found a lot quicker if the dog had been there. He would have alerted someone. I've seen that happen before."

"If this is Lloyd . . . Cooper, there's something I need to know. He was injured when I found him. Shot with an arrow."

Rocky heard the controlled silence on the other end of the line. "During bow season, I see about one dog every other week that's been shot. It's not uncommon," said the vet.

"But the dog was shot on the island. We don't have a bow

season here. I know Elizabeth was an archer. I can't help but put some of this together. Her death was probably a suicide; there is no reason to think otherwise, according to a police report. I'm asking you to speculate about something. Did you ever see anything that would make you wonder if the dog was mistreated?"

"This is Maine. We have people who still think that taking care of a dog means chaining it up in the backyard and throwing food to it once a day. Cooper is a great dog because he's got great genes and because he had an owner who trained him and took good care of him. Are you asking if I think Liz tried to kill her dog? Absolutely not. Not unless she completely lost her mind."

Rocky didn't say it, but she thought, don't you have to do just that to be twenty-eight years old and kill yourself?

"The other thing about bow hunters is that if they mean to kill a dog, they will. A dog won't bolt and run like a wild animal. They're an easy target. Any dog that I've ever seen that was shot by arrow had been in the wrong place at the wrong time. It was always an accident."

Rocky thanked the vet and hung up. She pulled on a jacket and the dog skittered to his feet and headed for the door. She wanted to clear her head with sharp air; an accommodating blast from the northwest welcomed her into icy arms. She pulled up the hood and walked with Cooper, crisscrossing every trail along the beach, through the dried beachgrass. They sat together in the twilight; Rocky uncomfortable on a damp log, the dog peacefully gnawing a stick, until the chill in her bones forced her up.

In the middle of the night, Rocky continued to feel the steady caffeine-driven thump of her heart. She had not been asleep since she turned out her light three hours earlier. With each turn from her back to her side, to her stomach, to the other side, the dog rustled on the floor, his sharp leg joints rearranging, claws clattering, sighing impatiently as if he wished he slept with a less rambunctious human.

Rocky's thoughts reached for the woman she had never met, who had stayed long enough on the island to leave a wounded, and loved dog, and then die in Orono. Rocky sat up and flicked on the light. This woman, Liz, had been young, twenty-eight, but right at the age where you can see the first plateau of adulthood, where a young woman might leave behind the tentativeness of being afraid to appear too serious, too sober. She had just purchased a house, how did everything go wrong? The first hint of daylight was still hours away. She got up and pulled on a sweater and her jeans. There was something wrong; this dog had not been mistreated, he did not display overly passive or aggressive behavior; he had not been afraid in his life with Liz. She looked at Lloyd who had risen stiffly and sniffed her pant leg. "I know what it's like to lose someone," she said to him.

Chapter 18

Property. That was the question. If the dog had been discarded, abused, or shot, couldn't he then come under the protection of the dog warden, or the ASPCA? Rocky watched the black dog dance enthusiastically around his food bowl like an overly large tap dancer with a limp.

"Hang on Lloyd . . . Cooper. I mean Cooper. Cooper, Cooper." She popped the top off the new garbage can and scooped three cups of dry food into his bowl. She put the bowl down and the dog looked up in what appeared to be gratitude, a slight tilt to his head, eyes softened, a three-wagged thanks.

The sky ignited with a blood red sun peeking over the horizon. She watched for what she knew would be brief moments of red before the sun settled into its daily dress of yellow. The shortest day of the year, December 21, had just passed, and by mid-afternoon, the sun would begin to depart. She had welcomed this time of year with Bob, the turning inward, staying indoors, abandoning all hope of yard work in the dark evenings. She loved driving up to their house when it was just dark, and seeing the golden glow of lights in the house welcoming her, meaning that Bob was home. If she was very lucky and it was his turn to get dinner, the house would be filled with smells of food and the promise of comfort.

Food. Right, she needed to eat. She made coffee and while it dripped, she shook cereal into a bowl, doused it with milk, and set it on the table. She ate and thought about the right thing to do with the dog. First she'd call Isaiah and tell him to hold off on calling the woman's family in Providence. There was no rush, no need to upset them at this time. Everyone needed to slow down and think. She put her bowl of almost finished cereal on the floor and Cooper licked the remainder.

"Need to go out? You go first, I'll be right there." She opened the door for the dog, who headed for the first tree and let loose with steaming relief. She picked up the phone and punched in Isaiah's number.

"Morning, Charlotte. Is this too early to call? Is the director of public works still drinking his decaf?"

"Rocky, he was just getting ready to call you. Before he gets on, I wanted to ask you about the holidays. Will you be staying on the island over Christmas?"

Rocky had tried hard not to think of Christmas, but it loomed with unbearable weight. She was determined to stay on the island, barricade the door, and wait until it passed. "I'll be here. You two off to see the family?"

"Our son in North Carolina wants to have the big family gathering at his place. Would you stop in and feed our cat? Isaiah is too shy to ask you."

"Give me the lowdown on the cat, when and what to feed her. She's an indoor/outdoor model, right? Let me know if there's anything else I can do while you're gone," said Rocky.

"You're a lifesaver. Here's the man about town."

Rocky was startled by the term lifesaver. A deep, sickening jolt ran through her legs as if her bones were dislodging. She wanted to tell Charlotte that she was no lifesaver.

"Morning, Rocky," he said.

"Isaiah, hold off on calling the woman in Providence about the dog."

"I already called the mother last night. They can't believe that you found the dog. And you know, she said the dog's name is Cooper," said Isaiah.

"I know about his name. You already called them last night? I need more time to check into a few things. I can't just turn him over to anyone after what he's been through. I think I found the vet in Orono who has taken care of him since he was a puppy. And I'm having trouble calling him Cooper. I'm thinking maybe we should give him a hyphenated name, like Cooper-Lloyd. But I want to take him up there just to make sure we're all talking about the same dog."

Even as she spoke, Rocky felt she was forcing a cheerfulness that made her sound like an idiot.

"Things are happening quicker than I expected," said Isaiah. "The parents, Jan and Ed Townsend, wanted to come today to get the dog. I hedged and said that we needed to finish up some paperwork at Sam's office. I talked them into coming tomorrow. And I figured you'd want one more day with the dog."

"Tomorrow? They're coming tomorrow?"

This is where normal citizens become renegades, tie bandannas around their head and go on the lam with big dogs. She pictured making a run for it with Cooper-Lloyd, quietly getting in the truck and heading for Canada.

"They're coming over on the first ferry. I know this is hard for you, but let's not forget what they're going through. This dog is their last connection to their daughter. You understand that, don't you, about trying to stay connected to someone who has died? I'll bring them by your place."

"You're bringing them to my place? I think we're making a mistake. Just because Cooper was Liz's dog, that doesn't mean this is the best solution. Why can't we try to do what's best for the dog?"

"Or do you mean what's best for you? Let me ask you, Rocky. Does it help to have someone tell you the best way to remember a daughter who has died, or a husband? This is not our call. I'm sorry. I know you've gotten attached to the dog," he said and his voice softened. "We'll come by after the first ferry."

Rocky put the phone down and turned to look out the open door. She saw Cooper leisurely delivering little spurts of urine. Her chest tightened as she pictured strangers coming to get him. She pictured a possible life for him with people who didn't care about him. They lived right in Providence, in the city, and he would become a city dog. She grabbed her jacket and joined the dog. "Come on, big guy. This is going to be a short walk." They headed down the trail to the beach. When they returned twenty minutes later, Rocky loaded water and food for the dog into the truck, along with an exuberant Cooper and drove to Tess's house.

Tess lived a full five minutes away by car. Nothing was far away on the island, except maybe the newer houses on the interior of the island, where developers had cleared trees and built new houses in remarkably mosquito-ridden areas. Rocky and Cooper jumped out of the truck. Rocky knocked on the kitchen door, and seeing Tess inside she pushed open the door.

"We've got trouble. How long does it take to drive to Orono? Elizabeth Townsend's people are coming up from Providence because they think Lloyd, I mean Cooper, is Liz's dog. They're coming to get him. They'll be here tomorrow."

Tess had not been awake long. She had told Rocky that she slept with the seasons and this time of year called for greater slumber, more time in the retreat of soft pillows and comforters filled with a long night of body heat. Tess's hair was still in a state of eruption and the skin on her face held wrinkles from the night. It looked like she had slept in the gray stretch-pants she was wearing. Rocky smelled cooked cereal.

Tess ran her hands through her hair. "His name is Cooper? Green and blue letters, robust form. Probably fit him better when he was a puppy. And why are we going to Orono?"

"I found a vet who thinks Liz was one of her clients. She says she'd remember Liz's dog," said Rocky.

"And do you want to find out about the dog or about Liz? Because you're starting to sound obsessed."

"I told you, this is about the dog. How long does it take to drive to Orono?" Rocky asked again.

"It takes about two and a half hours, three depending on your bladder. When are you going?"

"Now," said Rocky. "We need to go now. I want you to come with me. They're coming for the dog tomorrow morning and I don't want to let him go without checking out his identity. He could just be another abandoned dog. He doesn't have to belong to this woman who killed herself." Rocky thought she saw sympathy flicker across the older woman's face and the sight of it made Rocky step back.

"What? Don't you want to go? I just thought you . . ."

"I like this dog too. But you're on a life-and-death mission. I can smell it all over you. If you're going to ask me to join your rescue mission, you should tell me what else is happening. There's too much that you're leaving out," said Tess.

Rocky felt naked, like in dreams where she looked down and realized that she had no pants on and she was about to deliver a lecture. And life was happening too fast; she had planned on slowing life down, holding on to every shred of Bob, and now someone had just put a lead foot on the accelerator. Or maybe nothing that she had planned made any sense. She hadn't considered that possibility before.

Talking to Isaiah about Bob had not been as frightening as she had imagined. Something had loosened in her, as if her swimmer's muscles were warming up. Of course she could talk with Tess. Why hadn't she thought of that?

"Let's talk while we drive," said Rocky.

They decided to take Tess's car instead of the truck because Tess refused to ride for three hours with Cooper wedged under her feet, and neither one of them wanted him to ride in the back of the truck. And Rocky was worried about the truck on a long trip. Aside from the fact that it didn't have an inspection sticker, it had started with great reluctance for the last two days.

Rocky drove the first leg. They pulled up to the dock in the ten-year-old Saab in time for the 9:30 ferry to Portland. They pointed the car inland for an hour, then north. Cooper stretched out on the back seat, and aside from an unfortunate moment of bad dog gas, he appeared completely at home with the car trip.

"Please don't look at me while I'm telling you this. I don't want us driving off the road," said Rocky. This part of her throat was still rusty and it took longer than she imagined to tell Tess about Bob, about the day she was downstairs ordering socks and he was upstairs shaving and his heart seized up solid, and how she tried to force him back to life. Then she told her about the life they had, how finding each other had seemed like the perfect turn of the universe. She kept talking through Augusta and past Waterville.

"You're a psychologist? Please tell me you don't work with little children," said Tess after a much-needed bathroom stop at a McDonald's.

"No. Why do you ask?"

"When you told me that you were a preschool teacher, I thought, pity those poor children. Some people just don't have the knack to be with children, and I dare say you're one. I can't tell you what a relief it is to know that."

Rocky thought about being offended, but it was true. She had never been tempted to work with children. Once they hit college age, she could help them navigate around phobias and nightmares, she could understand where they could be stretched, and how they could learn to tolerate the precipitous drop of despair long enough to find the way out again. During the past year, she had even learned to understand and help students who threw up their food. But Tess was right, little children confused her. Her mother said it was because she didn't have children of her own.

Tess took her turn at the wheel. "Can I ask you something?" said Tess. They were back in the car and the signs on Route 95 said that Bangor was forty miles away.

Rocky sighed and adjusted her seat so that it tilted back slightly without infringing on the dog's space. "Go ahead. I think I've told you everything. Well, not everything. But you have the main highlights."

"What was the point in telling me you were something that you weren't? I thought we were getting on pretty well as friends. I never thought to tell you a lie about me; I never thought to hide myself." Tess rubbed her lower abdomen as if she had a big bellyache. "You are going to have to let me be angry and hurt for a while. I feel tricked and I don't deserve it."

"That isn't very Zen of you," said Rocky, but she knew Tess was right. "I didn't mean that in a snotty, sarcastic way, although it might be hard to tell. Could we talk about something else now? I am willing to accept my new status as a defective friend, the inferior model, but will you give me another shot at this? I don't want to lose you as a friend."

"You are on probation. Your penance is to be a little nicer to your neighbor girl. She likes you, although I can't imagine why," said Tess as she checked her rearview mirror before pulling out to pass a logging truck. "I hate to drive behind them. I'm convinced those logs will burst off the truck."

Rocky explained her strategy for going to the vet clinic in Orono. "I want to make sure this is really Cooper. They've got to have some way to ID him. What do they use anyway? They don't have fingerprints, and he doesn't have a chip in him. But if this vet took care of him since he was a puppy, she's got to be able to identify him. And then they might be able to tell us about Liz."

Dr. Harris's clinic was on the north side of Orono, between the town and the college. No cute names here, just Orono Animal Clinic. A sign at the front said, *All dogs must be leashed.*

"Okay Mr. Cooper-Lloyd, time to leash up," said Rocky.

She had a nylon lead for him, but she had discovered that he generally didn't need it, and in fact, she detected the slightest sense of embarrassment when she had clicked on a leash. Even now, he turned his head slightly away as she reached into the backseat to leash him.

Cooper looked at the building, got out and took a jumbo-sized leak on a little faux fence. It was colder in Orono and they already had the remains of several snowstorms piled up on either side of the walk. Cooper stopped to push his snout into the snow. He then headed straight for the clinic door.

"He knows where he is," said Tess.

When Tess opened the front door, they were faced head on by a receptionist's desk. The young woman at the desk stared at the dog, then at Rocky and Tess, then back at the dog again. She placed both hands on the desk and pushed herself up to standing. Her ponytail rested on one shoulder.

"Cooper, is that you?"

Chapter 19

Tess's first inkling of danger came in the rich moments before waking when she was filled with light and dark, warm under the comforter and cool on her face. The dark green rectangle was a bad shape to have in the abdomen, and the shade of green was not forest green, decorator green, or chlorophyll, but necrotic. Lower right pelvic bowl. She pulled herself up and wondered if it was a dream. But a part of her brain, the glorious multiwired part that she now so loved, registered the rectangle and she couldn't stop seeing it.

Tess's exacting memory for anatomy could not be called a photographic memory, since they were not based on photos of the interior world of the body. What she learned about the body was not just to be found in textbooks. Her vision of the body looked more like Michelangelo's sketches, someone she long suspected of being a synesthete. That would account for a lot.

In her world, the kidneys and liver were orange brick factories with reliable workers who continually brought in boxes and bags of goods to be sorted. Some were used for fuel, some were trouble, and some were stored. A big recycling effort.

Brick, two story, with a continually turning waterwheel.

Or take the heart. It was ruby red and midnight blue, a creature from the sea, a sightless fish that heard everything, vibrated to sad movies and disappointed lovers, and sent its messages in flowing movement, undulating from its core. And the whole uterus, fallopian tubes, and ovaries were one continent with a long string of islands on either side book-ended by volcanoes that erupted with a glistening egg each month in an unerringly egalitarian manner, one volcano nev-er taking two turns in a row, a perfect Ping-Pong game across the continent.

Tess knew the inside of her body, or anyone's body, but hers in particular. The green rectangle had set up shop, had slipped in under cover of darkness. Had a switch been flipped somewhere else in the thin dolphin glands or the round star-shaped glands? She was sixty-eight. Was this going to be all she had?

She would wait before going to see a doctor, before the long series of tests that would no doubt be run to tell them what she already knew. She wondered how long it had been lodged in her body and what damage it had already done. She gave herself permission to not let it intrude yet on this full and happy part of her life. Tess fit perfectly inside her body. If she glanced at her reflection in a shop window, she was momentarily startled at her white hair, but not judg-mental. She was done with the criticism of her harsh youth; was she pretty enough, smart enough, good enough. Now she walked a full life of yes, yes, and yes. Even her ex-hus-band had emerged, yellowed and gasping from half of a life soaked in vodka, blinking at the bright relentless sunlight of clear-headedness.

Every Thursday they met for dinner and a game of darts in Portland. If they had stayed married, it would have been forty-six years in February, but they had not. His drunkenness culminated in a desperate divorce decades ago, so long ago that Tess realized that they had been friends through nearly four lifetimes. The first lifetime was college and romance, marriage and babies. The next was the terrifying part, watching Len slip further and faster into catastrophic binges followed by a steady diet of more alcohol than she thought one human could ingest. The next lifetime was the divorce, Tess and the two kids without Len, going back to school and loving it, and then the kids grew up. Somewhere in there Len got sober after two bouts at a treatment center. He couldn't practice medicine anymore, and hadn't for thirty years, but he worked three days a week at the Chamber of Commerce in Portland, telling tourists what time the ferries left and where to park their cars. The fourth part was sober darts once a week.

She felt the pain again in her lower abdomen, saw the hard edges. She was driving to Orono with Rocky and she could smell the panic coming off the younger woman's skin, a scent like cider vinegar and mangoes that had gone too far past ripe. Tess shifted in the driver's seat and put her left hand on the wheel and placed her right hand on the crease between torso and thigh. With her thumb, she pressed with curiosity to see if the dark angular shape could be felt from the outside. Rocky was absorbed in her own cold fear and wouldn't notice a little tummy prodding. Tess felt sure of this. No, of course she couldn't feel the outline of anything, but somewhere deep inside responded with a honeycomb of orange pain.

Tess put her right hand back on the steering wheel but part of her brain fell through her body, tumbled down into her lungs, slid past a kidney and liver, made its way around a maze of intestines large and small, and settled in the neighborhood of the unwelcome intruder.

No you don't, not now, I'm not ready.

Then she left the intruder as she listened to Rocky tell her who she was and how death had robbed her. The irritation she felt at Rocky for not trusting her felt good, felt like life compared to the destruction going on in her body. She reveled in the chance to spar with this new friend and she gave her a suitable lashing.

"I feel tricked and I don't deserve it," said Tess. Was this for Rocky or her own body?

They drove to the edge of Orono, to the town where Liz Townsend had lived. Tess pulled up to the clinic and Rocky leashed the dog. Once they were inside, a receptionist called him by name. The young woman behind the desk looked stunned. Tess could see a healthy skeptic, a scientist ensconced as an office manager. She moved away from the counter, walked slowly to the dog. She looked like part of her still had the brakes on. She slid a hand into her pocket. "Cooper, I have a biscuit for you." As soon as she said this, the dog walked up to her, sat down, and then lay down. This must have been her test and with the success of her experiment, she crumbled.

"Oh, Cooper. I was so worried that we wouldn't see you again."

Chapter 20

Dr. Harris clinched the dog's identity.

"I had forgotten this when you called yesterday. Liz's dog had a dewclaw missing on his right front leg. He had snagged it badly when they were hiking through some pretty tough underbrush. I had to remove it."

The doctor knelt by the dog. He was too big for the steel table. She ran her hand along the back of his leg.

"Yup, no dewclaw, but I would have known him anyway. I know my patients. This is Cooper. Liz didn't want him to have a chip installed, no matter how much I tried to convince her. He was pretty popular here. Some dogs just are. Other dogs get traumatized by a medical procedure and for the rest of their days coming to the vet is an ordeal for everyone. Cooper always acted like he knew we were doing the best that we could. The dewclaw was the worst we had to do to him, and it wasn't that difficult."

The doctor checked the shoulder area where he had been injured over a month ago.

"This is what you were talking about, right? Dogs heal so quickly. Once they begin to mend, you might never be able to tell they had surgery. But I can see he lost some muscle and he might keep the limp." She explored the area with fingers that read his body like Braille. She stood up.

"So now what? You've identified the dog. What are you going to do with him?"

Rocky had hoped that bringing him here would clear something up, and it hadn't. She had dragged Tess and the dog all the way to Orono for nothing.

"Liz's parents are coming to the island tomorrow to get him. Right now he's under my custody," said Rocky. She was startled by her use of the word custody, as if this was a divorce case involving children, or as if Cooper was in prison. "Do you have any idea what Liz's wishes would have been?" asked Rocky.

"She was a good pet owner, one of the best. She seemed like she might be sort of impulsive in other parts of her life. But not about taking care of Cooper. They were devoted to each other. Sometimes you see that with a dog like this; they become companions. So I guess she would want him to have a home where people cared about him. What about the boyfriend? The last time I saw her, which was back in May, she had a boyfriend living with her. I only know this because she said he tried to make Cooper sleep outside the bedroom, but the dog made such a fuss that even the boyfriend gave in."

Rocky looked at Tess at the mention of a boyfriend and they both factored in one more person.

"Did he get along with the dog? I mean was he jealous?" asked Tess.

The doctor took the moment to check the dog's ears. "No, Liz said he wanted the dog to like him more, but Cooper politely ignored him. Wouldn't do one thing he asked him to do. Are we done here?"

Rocky remembered what she'd brought, what she had thrown in her pack at the last moment.

"I brought the arrow," she said.

Both Tess and Dr. Harris looked at her.

"The arrow that was surgically removed, the one someone used to shoot him." Rocky took her small black daypack off her shoulder. She put it on the examining table and unzipped it. She pulled out a manila envelope, straightened the two arms of the clasp and held it up so that the arrow slid out with a sharp clack from the point and a more stunted sound from the shaft. Only about four inches remained of the shaft. The doctor picked it up.

"Traditional bow hunter. I have to say that I admire this more than the other type. If you can be accurate with a traditional bow, you are part of an elite group. But you don't have the power of a compound bow, which is what may have saved our friend here." She nodded her head at Cooper, who had decided to sit on Rocky's feet. "If you're wondering if I knew anything about Liz's archery, I don't. When people come here, they only talk about their animals, or that part of their life that relates to their animals. She was a good, responsible pet owner." Dr. Harris looked down at the dog. "He's taken you on, hasn't he?"

Rocky noticed the weight of his rump on her feet and how he kept her from floating away.

"Yeah, we seem to be operating hip to hip these days. But that's one reason why I really want to find out if Liz would want him to go to her parents. Wasn't she out of touch with her family?"

Dr. Harris put her hands in the pockets of her vest. "You're an animal control officer? You've got a couple who want this dog and you drove three hours to make sure it was truly Liz's dog. You are either the most dedicated dog warden I've ever seen, and I've seen some of the best, or something else is bothering you. What are you worried about?"

Tess and Dr. Harris faced Rocky. The dog, sensing a change in the atmosphere, tilted his head up and also looked at Rocky.

"I needed to hear you say that Liz wouldn't have hurt him. I thought that would have been enough. But something is wrong here and we're all missing what it is. You're a scientist," said Rocky, pointing her head at the vet. "There's a certain order to things, A leads to B, causality of certain events, but something is out of order here."

Ann Harris looked puzzled by Rocky.

Tess said, "She's a dog warden now, recently vacated from her life as a psychologist. Some sort of career move."

"Liz didn't say anything about that to me. I wasn't her confidante. Ask me anything about this dog's health, and I can tell you that," said Dr. Harris.

"Can you tell me where she lived?"

The vet paused for a minute. "Well, there's no standard of confidentiality about to be breached. I guess there's no reason not to," she said. She opened up Cooper's file on the counter. "Liz lived over in Old Town, near the college. It's really still Orono, but they like to have their own name."

Rocky wrote down the address and suddenly something shifted. She realized that she was in a veterinarian clinic, really in it, and her first thought, and second, and third had not been about Bob. But her reprieve was over. The smells thundered in on her, the oily scent of water dogs, the familiar disinfectant to cover up cat and dog accidents, even the lingering scent of a poodle's anal glands that had been recently emptied out, all joined forces to drag her back to the empty well of Bob's death.

Her heart began to pound and drum blood through her ears. Her breath turned shallow, as if she didn't want anyone to hear her, and she could no longer hear the words that Dr. Harris was saying.

"I need some air . . . must have been the drive," she said as she headed with determination for the door of the examining room. She heard Cooper's claws scuttle to standing as she touched the doorknob.

"I'll be outside," she said in a small, dry voice. She walked past the receptionist and pushed open the front door. Cooper followed with his leash dragging on the floor. Outside, she leaned on Tess's car and gulped in fistfuls of cold, biting air, filling herself back up. She knew how to handle this; she had taught countless people how to counteract anxiety attacks. Take even, steady breaths, and slow your breathing. Inhale for four, hold for four, breath out for eight. Slow and steady.

Tess joined her. "You don't look so good. You are exactly the color of wet ash. I said our goodbyes in there. And here's the arrow." She handed the envelope back to Rocky.

"It's just being in a vet clinic again. It took me by surprise, that's all."

"Smells. Happens to me all the time. The olfactory sense goes to a part of our brain that lights up memory. Being in a vet clinic must be like standing in your husband's pajamas. Take a few deep breaths of fresh air," said Tess.

Tess pulled a blue Polartec hat out of her coat pocket and

pulled it on; her white hair jutted out beneath it. She extracted gloves and pulled them on. It was early afternoon and a storm front from the northwest was steadily approaching. "This would be a good time for us to head home. I don't want to drive in a blizzard," said Tess.

Rocky straightened up. "Not yet. We've got her address. I want to drive past her house. Look, I don't exactly know why . . ."

The clinic door opened and the receptionist waved an arm at them. "Hey, wait up a second." The young woman did a little jog to the car, and wrapped her arms tightly around her torso. She had on a T-shirt and a green lab coat over that. "Whatever you do, don't let Peter talk you into giving the dog to him. Liz was done with him."

Tess and Rocky exchanged glances. "I didn't catch your name," said Rocky.

"Sorry. I'm Shelly. I was a friend of Liz's. Or we were just starting to be friends again. Nobody could be friends with her when Peter was around."

"Was that her boyfriend?" asked Tess.

"He had been, unfortunately, for about six months. And then she spent the next three months trying to get rid of him. She never really understood the effect that she had on men. It was like a chemical reaction. They got addicted to her," said Shelly.

"Was he an archer too?" asked Rocky.

"No. And he tried to get Liz to quit spending so much time with archery. He didn't like that she competed with men. He didn't even like that Cooper was so close to Liz. I told her that he was pure trouble. She told me later that she wished she had listened to me." Shelly's chin quivered and blood vessels swelled in her eyes as she tried not to cry. "I went to the memorial service. I can't believe she's gone. That asshole was there, he had the nerve to come to her memorial. He slithered in like the snake that he was. Didn't speak to anyone."

"I'm sorry you lost your friend," Rocky said. She waited until Shelly could talk again. "Did Dr. Harris tell you how I found Cooper? Someone used a traditional bow and arrow to shoot him. Is that what Liz used?"

"That's what I wanted to tell you. Liz would never, no matter how whacked out she could get with her bipolar disorder, hurt Cooper. Did you know she was bipolar?"

"I wondered," said Rocky.

"Until she met Peter, she had her meds figured out and it was like she finally got it, how to manage meds with sleep and diet. She hadn't had a manic episode for ages until he convinced her to go off her meds and let him take care of her. He was against all medication. And yeah, she was way into the traditional bow and arrow stuff. She got her equipment from some guy out in Nebraska who made everything by hand."

Two cars pulled into the parking lot to the side of the clinic. An agitated Doberman wearing a plastic cone collar jumped out of one car accompanied by a woman with a wool plaid jacket. From the second car, a silver-haired man lifted an animal carrier from which the howls of one cat, possibly two, could be heard.

"Look, I've got to go. Just don't let Peter have Cooper," said Shelly. She turned to go back inside.

"Wait. What about Liz's parents? They're coming to Peak's Island tomorrow to get him," said Rocky.

Shelly stopped. "I don't know them. Only heard her talk

about them. But let me ask you. Would you want your dog to go to someone who hadn't talked to you in almost two years? It wasn't Liz who cut off the relationship. It was her mother. I've got to go."

Tess, Rocky, and the dog got into the car. Rocky unfolded the map of Maine.

"We're in the neighborhood. How long could it take?" asked Rocky.

Chapter 21

The first thing they noticed was the green Dumpster in the driveway. The supersized kind, the ones that people use when they are going to gut an entire house to remodel. Two pickup trucks were parked in the street, both with ladders sticking out the back ends and silver toolboxes that took up half of the bed.

"What should we do with Cooper? He already knows we're back in his hometown and apparently in front of his former house. We can't do this to him, it would be too upsetting," said Tess.

Cooper stood up in the backseat and began to pant.

"Don't stop. Drive a couple of blocks away and let me out. I'm going to talk to the carpenters. Just drive around for a while. Maybe there's a park near the college where you can walk him," said Rocky.

Tess pulled to the curb several blocks from the house and Rocky quickly slipped out. Cooper made a dive for the front seat. Tess grabbed his collar.

"I'll be back at this corner in thirty minutes," said Tess.

Rocky jogged back to the house with the Dumpster. It was a

white bungalow from the 1940s, a solid house with an inviting porch, two dormers on the second story. The rest of the houses on the block looked similar, and Rocky figured the houses were all built around the same time. She heard the shrill whine of a Skil saw from the house. As she passed the Dumpster, she noticed a couch sticking up and old paneling and kitchen linoleum that had been ripped out.

She knocked at the open door, although she doubted anyone could hear her above the racket. She stepped inside and headed for the source of the noise. A blond-haired man with a flannel shirt hollered to someone, "All these cabinets got to come out. That Dumpster is leaving in two days, get the lead out!"

"Excuse me," said Rocky.

The carpenter whirled around. "Hey, I didn't know anyone was there. I don't suppose you brought us hot coffee and a late lunch?" he asked.

He was built low to the ground, thick arms and legs. His boots had a stout two-inch heel and Rocky suspected that without them, she would be taller than he was.

"Sorry, I'm not the lunch lady. I have possession of the last owner's dog. I'm the Animal Control Warden from Peak's Island. Elizabeth Townsend owned this house, didn't she?"

"She used to. Then she sold it, and she must have rented it from the new owners for a couple months. People do that a lot if they need extra financing time on the other end of things. So what can I help you with?" He held a small, claw-headed crowbar in his right hand.

"I'm not sure. Her dog is in my care and I need to place him in the best home. Her parents are meeting me tomorrow to get the dog, but I don't have a really great feeling about them. Did you find anything, I don't know, that stands out to you?" Rocky knew this sounded too vague.

"All I can tell you is that she killed herself and unfortunately, she wasn't found for close to a month," he said. "After the police left, a crew that specializes in that kind of thing had to come in. They're the ones who clean up after a messy death. That was news to me, cleaning crews who specialize in homicides and suicides. How would you like that for your job? Anyhow, then the parents came up here and took a couple of things, pictures I think, that's what the present owners said, then we were hired to gut this place. They're thinking of selling it. No one wants to live in a house where someone committed suicide," he said.

"Did you know her?" asked Rocky.

"No. I heard she was a university type. Hung out there, taking classes. We have to finish emptying out this place; you got anything in particular that you're looking for? I can't see how I can help you."

"Could I just look around the house?"

"For what? We're down to the walls and floors upstairs. We only have the main floor left for demolition. What did you say that you did?"

"Animal Control Warden. When you were throwing stuff out, did you find anything that made you stop? Anything that had to do with a dog?" Rocky said.

"Nothing about a dog. I did save something, though. She had sawed right through a bow-and-arrow rig. Nice too. Didn't know what it was at first, then I started putting it together like a puzzle. She sawed it all up into pieces about three inches long and stacked it in neat little piles right on the kitchen table. But I already gave that to her old boyfriend. He came around the other day and I figured it meant something to him. Couldn't hurt to give it to him. He looked pretty broken up."

She remembered the man at the convenience store parking lot in Portland, the one who sent Cooper into a fit just by getting out of his truck. She remembered his strut and the way he had slammed the door on his SUV with enough energy to rock the vehicle.

"Did he say anything else?" she asked.

"No, just that he had lived here for a while during the summer, and they split up," he said.

"What was he driving?" asked Rocky.

"Some kind of dark rig. It was almost quitting time when he got here, too dark to really see what it was," he said.

When it looked like there was nothing left that the carpenter wanted to say to Rocky about the state of the house or any visitors, she asked if she could look through the downstairs rooms. He had already told her that everything had been stripped from the upstairs.

"Don't fall down and hurt yourself," he said.

Rocky caught the sudden tone, the inflection, that he had been unable to contain, a way of being with a woman that he had learned way back in high school that might have worked for him then but now looked like a sweater that no longer fit.

"I won't be long," she said. She was positive that he watched her butt as she walked out of the kitchen.

She went into the small dining room and living room, the bathroom, toilet and sink only, and she felt the brakes go on in her head. She looked again in the dining room with the six-over-six wood casement windows. Out in the backyard were bales of hay stacked with the archer's target. Of course there was a target, no secret there. But something was familiar, something pulled at her and she used the edge of her jacket to wipe at the dirt on the windowpane. Sawdust and explosions of dust had been created by days of demolition. She peered out, trying to understand what it was she saw.

"Jesus Christ!" yelled the carpenter from the kitchen. Over his voice a clatter of claws burst from the kitchen when the carpenter had dropped his crowbar. Rocky tore her face from the window. She heard the man scuffle more and curse as she headed for the commotion.

"Hey, hold up there. Is this your dog?" he asked.

Cooper careened into the dining room and when he saw Rocky he pulled his lips back in an anxious smile, lowered his head slightly, and wagged his entire back end furiously.

"Lloyd, Cooper, how did you find me?"

The dog whined in discomfort, as if his bad leg had suddenly gotten worse. But Rocky knew it was the house filled with smells of Liz and the terrible smell of death that would be exploding in his nostrils like fireworks. More footsteps, heavy breathing, and another blast of cold air. Tess entered, breathless from running. She quickly put her hands on her knees and bent over to take in as much air as she could.

"I'm too old for this," she said as she nodded to the man in the kitchen. "I took him over to the college and as soon as I let him out, he bolted. I knew where he was going."

"I'm sorry to interrupt, but we now have a small crowd, which is never a good thing with demolition work," he said. He looked at Rocky. "Are you done?"

"Done," she said. "Come on. Cooper." The three of them headed back out the door. When they reached the sidewalk, the dog stopped and did an about-face. Before Rocky could grab his collar, he ran to the backyard and quickly rounded the corner, barking an alarm. Tess put her hand on Rocky's arm. He circled again

"Let him go. He's getting something out of his system."

After his third time circling the house, Cooper stopped at the cross of the sidewalk and the path to the house. He looked expectantly at the two women.

"We're coming," said Tess.

He led them back to Tess's car. When he got in the back-seat, he put his head on his paws that were folded in front of him and closed his eyes.

The first snowflakes began to fall. By the time they arrived back in Portland, they had driven six hours through a blizzard, which had turned to icy cold rain as they neared the coast. They took the 8:30 ferry back to the island. When Rocky collapsed in bed, the last thing she heard was the deep sigh of Cooper.

Chapter 22

Isaiah's truck pulled up to the cottage midmorning. He was closely followed by a beige sedan. Rocky watched from her kitchen window. A man and a woman, both fiftyish, climbed stiffly out of their car. They were heavy, solidly shaped and did not look like physical movement was easy. These people would never walk him; they didn't walk themselves. Rocky suddenly realized that she should have kept driving to Canada with Cooper. They could be happy in a small border town or perhaps outside Quebec City. The threesome climbed the few steps to her deck. Before they could knock, Rocky opened the door. She had told Tess to stay home and sleep; the older woman had looked unusually exhausted when they returned, and she was leaving later in the day to spend the holidays with her family.

She locked eyes with Isaiah in desperation. It was possible that she could appeal to a wild streak in him and he would use his authority to send this couple packing and Cooper could stay with her. But he gave her a stern, resolved look. He held open the door for the Townsends. Rocky noticed that his hand on the doorknob had the slightest quiver, his knuckles pressing light points against his dark skin.

"There he is, there's the good boy," said the man.

Cooper gave a polite show of interest. He rose and sniffed the man's hand.

"You remember me boy, don't you?" he said.

"Rocky, this is Ed and Jan Townsend. This is our Animal Control Warden who saved Cooper and has been taking care of him for the past month or so."

"I'm sorry about your daughter," said Rocky. She remembered to say this when she saw the familiar grip of grief in the man's eyes. Jan looked more complicated; her lips were pressed together in ancient anger and Rocky suspected that the strong aroma of cigarette smoke came from her. Her husky voice confirmed it.

"Thank you for taking care of the dog. It hasn't been easy closing an estate with someone like Liz. We've had to take care of a lot things that Liz tried to destroy," said Jan.

Rocky knew that the relationship between mother and daughter had been ruptured by Liz's disorder, but she had expected death to soften her. Rocky was jolted by the anger that washed over the woman.

"Do you mean Cooper's injury? No, no. I'm sure that Liz didn't harm Cooper, if that's what you mean. I was just up in Orono yesterday and spoke to a friend and the vet who took care of him. Liz loved this dog—" said Rocky.

"You don't understand," said Jan. "Our daughter was very sick. She had a bipolar disorder. Manic depressive. You don't know what we have gone through with her since she was first diagnosed when she was nineteen years old. Hospitalizations,

calls at three A.M., our credit cards maxed out," said Jan. Neither one of them moved to take off their coats.

"When was the last time you spoke with your daughter?"
asked Rocky.

Jan had not made one move to the dog even when Cooper
sniffed her shoes. When he attempted to sniff her crotch, she
pushed him away.

"I don't see the point in this, but we hadn't talked with
her in nearly two years. We offered to let her live at home
so we could monitor her medications and make sure that she
attended therapy. Once Ed's father died and left the house in
Orono to her, we didn't have as much leverage. We had to set
boundaries with her to keep our own sanity. She refused to
abide by our rules and we had no choice," she said.

Ed cleared his throat. "We're going back on the next ferry,
so if you could hand over the dog, we'll be on our way. We can
manage from here."

Cooper sat down with his haunches wedged against Rocky's
feet. Her running shoes still held the sand and salt from this
morning's walk. Her hand went automatically to his head
and she rubbed the loose skin of his scalp. The cat, in a moment of rare congeniality, rubbed up against Cooper's leg.
The dog tilted his head to one side and peeked down at the
cat in surprise.

"I suppose there are vet bills to take care of. How much do
we owe?" said Jan.

"That bill was taken care of. I paid it, well most of it. We
got a deal from the vet. He lives on the island," said Rocky.

Isaiah rolled his eyes. "I didn't know that you paid his vet
bill."

"I've gotten sort of attached to this guy and I want to let you know that I would be willing to keep him. If you two don't really want a dog, I mean, they're a big responsibility, and not everyone really has time for a dog like this—"

"We take care of our own. We're cleaning up after our daughter and this is part of what she left," said Jan. Had Liz's illness washed all the life out of this woman? Or had Jan always been this way?

"Cooper is not part of a mess. He's a dog who loved your daughter and was loyal to her. If you think that you're not going to have time for him, I'll take him. He likes it here. He likes me," said Rocky

Ed unzipped his jacket several inches. "This might not be a bad idea, honey. He did overpower the house the last time he was there."

"No. I just hired someone to put a run in the backyard and we have a new barricade fence. He'll do fine out there," said Jan.

Isaiah moved toward the door. "We've got twenty minutes to the next ferry. The Townsends have made up their mind Rocky, and they have heard your offer. They have declined. The dog is leaving with them. Let's not make this any harder on them than it already is," he said. "You've taken good care of him, Rocky. That's the job."

Ed took the leash off the kitchen counter and snapped it onto Cooper's collar. The dog's ears dropped and the center of his eyebrows rose. Everybody, including the dog, looked at Rocky for the next move.

"Come on, Coop," said Rocky. She moved slowly, dreamlike, wishing herself anywhere but here. She followed the couple and the dog to their car. The coffee that she had been drinking since six A.M. started to form sharp gravel in her intestines. Ed opened the back door to the car and urged the dog in. Cooper looked back at Rocky as if she were coming with him. She bent down and put her arms around his neck, scratching his chest the way he liked and kissed the top of his head. Her throat tightened.

"Get in, Cooper," she said.

The dog hesitated, then leapt with surprising ease into the backseat that had been covered with a ragged towel. Rocky winced when she saw that Cooper's fur was still damp from this morning's walk. The Townsends wouldn't like that.

The Townsends backed up their sedan, turned around, and drove off. Cooper was sitting in the backseat and as they pulled out, he turned his head to look toward Rocky.

She stared at the departing car long after it was out of sight, frozen to the spot.

"You did the right thing," said Isaiah. He cleared his throat and pushed his hands into his pockets. Rocky spun around at him.

"Don't talk to me today, or tomorrow! This is not the right thing and you know it. This stinks. A dog run! A fucking dog run! He's not that kind of dog. He's a people dog, he has to be with his person. That's me."

Rocky felt the last two words settle into her as the shocking truth. She turned her heel on Isaiah and walked back into the house and felt the unstoppable convulsions of sorrow howl out of her as she leaned against the door. Isaiah knocked.

"Go away!"

He was quiet outside her door, then slowly scuffed off the deck. She heard his truck pull out. After her sobs emptied out, she splashed cold water on her face. It wasn't fair that she had to keep losing everyone she loved. She could stop this disaster from happening; she had a choice this time. Her keys to the truck hung on a nail by the door. She grabbed them and ran to the truck. The battery, which had been acting peevish, gave its death rattle, the reluctant sound of a battery that would like to oblige, but has lost its juice. She kept turning it over until there was nothing but a click from the ignition.

She pounded the steering wheel with her fist. "No, no, no!"

The dock was one mile away. She had five minutes before the ferry left. Sometimes in the winter their schedule was less than exact. She pulled off the backpack, and started running. These were different muscles than walking muscles but she hoped they were in working order because she was going to take them to the limit. She could make it and she would stop them. She was the Animal Control Warden. She had some authority.

Her legs responded to the emergency. The sandy gravel tried to drag her down, but she pushed off with each step as if nothing else mattered. She hit the paved road just past Melissa's house and she got up on her toes and ran like she had seen sprinters do. There was one hill as she rounded the main island road and gravity took an extra measure from her. She heard the ferry blast its departure horn. She tilted her head back to suck in more oxygen and pumped her arms as she blew past the closed fudge shop and T-shirt shop. She skidded around the corner to the dock. The ferry was already churning up water and was fifty yards out. There was only one car on the ferry, and she could still see the top of Cooper's black head through the window. She reached the end of the dock and without wanting to, she yelled, "Cooper!" The cold restraint of the metal chain barricade pressed against her thighs.

She thought she heard his deep, resonant bark over the wind and the engine as she collapsed to her knees and the ferry carried him away.

Chapter 23

Melissa knew something was wrong when she saw Rocky running, really running, not jogging for exercise. It was not normal for adults to run unless they had on running gear: slick running pants, matching shirts, and windbreakers. But she was quickly diverted from anything that might be happening in Rocky's life. This was a weekend when her father was going to be away, so she could stay home. She would stay home more often on weekends, but she didn't want to hurt her father's feelings.

Her room, and all her stuff, was here; this is the house where she was born. After the divorce, when she had been eight, her father hadn't really known how to set up a house so that it felt like a home, although he had tried. And her mother had offered to help him at first, buying him dishtowels so that he wouldn't keep using the same two that he left with. But her bedroom at his house never felt like she could escape into it; she was a guest.

Later in the morning, she noticed Rocky walking back. Rocky looked pissed off in a major way, but oddly shrunken, like she was caving in on herself. Melissa didn't dare approach her when she looked that mad. She already knew what Rocky was like when she was just being her regular annoying self, and that was bad enough. Melissa tried to think of reasons to ridicule the woman so that she wouldn't think about the reaction that she had to her at the athletic club, or that she had taken Rocky's lingerie and kept it for days before sliding it back into the laundry basket on one of her dog-feeding missions.

She waited until late in the afternoon of the next day and knocked on Rocky's door. Lloyd loved to go with her for slow jogs on the beach and she needed a break from studying. Rocky answered the door in what looked like the clothes she had slept in, dark blue flannel pants. Melissa considered that the woman might be sick. She peeked around her to see the inevitable rush of appreciation from Lloyd.

"I'm going for a run, a slow run, I know you don't want Lloyd really running until his leg is all the way healed, so I'll make it a slow jog," said the girl. "Where's Lloyd? Can he go with me?"

Melissa didn't like speaking with adults and her words came out in a rush. Then she remembered Rocky's journal and the rambling entries and wondered if she was still suicidal because she didn't look right and she took too long to answer. She wondered if Rocky was crazy and if she was, that somehow made it easier to be around her.

"Oh my God. You don't know. His name isn't Lloyd. Melissa, a lot has happened in the last two days. I found out that his name is Cooper. And he left the island yesterday," said Rocky.

"He left? You mean he's gone? With who?"

"His owner died, that's why no one was looking for him.

She had died over in Orono. Her parents came to collect Lloyd . . . Cooper, yesterday."

Melissa put her hand on the doorframe to steady herself. She had been caught off guard. Despite her best efforts to control her world, she was assaulted by the news, struck hard in her midsection and it felt like her ribs were going to break.

"You let him go? I would have taken him! If you didn't care about him, then I did!"

"Do you want to come in? I can tell you the whole story. I didn't want him to go, but they were the dead woman's parents and Cooper was part of the estate, he was their property," said Rocky.

Melissa didn't make a move to come in. Her eyes filled with hot tears and her skin flushed red, starting low on her neck and racing up to her cheeks.

"You have ruined everything! I wish you'd never come here," she cried and ran off the deck and down the dirt road, her body exploding with the urgent need to fly apart. She took the path to the ocean first. She knew all the paths that twisted and turned, that invariably confused tourists during the summer. Melissa did not want to remember her life before the dog; she did not want to remember who she had been before he had come to the island. Why had Rocky done this? Even Rocky, stupid, horrible Rocky had loved the dog. How could she have let him be taken away?

If Melissa had known, she would have taken the dog, she would have broken into Rocky's house, slid like a shadow through a slit in the door, through a mouse hole, down the chimney, and taken the dog, Cooper, and hidden him away. Even on this island, there were hiding places. She and Cooper could have lived in the dense bittersweet jungle, or the barn at the old Hamilton place, deserted since early fall, or she could have taken the ferry to Portland and gone to her father's house. Would he have understood? She had not tested him with anything important, anything that came from the dark, empty tangle of her foodless center, and like the guerrilla fighter that she was, she wondered if he was friend or foe, enemy or comrade, and she didn't know if he could be trusted. Could she show up on his doorstep and say, "This black dog is Cooper and I eat four kibbles from his dog dish and he is teaching me to eat again and when I am ready to scream in terror at the food sliding down my throat into my stomach, this dog presses his head into my palm."

When she got in from running along the labyrinth of trails, her mother was on the phone in the kitchen and looked up at Melissa with dark eyes.

"That was Rocky. She told me about the dog. I'm sorry he's gone," said her mother. And for the first time in nearly a year, Melissa let her mother wrap her arms around her.

Chapter 24

Cooper was stunned by his exile. There had not been one minute with the woman, the one who had saved him, that he had doubted her. And then she sent him away. The First One was gone. Liz, Liz. He knew the sound of her name. He had known of her death, felt it, but the waves of death scent in the old house had confirmed it. That was where she had died, in the house where they had lived together. There had been a human death and it was the First One, Liz, the one he had known since leaving the litter, the one who had urged him on, trusted him, loved him beyond all others. She had been tremulous at times, speeding up like a storm, making her unaware of simple things, and he had learned to sniff the change before it came and he increased his vigilance then and would refuse to leave her side. He knew that he held some power to calm her, even as her illness raged.

A good life, a very good life, is finding one person who knows you, who shares the joy in chest rubbing, the pleasure of eating, of running damp and happy in the heavy dew of morning, of sitting with you while you chew with abandon on a fresh stick. But it is more than that, it is a look in the eyes of the human, and the smell, the thousands of smells that they offer. A good life is finding one such human. And he had found two.

The death scent was old but unmistakable. He had run around the house three times in the ancient way of saying goodbye that he had not known before that moment, but which came to him out of the merging with all the canines before him who had come in from the wild to be with humans. Three times around the site of death, barking a heralding cry to let the other side hear of their coming. She was no more.

Now the New One, the woman who was a tracker in her dreams, had changed course. She had been another miracle; she had found him when he was broken and feverish. She also needed watching and as soon as he was able, he took up his post with her. He dreamt with her, nudged her awake when her dreaming went badly, and he had been calmed by her touch as well. She offered a new rhythm, older than his Liz, without the perilous spirals of energy that kept Liz from sleeping for days and days. And the look, he could hardly believe the New One had the look that canines seek, or at least those who have their wits about them.

He had settled into his new life with the New One. And then suddenly, she let two people, the man and the woman, take him. She had hesitated, she struggled, her scent turned to fear and sadness, yet she did it. He heard her say it when the man and the woman opened their car. She said, "Get in, Cooper," and he had obeyed.

These two are Liz's parents. He had been in their house long ago. The house held ghostly scents of memories for him, when there was rage and frustration between his Liz and her parents. They did not know how to soothe her like he did and he has taken a protective stand between Liz and her parents.

As soon as the long car trip ended, during which they did not stop so that he could relieve himself, he was led through the house and taken out through sliding glass doors in the kitchen where he was put outdoors, tied to a lead that ran along a high wire. The yard was surrounded by a solid wood fence, higher than even he could jump, and he could see nothing of the surrounding area.

He had never been tied before and he was ashamed. There was no one else to see him and for that small gift, he was glad. They brought food outside and placed it in a bowl. They brought water as well. They left the house during the day and did not return until the light began to fade. When they returned they came to look at him and brought him more food. More time passed, darkness settled, and they allowed him into the kitchen. He made the mistake of trying to follow them as he thought he should, down the hallway to their bedroom. But the woman scolded him, smacking a newspaper with her hand to make a sharp noise, and put up a barrier to let him know to stay in the kitchen. It was a minor thing, this barrier, he could have easily jumped it, but he understood the message to stay away.

The next night, after the man brought him food and left him in the yard, he saw the glow of the woman's cigarette in the kitchen. She sat in the dark smoking. Cooper could feel her looking out and wondered if she could see the nightshine from his eyes. If allowed, he could help her. He would permit her to weep as humans did and to drain the anger and sadness from her blood by stroking him. He could urge her outside and drag her senses to stick throwing and the thrill of physical exhaustion. But she would not permit it, she would not see him as he was.

He knew this was it; there would be nothing else. Already in this life he had had two people who were beyond what he could have hoped. He had seen other dogs who had not fared as well, and he was grateful. But the New One had sent him away to this place and he could not understand why. He stopped eating on the second day and no longer hoped for the New One to come for him.

Chapter 25

They were all gone. Isaiah and Charlotte were in North Carolina for the holidays, Tess was on the mainland with her ex-husband and their two children and grandchildren, and even Hill had disappeared to points unknown. Rocky had not asked him where he was going when he called to say that their lessons would not resume until after the New Year, and she hoped that her disappointment did not show and if it did, that it meant she was dedicated to archery, not that she would in any way miss him. In reality, she had wanted to tell him about Cooper and the terrible mistake that she had made.

Rocky had refused to meet with her family over the holidays. "I just can't. Not this year. I refuse to pretend that I am celebrating anything," she told them. Caleb and his wife went to California to be with their mother. Rocky assured Caleb that he could come to the island in the spring.

Isaiah had replaced the battery on the truck for her the day after the Townsends took Cooper. Rocky watched him from the house. She had refused to speak to him, and he knew not to come to the door. She called Charlotte and said, "I'm not mad at you, and I probably won't be able to stay mad at Isaiah

ot been able to go to sleep the first night until
dawn and the second night was not much better. She napped
during the day. She missed Cooper's breathing, his scent, his
demand to go outside, to draw her out, his soft eyes, and his
need of her. She missed the sprawl of his body, his satisfaction after his meal, his enthusiastic tail wagging when she
walked in the door, or watching him gnaw on a stout stick
until some artistic culmination caused him to stop and add
it to a pile of similar sticks on the deck. She kept picturing
him running around Liz's old house in Orono three times.
Had he really done that? He came and stood by her when he
was done. She spent days picturing his ritual and in an early
morning bout of insomnia, she suddenly realized what had
happened. He had completed what he needed to do with Liz
and then there was nothing old between them; he had signed
on with Rocky completely.

This was a miserable job and she regretted taking it. When
Isaiah returned, she would tell him that she was resigning
before she did any more harm. She had hurt Cooper by getting too close to him and letting him get too close to her. He
couldn't understand about property laws and estates.

The island was muffled in the silence of empty houses.
Christmas came and went. She drove the truck around the
island twice each day. No stray animals were reported, no
lost animals needed finding, and no dead animals needed re-
moval.

She went to Tess's house and practiced archery for hours
each day, letting her thumb slide along the edge of her jaw as

Hill had demonstrated. She wore silk long underwear under her jeans so that she could stay outside as long as possible to shoot again and again at the target. Pull and release. Fewer arrows strayed to the outer edges. She allowed her muscles and bones to take over. Nothing was going right in her life; there was no reason for archery to be any different. The light was fading and she wanted a few more shots.

She pulled back her right arm, and the arrow and the bow became a part of her, extra appendages that attached firmly to her ligaments. She sighted the target and saw, before she released the arrow, exactly where it would pierce the target. Rocky took a breath and released the air in a slow and perfect stream. She suddenly saw it, the place between breaths that Hill had talked about. What he had not told her was that it was as real as a spot on the map, like Portland or Boston, and that she could step into it. There was nothing between her and the target. She released the arrow and followed it to its certain home, dead center. Rocky felt a tingle of exquisite light run up her spine, unimpeded from her tailbone to the top of her head. She shot for several more minutes before the new and strange sensation left her as unannounced as it had arrived.

When she returned home, she called information for the Townsends' phone number in Providence. It was still her job to see how Cooper was doing. They were unlisted. When Isaiah and Charlotte returned, she'd get their number from him. How else could she reach them? Then she remembered that she had the obituary from the newspaper. She'd send them a note in care of the funeral home who would forward it to the Townsends. She tore a sheet of paper from her black journal that she had not touched in days. The edge of the paper bore ragged tears from the metal spiral binder and she evened it out with a scissor.

Dear Mr. and Mrs. Townsend,

If love is the reason that you want Cooper, then I am glad and I wish you well. But if you took Cooper in order to repair something that was broken between you and your daughter, then I ask you to look into your hearts and think about what Liz would want and what the dog wants. I think you know. I think he belongs with me. I will take him back any time. I will come and get him and I will take care of him for the rest of his life.

She dropped the letter in the mail drop box outside the grocery store. There were a few more hours of thin daylight left and she didn't want to go back home yet. Even Peterson the cat seemed disgusted with Rocky and avoided her, refusing to sit on her lap.

In the evening, she tried Hill's number again and this time she left a message, and then wished she hadn't.

"Hill, this is Rocky. I know we don't have another lesson until next week, but would you like to meet me in Portland, um, for coffee? Oh, you probably don't go out for coffee. Could you agree to meet me on a street corner? What I mean is, that the dog that I told you about, well he's gone . . ." Beep.

Hill had his message machine on a timer to keep messages short. Why didn't he say so upfront, as in, "Leave a message and make it short. You have thirty seconds starting now." Rocky called back.

"It's Rocky again and I think you should warn people about

the time limit. Aren't people in Maine the slowest talkers in the country? Most people will just get to hello when they are beeped out. But here's the thing, everyone on the island is gone, or everyone I know, and I'm going to resign my job and I wanted to talk it out with someone . . ." Beep.

If he put those two messages together, he would get something, but she wasn't sure what. He already had her phone number; he had it on the checks that she had written to him, so he must have written it down. Or did he? She admitted that she was a bit flustered when she was around him, and she couldn't for the life of her remember if she had given Hill her phone number. No, wait, he had called her last week and left her a message so he had to have it. She did not want to sound one bit needier than she already did on the other two messages.

"Hi, it's me again. I hope this message comes before the other two that I've left you. If so, don't listen to the next two messages from me. It's not that it was hard being Christmas and all and this was the first Christmas since my husband died, which I hadn't told you up until this moment, but it's that I had to give the dog to people who won't understand him. Some people shouldn't have dogs; they shouldn't have gerbils. And I thought I could stop this one bad thing from happening . . ." Beep.

She would not leave him another message.

Chapter 26

Rocky heard the solid sound of a truck door closing. Everyone was gone until the end of the week. Only the girl, Melissa, was still on the island with her mother. That's what Eileen had told her when Rocky called to tell her that Cooper was gone. Melissa had already informed Rocky that she had ruined a perfectly good existence by coming to the island. The girl had started to be a regular visitor, but Rocky was sure that if not for the black dog, Melissa would have ignored her with precise adolescent stonewalling. But even in her dark spiral of grief, Rocky could see that the girl was shattered when she learned that the dog was gone.

Rocky was not expecting anyone, which meant that this could be a drop-in call about a missing pet, or raccoons on the prowl. She looked out the small kitchen window and saw Hill hefting his bow and arrows, running his fingers through his hair, squaring off his shoulders, and looking at the little house as if he had already decided something.

She had on the same dank jeans that she had worn for three days. Her hair was unwashed, and there was an empty, unrinsed can of tuna in the sink. She wished she had on clean underwear, which she did not, and that she had brushed her teeth, which she had not done either. She heard his boots on the deck and without hesitation, the knock.

When she opened the door, he was framed in cold air. His eyes blinked in their odd blue and green, and she thought they were startled, registering an alarming sight. She worried that what he saw was stale, rumpled clothing, a tinge of grease in her hair separating it into limp sections. Could he see that she was coming undone? Was it alarm that she saw on his face?

She ran her fingers through her hair and said, "This is my new camouflage outfit. How do you like it? It's what all the hunters are wearing this year."

"When did you become a hunter?" he said, softening his face, the right side of his mouth lifting before the other side caught up.

She took in a larger breath. "I haven't yet. Just checking out the clothing options. I was wondering what it was like to be a hunter, what it would take." She took one step backward.

"We can start by practicing. Where do you practice?" he finally asked, scanning the area from left to right.

"At a friend's house. I set up a target behind her house."

It was early afternoon and they might have an hour or two of strong daylight left.

"Show me where. Let's go there," he said.

"Give me a minute," she said without hesitating, as if it were the most natural thing for him to request. She closed the door with him on the outside. She needed one more moment without looking at him, but this was wrong; she realized that her interpersonal skills were not up to par and she yanked open the door.

"Sorry. Come in. It'll take me five minutes to get ready."

He came in and stood in her kitchen with faded yellow and orange linoleum, aluminum strips around the chipped Formica countertops. She retreated to the bedroom, and every sound that she made clattered in naked disclosure throughout the house. Her scuffed steps in the bedroom, dresser drawers opening, a metal coat hanger clanging along an iron rod, the flush of a toilet, the ping of pipes as the sink faucet was turned on. When she came out of the bedroom, Hill stood in front of Caleb's sculpture, a woman playing the saxophone, her upper torso tilted back in euphoria, her eyes squeezed shut in crinkled joy, her knees spread wide under the folds of a dress. Rocky wished the statue would press her knees together.

He turned slowly toward her. "I didn't learn to hunt from men. It wasn't like that. Whatever you're thinking about hunters, I'm probably not it. I learned first from my grandmother, then later when she was gone, my father took over."

Rocky rested her bottom on the arm of the couch. She wasn't sure why Hill was telling this, but she knew that she wanted to hear him.

"Tell me," she said.

"I learned to hunt early on with my grandmother, and she taught me smells and scat, and broken twigs. She refused to use a compound bow, said it was unfair to the animals. She said anybody could use a compound bow. She told me that if I learned to use a traditional bow, I'd understand the prey better. And I'd understand myself better."

Rocky pulled one knee up and wrapped her arms around

it. "My Italian grandmother taught me to make ziti. That feels a bit tame in comparison."

Hill put the archery gear on the counter. "She taught me to find deer scat, dried in neat little piles of pellets, and to put it on a flat stone and grind it with another stone until she had a fine dusting of powder which she put on our boots, jackets, and our hats. It masked our scent. She taught me to construct a hunting stand."

"What exactly is a hunting stand?" asked Rocky.

"They're different, depending on what you're hunting and what weapon you're using. She was a bow hunter, so hers was a small platform of roughly bound branches about fifteen feet up in the lower branches of a tree, a place to wait for deer traffic. She taught me to wait in complete silence when I was ten years old. She claimed that she had never wounded a deer; all of her kills had dropped to the floor of the forest within seconds. It was the surest place to shoot from, both for the hunter and for the sake of the deer."

Rocky pictured young Hill and his grandmother, covered with dried deer poo, unseen and undetected by the flickering nostrils of the deer that walked undisturbed beneath them until they selected their kill and shot the animals from above. Now Hill stood before her with his hunter's weapons and she felt like both the prey and predator at the same time, covered with a scatlike covering of insomnia and longing.

Rocky stood up and tucked her hair under a fleece hat. "Let's catch the last of the light."

She was glad that they were leaving her house. They had already expanded so fully that the walls of the house were bending outward to contain them.

"I set up a target behind Tess's house. I never wanted the

dog to see me shooting. I didn't want to scare him," she said.

They climbed into his truck. "I came as soon as I heard your message. There's a pile of unopened mail sitting in my kitchen and a refrigerator with bad milk. I got in my truck and came straight here. I'm sorry about your husband. What happened?"

Rocky clicked her seat belt into place and her hands trembled. "His heart. I thought I could have saved him. I tried to, I did CPR as soon as I could get my hands on him. He had this thing that he said, that he married a woman who could save him."

Hill backed up the truck. "What was that supposed to mean?"

"It was a joke about me being a lifeguard when we met. He wasn't the kind of guy who needed saving, not like a wreck of a person, you know? That wasn't it. Only it wasn't a joke and I really did need to save him and I couldn't. A couple of months after he died, I came here and then the dog came here and I let him go without a fight, and I want to get him back because he needs me, or I need him. Can we talk about this after we practice? I hate to say this, but I need to shoot something."

He patted the steering wheel. "Lead on, and we'll shoot the daylights out of that target."

They drove the short distance in his truck to Tess's house. The faded prayer flags settled to a steady sway from a quiet breeze. They were tied on a line from her front door to a rhododendron bush beyond the porch.

Rocky smelled the man scent of Hill's jacket when he reached over to grab his quiver of arrows and his bow in the truck. Each round molecule of his scent got off on her upper lip and rolled with urgent desire up her nose, dove into her bloodstream, and took the express to her brain. Her body responded in a jet stream of warmth cascading between her eyes and spiraling with alarming speed through ribs, pooling between her hip bones, pausing for a decided message between her legs, gaining speed in flourishing agony down the insides of her thighs and thinning past the knobs of her knees, shooting yellow light out the tips of her boot-covered toes. She reached for the door handle and pulled it open with a click.

Hill opened the gate to the backyard, and it screeched with a heralding cry. He held open the gate for Rocky and she passed through holding her breath, avoiding the chance to inhale any more of him. She pointed to the ringed target fifty yards away, attached to a stack of three hay bales. He had a fresh paper target rolled up in the quiver of arrows that he slid out. "Let's start fresh," he said and he covered the old target, tacking it with the pins that held the old one in place.

"You've been practicing," he said. "I can tell by the way you carry your bow. There's a turning point with students, when they stop carrying the bow as if it will take a bite out of them."

In fact she had passed over a threshold, faster than she thought she should have, when the arrow, her arm, the bow, and the target all flowed together and when it happened she felt like she had skipped a grade. She had felt her heart beat steady at the command of the bow and arrow. She noted the calmness of the release and the whole thing was over in a few moments and she had wanted it back. She told Hill about it.

He listened as he paced out a distance.

"The kinesthetic memory of your body is taking over. The times of not hitting the target, all the failures, have to be fully felt, again and again to get just one of those moments of flow that you got. I don't know why that happened for you this soon. I've had students practice for a year before they step into a space where all the parts work. Did it just happen that one time?"

"Yeah, this week. So I shouldn't count on it happening again soon? I got a peek of something happening in the future, like time travel," she said.

He put his bow on a small section of stone wall. "I can't predict how it will go for you. For most of us, those moments are hard earned, inch by inch with a lot of outright humiliation, followed by lagging self-doubt that leaves a taste like rank meat. Then it starts to change. First the arrows hit the outer rings, then a few strays dive toward the center, then that bad-boy voice quiets down to a murmur and a new voice opens up who says to take a breath, release the breath, hold very still. And in the opening between breaths the world opens wider, clear like glass, all seen with excruciating clarity. And suddenly the eye of the target reaches out to you and the archer only has to let go. And I have never told anyone that before."

He had stepped closer to her with each word and he suddenly reached out and put his hands on the edges of her jaw and into her hair and she wasn't sure how he had gotten there, whether he had been pulled or he had been shot out of an archer's bow. Rocky's hat popped off and she grabbed both of his hands.

"I want to tell you about why I'm here and about the dog and about this woman who was an archer, who used to own him and how she killed herself after something terrible happened to the dog, and now the dog is gone, her parents came to get him and this is such a terrible mistake . . ."

A look of bewilderment followed by horror came over his face. He dropped his hands and stepped back.

"I can't believe this. Why didn't I put this together?" He sank down on the stone wall, put his head into his hands, and then looked back at the stunned Rocky.

"I need to tell you something, and I'm going to do it quickly." He swallowed hard and pressed his lips together when they had started to quiver. "The world of archery competition in Maine is a small community and the number of women archers is an even smaller piece of the pie," he said.

Oh, no, thought Rocky, already skipping ahead to a likely conclusion, I am such an idiot.

"The reason my wife and I are separated is because I went to a competition about a year and a half ago in Orono and stayed the night. I met a woman there. I'd never seen her before at any of the competitions and she was good, really good. I couldn't help but notice her and she had it, she really had something. That flow that we were just talking about? She could step into it like no one I've ever seen. Anyone could see she loved everything about archery. I stayed with her for one night at my motel. After that I dragged myself home and Julie knew it the first minute I walked in the door."

A gust of wind found them and Rocky's hair blew into her face. She reached down to get her hat and rammed it on her head. "You knew Liz Townsend? Does everyone but me know this woman? Am I suddenly her receptacle for dogs and old lovers? Why didn't you tell me?"

"Tell you what? That I cheated on my wife once and everything went to shit after that? I'm not proud of what I did. And I didn't want my wife to leave me."

"No, I mean, yes, you should have said something. But you should have put two and two together about the dog. I told you I had a dog that had been shot. You knew, didn't you?"

Everything that had opened in Rocky was closing down and it felt like a river was changing course from north to south. How could she have been so wrong about him?

Hill stood up. "How could I have known anything about her dog? She might have mentioned that she had a dog, but we weren't really talking about dogs then. Rocky, this was a one-night stand. I told her the next morning that we couldn't see each other again."

"This whole thing just got too weird for me. Forget that I left you a message, forget about lessons, forget that you ever drove out here," said Rocky. She wrapped her arms around her torso.

Hill took a step toward her and she wondered how much of a mistake she had made. There was no one else around within shouting distance. Rocky knew she was not a poker face; whatever he saw made him stop abruptly. Hill stopped and opened both his palms toward her as if she were a stray animal that needed reassurance. That's what she did before she captured a stray.

"Okay, Rocky. I'm not exactly sure what happened here, but try not to blame me for something that happened before you even met me. I did read about Liz's death, but I never put it together with your dog that was wounded."

Rocky knew that for the most part, it's impossible to tell if someone is telling the truth. But she suddenly had zero idea if Hill was telling her the truth or if the world had gone sideways and she was the last to notice.

"You should go," she said.

"Let me give you a ride home," he said.

"No. I'm going to stay here."

He nodded and seemed like he was going to say something else, but then he gathered up his gear and walked away, pulling open the gate with an iron screech. She waited until the sound of his truck faded before she pulled out some arrows, set one in the notch, pulled her hand along her jawline and released. Nothing was right. Her arrows stuck around the outside perimeter of the target as if the center were covered in a glass dome. She tossed her bow on the ground and went to get her arrows. As she approached the target, her eye was drawn to the mark that Hill made on all his targets on the bottom left corner, a stamp that one of his students from high school made for him of a hunter with a fully drawn bow. He sometimes gave students a new paper target.

"Oh, Jesus," she said. That was what she had seen at Liz's old place. That's what had caught her eye when she looked out the window. The target with the stamp on the bottom left corner.

Chapter 27

In Providence, Rhode Island, Liz's mother smoked the last cigarette in her pack and smashed the stub in an ashtray cluttered with the remains of filtered menthols. Her daughter was dead and she was raging day and night, smoking two packs of cigarettes per day, cauterizing her lungs in the deepest places, and coating them with an anesthetic of tar.

With every breath that she had taken during the two-year strain of not speaking to her daughter, she had imagined Liz and what she'd be doing at any point in the day. Would she take her medication, did she know how angry Jan was, that her mother was right? She had pictured a future when Liz would ask for forgiveness, when the time of punishment would be over, and Jan could have her daughter back. But the side effects of shunning her daughter, not taking her calls, not reading her imploring letters, refuting even her husband when he said, "Come on now, Jan, that's enough," was that her world had grown darker and smaller and even the sweetest sounds from birds in her backyard had turned into jagged points of scratching.

She had busied herself with the logistics of death: arranging for the cremation, writing the brief obituary, discovering that the house in Orono had been sold and Liz was only renting it, and suffering the tangle of paperwork that comes with death. The property on Peak's Island would have to wait for the slow grind of probate court before they could put it up for sale.

Jan pulled another cigarette from the pack and clicked on the plastic butane lighter. The dog was still outside tied to the zip line that allowed him what Jan thought was a perfectly fine run of thirty feet. He had stopped eating his food. He was stubborn like Liz. She'd let him inside when it was time for her to go to bed. The weather report predicted freezing temperatures. She was not impervious to the suffering of others. Liz had loved this dog. Even Jan had seen the cord of connection between Liz and her dog, a braid of fuchsia and green, and fragrant like pumpkin vines, yes something that had slowed Liz's manic moments in the worst of times.

Jan was drowning in the deep gash created by Liz's death. This is not how life had started with Liz, this was not the flutter of joy she had felt with her daughter before Liz's bipolar brain had torn them in half. She closed her eyes and dared to remember the tender joy of holding Liz in her lap when she was three years old, sniffing her hair and thinking that, like a mother bear, she could smell her own child blindfolded. Hers was the child that smelled like fresh hay, earth, and almond oil.

She felt a flutter near her armpit that was soft like a child's hair. A tendril of scent caught her attention. It was the musky almond smell of her daughter's hair when the girl had been small, when the world had been theirs. For one agonizing moment, she felt the cupped palm of a child against her cheek. As if lancing a gangrenous wound, the years of poison released from Jan and the green squirt of liquid shattered. All that was left was the deep ember of mother and child.

Outside in the yard, the dog sat up, tilted his head back and howled as if a fire truck was splitting the night with its siren.

Chapter 28

Rocky hit the redial button. She had already left a message at the funeral home ten minutes ago. She wanted to speak to a person, not a recording. She wanted the phone number of Liz's parents. The funeral home had been listed in the obituary and that was all she had. The Townsends were unlisted; she'd already tried calling Information. She'd gone into Tess's house and tried everything to search for them on the Internet. Nothing. Isaiah was still out of town and he had been the only one to talk to them on the phone. As a last-ditch effort, she tried the vet clinic in Orono, but they were closed for two days. "In case of emergency, leave a message for the doctor on call and he'll get back to you." Rocky had tried the doctor on call and he said he couldn't give her information from another veterinarian's office.

Cooper had been gone for four days and Rocky was frantic. She had never been this clear about anything. She had made a terrible mistake and now she was going to fix it. She hit the redial button for the funeral home in Providence seventeen more times in the next hour. Then on the eighteenth time, a voice said, "Harsdale Mortuary."

Rocky's voice stuck in her throat, then she swallowed hard and spoke. "I'd like to call the Townsends in Providence to offer my condolences and I believe you handled the arrangements of their daughter Elizabeth. Do you have their phone number?"

"Who's calling please?"

"This is an old friend of Liz's from Maine. I just found out about her death," said Rocky. Why had she fabricated this lie, why didn't she just tell the man that she was the dog warden and that she needed to get in touch with the Townsend's about the dog?

"We can't give out phone numbers of our clients. But you can send your condolence card to us and we'll be sure to get it to them," said the as yet unidentified man.

"I've already done that. Now I want to call them. Calling is better. I mean I used to have their phone number, but I've changed address books and that was back when Liz lived with her parents. I just don't have the address now, it's not like I never had the address and phone number. So could you just give me the street address? I'd like to send flowers too," said Rocky.

"We can handle the flower arrangements also. What would you like to send? Do you have a price range?" he asked.

Rocky hung up.

Because she was desperate for any connection to Liz and Cooper, Rocky decided to drive over to the old Hamilton place where Liz had so briefly lived, possibly for only a few days. Tess had described it as one of the few old houses that had ventured toward the center of the island. Almost all the old vacation houses were built as close to the shore as possible, but this house was the last house on a sandy road that plunged inward, crossing a small bridge over a marsh, surrounded on both sides of the lane by impenetrable growth, tangled and dense.

The road ended in the yard of an older house that had gone through a series of additions and remodels. Like so many of the houses, it was built on the uncompromising waves of rock that layered much of the island. The core of the weathered house was tucked behind a façade of screened in porch. On either side, newer additions had been attached with limited regard for symmetry.

She opened the door on the truck and the groaning creak of door hinges sounded louder out here. She made a mental note to blast the hinges with WD40. The owners of the house had made a heroic effort to keep about an acre cleared of the encroaching undergrowth. Rocky looked at the large outbuilding where a riding mower was likely to live. She grabbed her gloves from behind the front seat and slammed the door shut. A damp wind whistled in the clearing. She was not going to think about Hill today.

Had this been Liz's dream, to come here with her dog? And do what? It might have been the impulsiveness of youth, the result of manic buying, or the simple desire to live within an easy commute of Portland. Rocky zipped her jacket and walked to the outbuilding, a small barn that was rapidly rotting into the ground. Stone-lined garden spaces graced either side of the large barn doors. With a forceful heave, she slid open one of the doors. Air that was even colder than the outside temperature escaped and ran over her, chilling her to the core.

The flashlight was in the truck, and if the dog had been

with her, she would have gone to get it. Or if Tess was with her, she would have gone to get it. But here alone, not needing to take care of anyone else and not caring very much what happened because all the worst things had already happened, she stepped into the barn and waited for her eyes to adjust to the gray light. Late-afternoon sunlight came in through two dust-covered windows. She sat gingerly on a wood chair that needed webbing on the seat.

Someone had shot Cooper out here. He had to have been shot on the island. And by all accounts, no matter how difficult Liz's life had been at times, she loved Cooper more than anything or anyone else. The two of them must have had just a few days of their new life on the island before things went terribly wrong. Rocky scratched the heel of her shoes along the dirt floor and the low rays of sun caught the disturbed dust. She sat until her bottom ached from the cold.

Her heart double-timed as she heard a truck pull up. She was terrified that it was Hill, because if he knew about the Hamilton place, then he had lied about everything. Could he have shot Cooper? Rocky went to a dust-covered window and peered out.

Rocky knew it was Peter, the boyfriend of the dead woman, the minute he stepped out of his SUV. The windows were tinted dark, the color of the vehicle was dark; she still couldn't tell exactly what color in the approaching twilight. She was obviously here; her truck was outside. She walked out of the barn, mustering all of her best body language to appear confident and official.

What was it, how did neediness and obsession get exactly translated by the way he held his shoulders in so tight that she could see it through his jacket? And the way he walked straight toward her, and smiled with the bottom half of his face while his eyes hooked into her.

"Shit," thought Rocky.

What do you do if you meet a bear on the trail, or a mountain lion, or any of the big predators? Those were the only two she could think of, and she was pretty sure that most black bears were more interested in bird feeders and compost. You didn't run, she remembered that much. Bob had told her that in the animal world it really is about size or about perceived power. Make yourself bigger, turn and face them, maybe back up slowly, which she didn't think was such a good idea in this instance because that would put her back in the empty barn, and more than anything she didn't want to be in the barn with this man. She scanned the area for something large to pick up, like a thick branch, all without moving her head. Turn and face him and make yourself bigger. No backing up.

"I saw your truck. Are you the animal control lady? Someone at the dock said you drove a yellow truck. I think you have a dog that I'm looking for."

He stopped four feet from Rocky. She didn't know if he remembered running into her for all of thirty seconds that day in Portland. She'd had her car, and Cooper and they were in the parking lot of a convenience store, when this guy pulled in and Cooper went off like a grenade in her car. But before Rocky could hold on to this shred of temporary comfort, Peter drew in closer and pointed a finger at her chest, dead center.

"Hey, that was you, wasn't it? About a month ago, over in Portland."

Rocky felt one of her fingernails pierce her palm. She was

with a predator. Stand and face him, make yourself bigger.

"Yes, and I recall the dog didn't seem to take to you. He went ballistic, didn't he?"

Peter kept his arms at his sides, not folded in front, not hands in pockets, but at his sides as if he had guns ready to go off.

"That dog belonged to my girlfriend. I know how to handle him. A dog like that, you have to be firm, show him who's the alpha. She'd want me to have him. She's dead."

Rocky willed herself into being a therapist again and not a woman alone with a crazed ex-boyfriend of a dead woman.

"I'm sorry," she said. "It's so hard to lose someone."

She saw a flicker near his eyes, a moment of hesitation, a moment of who he had been before he had turned into the bad boyfriend who couldn't let go. Now he was stalking the dog because that's all he had left.

Rocky had only worked once with a man who stalked his ex-girlfriend, and he came to therapy because he was convinced that going to therapy would get his girlfriend back. She had been struck by the absolute singularity of his pursuit; he became a laser beam, breaking into his ex-girlfriend's computer, accessing her e-mail, her post office box, even tapping into her parent's phone messages. Rocky realized that Peter had something that she wanted more than anything right then, the address and phone number of Liz's parents in Providence. She became the predator. She became very large and faced him.

"I brought the dog to the shelter in Portland. I didn't know about other family. Why don't you check the shelter tomorrow. And I'd like to send the family a sympathy note. What's the street in Providence?" said Rocky. She kept her gaze soft, remarked on the shockingly early arrival of night at this time of year, and jingled her keys as a cue to leave.

The address and phone number slid off his lips so easily. Rocky knew instantly that he had prowled the neighborhood in Providence searching for the dog. She thanked him like she meant it and walked past him to her truck. She held the car keys as if they could save her.

Rocky locked both doors of the truck and pressed her palms against the steering wheel. She suddenly had to pee worse than anything, but she was too afraid to get out of the truck, too afraid that he'd come back, that he would have caught her lie. He was on a mission, and his senses were shined up like silver. Any minute now he'd guess what had happened. Somehow Rocky had gotten what she needed from him, the phone number and address of Jan and Ed Townsend in Providence. Rocky had lied to him, said that the dog was being held at the shelter in Portland. She had until he took the ferry to Portland and drove to the animal shelter, worse yet he probably had a cell phone. But the shelter should be unstaffed at night. She had until tomorrow. He might call and find out that Cooper had never been there. It wouldn't take him long to figure out what she had done.

She stopped her hands from shaking and drove the truck to her house. She drove right up on the winter grass, left the truck running and jumped out. She hadn't locked her door, half the time she forgot. She grabbed the phone and punched in the number for the Townsends. The answering machine picked up and Jan's dusky voice came on. Why weren't they there? It was six P.M. and they didn't look like the kind of people with either friends or hobbies.

"This is Rocky on Peak's Island. This is very important.

Your daughter's former boyfriend is going to try and convince you to give him Cooper. Liz didn't want Peter to have the dog. Look, it's worse than that, something is off with this guy. I have a feeling he had been stalking Liz. Don't let him in your house." She hung up the phone.

She still had to pee. She didn't want to. She knew it would take too long, but she had to. She marched into the bathroom and slipped her jeans down and sat on the cold toilet seat. Faster, go faster, she willed herself. She pressed on her belly. The next commuter ferry would be leaving in thirty minutes, and then not again until seven o'clock. She hauled up her pants. She couldn't miss the ferry. Peter would have taken the ferry that just left. She grabbed an atlas, turned the pages to Massachusetts and Rhode Island, and in two running steps she was out the door and back in the truck. As she drove past Melissa's house, she paused, and without knowing why, she stopped and knocked on the young girl's door. Melissa and her mother both answered.

"Melissa, I just wanted you to know that I'm going after Cooper. I'm not coming back without him. You keep an eye on my place and feed Peterson, OK?"

Melissa's eyes softened slightly, going from rage to hope and settling in at caution. Rocky saw that Melissa's skin was pulled even tighter around her face than the last time she had seen her.

Rocky turned and ran back to the truck and drove to the ferry, waiting impatiently for the 6:30. She prayed that she wouldn't see Peter standing at the dock in Portland. She stayed in the truck for the crossing, kept the doors locked and was prepared to drive over him if he stood glaring at her on the dock. But he wasn't there.

She changed vehicles in Portland. The yellow dog warden's truck hadn't passed an inspection in five years, so she picked up Tess's car in Portland.

She figured the trip would take two and a half hours. She flew onto the highway out of Maine and watched the digital clock glow the time at her, watched the odometer tick off the miles. She had to stop in the notch of New Hampshire before Massachusetts to get fluid for the windshield wipers to keep her windshield clear. When she hit Massachusetts, she started imagining what she would say to Jan and Ed, wondered if she'd have to wrestle them to the ground, if they'd call the police, and what she could say so they would just give Cooper back to her. She slipped into the eastern edge of Connecticut and had to pull over once to turn on the overhead light and chart the fastest path into Rhode Island.

When Rocky hit the city limits of Providence, she stopped at a gas station and asked where Clementine Drive was. The two high school boys running the place didn't know, so she bought a city map and found it on the northern edge of the city. When she pulled up to 63 Clementine Drive, the house was dark except for a bluish glow coming from what Rocky imagined to be a kitchen fluorescent light.

The neighborhood was filled with sixties' ranch-style houses. Rocky turned her car around and parked across the street several houses away. She remembered what Jan had said about a new fence and a dog run in the backyard. She stepped out of her car, closed the door, and looked at a new fence that started at the edge of the garage and connected with the property fence, butting up against a neighbor's hedge. The lumber was still fresh, a barricade type of fence, the sort that Rocky connected with prison yards minus the razor wire.

First she gave a firm knock on the glass storm door. Then she pressed a doorbell and heard the muffled echo in the house. Knocked again. It was nine o'clock at night, where were these people? Wherever they were, they wouldn't have taken Cooper with them. She couldn't picture them taking Cooper for a ride in the car.

Rocky looked at the houses on either side and across the street. The nearby houses had their curtains drawn. She went to the darker side of the house, away from the entrance and the garage and slid around to the outside of the barricade fence and hoped that the Townsends had done the unfriendly thing and presented the neighbor with the side of the fence with horizontal 2x4s. They did not disappoint her. Cooper would have heard her by now. She pictured him with his ears turned toward her and his eyes reflecting green light. She chanced calling to him to let him know it was her so that he wouldn't bark. She spoke softly.

"Cooper, Cooper. I'm coming in, Big Guy."

As she got a foothold on the lower 2x4, her nose filled with the smell of fresh lumber. For a moment she was filled with images of her brother Caleb and wished he were with her, giving her a strong boost up with his fingers intertwined into a stirrup. She grabbed on to the top of the fence and hoisted one leg over, felt the top edges of the roughly cut wood grab the inside of her pants. Then she lifted her other leg over and hung ungainly with her legs dangling as the fence pushed hard into her belly.

"Cooper, don't worry. It's just me." She knew he'd recognize her scent as well as her voice. She dropped into the yard.

"Cooper?"

Her eyes adjusted to the combination of night and filtered light from a streetlight in the next block. The yard was rectangular and unadorned by anything except several trees and a shed tucked into one corner and doghouse close to the house. She saw the reflection of light coming from sliding glass doors leading to the kitchen. As she approached the plastic, igloo-shaped doghouse, she was swallowed by the total absence of life in the yard. Above the doghouse was the dog lead that ran from a wire strung from the house to one of the trees. A wooden pallet had been placed in front of the doghouse to keep the dog off the ground.

Rocky knelt near the pallet and bent over, sniffing the wood. She smelled his damp wonder, the oil from his skin, and saw the one stick that he had managed to find in the scrupulously groomed yard. It was either a newly acquired stick, or Cooper had been too sad to properly gnaw the stick to tiny bits.

She repeated to herself, "I am not coming home without Cooper." If he wasn't in the house, what would she do? She was surprised at how easy it was to decide to break into their house. She went through no moral dilemma, no painstaking choice, just a flicker of concern about possible alarm systems that the Townsends might have installed. This was her moment of redemption for the crime of letting Cooper go and alarms and glass were incidental.

She tried the sliding glass doors. Locked. She had read about how easy it was to break into the average sliding glass doors, but she couldn't remember the exact method. She tried several aluminum cased windows, and unless she was willing to cut through the tight aluminum screening to get to the inside window, she was roadblocked. She wasn't opposed to slitting the screens, but she had nothing sharp enough with her to do the job. She looked at the door leading into the back of the garage and pictured the knob turning effortlessly in her palm, going into the garage, into the house. She willed it so.

The knob did not turn. Why couldn't they be forgetful like she was, why couldn't they walk out of their house this one time without locking the house down like the inner sanctums of the Pentagon? It was a simple door with paned glass on the top half. Rocky took off her jacket and wrapped it around her fist, and without pausing, she smashed the pane nearest the handle. The shattered glass sent a muffled sharpness into the air; the glass had hit something thick and absorbent, like a doormat. She shook her jacket and put her hand through the opening until she felt the simple doorknob lock and opened the door. She crunched over the broken glass, noted that the sedan that Jan and Ed had driven to Peak's Island was gone, and went directly to the door leading into the kitchen, which was unlocked, and she walked into their house. This time she didn't care. She spoke firmly, "Cooper, come here boy." She went into every room in case he had been shut in, or stuck in a crate. But she knew he wasn't there, any dog would have barked by now. She saw no evidence of dog food, no water dish. Everything from Rocky's ribs down began to crumble. They had gotten rid of him. They wouldn't have given him to someone else. They would have had him put down. How much could Jan hate her dead daughter? Everything from her ribs up began to constrict and twist.

She walked out the front door. A light across the street went on, and she saw a face look out into the darkness from a front door, peering uselessly from the ocean of light in their house. Rocky got in her car, and as she drove back to Maine, she realized this is what it felt like to lose everything. She had lost Bob and her life was a continual spiral of losing everyone. Rocky did not think she could face Melissa, but when she ultimately did, she would tell the girl that she had been right; Rocky should never have come to Peak's Island.

The small bit of New Hampshire that she had to drive through offered her a Motel 6, and by midnight she had slipped off her shoes, wrapped herself in the bedspread, and dove into a punishing sleep. Tomorrow would be her last day on Peak's.

Chapter 29

Checkout time was noon, but Rocky had been awake since seven. She drank a glass of heavily chlorinated water from the tap and thought that New Hampshire didn't go for things like chlorine. Maybe this part of the state was too close to Boston. Then she sat back on the bed with the spread wrapped around her and planned her departure from the Island. She'd wait until Isaiah returned. He was, after all, her boss. Or she could just leave the truck and the keys to everything at his house. No, she had promised to feed their cat. That was the last attachment that she had left and she was not going to fuck that up.

She heard a voice say, "Feck. *Feck* that up. No need to be vulgar."

She threw off the blanket and stood up. "Bob? Oh my God, I'm going crazy in a Motel 6." She knew that it was not uncommon to hear the voice of a loved one who had died. Sometimes the effect was soothing, but more often it was startling, and clearly she was startled. She had been searching for him in her dreams for months, and she had been comforted by the one dream of him that she eventually had, but the clear tone of his voice in his mock Irish accent shocked her.

When Bob said that something was fecked, there was the barest chance of hope; and one could say it in front of one's mother. He clearly had not said *fook*, which was a more serious condemnation. Was there hope?

She said to the empty room, "You've got to give me more than that. I'm looking everywhere, and hope isn't in the picture."

She waited until noon in exactly the same spot, on the bed, in the same position with the bed cover wrapped around her shoulders in case she heard the voice again. The only sound Rocky heard was the coming and going of other travelers, cars starting up, doors slamming, and finally silence. She drove to Maine, picked up the yellow truck in Portland, and headed for the ferry. She had not eaten in over twenty-four hours so she bought a bag of barbecue chips on the ferry and after eating them, wished that she hadn't. The grease and salt met in an unfriendly tangle in her stomach. She'd pack up quickly before the day was done.

The sky was thick with high clouds, the kind that foretold snow. It was a shadowless day. Rocky wasn't ready to stop at Melissa's house yet to tell her that Cooper was now beyond their reach. He'd never be coming back. She would have to work up enough courage to tell Melissa.

It was midafternoon as she pulled up to her cottage. A light was on inside. Oh yeah, she thought, I told Melissa to look after the place. She prayed that Melissa wasn't there waiting; she wanted a few more moments before she had to tell her. Dread grew in Rocky's throat and wrapped around her heart. Fook, she thought, Melissa is inside, I can hear something.

As she approached the steps, she turned her head slightly

to one side as she tried to discern a familiar sound. After the startling voice of her dead husband earlier in the day, she was cautious. Rocky turned the knob and pushed open the door. She saw the great black shape of Cooper wagging and twisting toward her with his lips pulled into the biggest retriever smile. Tess and Melissa stood on the far side of the island counter with jubilant faces, eyebrows high, eyes glowing, their cheeks spread wide and high from smiling. Cooper took one huge lunge and put his front paws on her chest and flattened her against the wall. He made a high sound like singing.

"Oh, Cooper! Oh my God, Cooper-Lloyd." Rocky slid to the floor and dug her fingers into his thick winter fur around his neck. "What are you doing here?" she asked him. Getting no answer, she looked at her two guests. "How did he get here? What's going on?"

Rocky had never seen Melissa excited before. The girl spoke rapidly.

"I was here bringing in the mail, leaving some cat food out, and this car pulled up. It was those people who took Cooper. They brought him back. I couldn't believe it!" Melissa said. Her face lit up, and for one second Rocky got a glimpse of how Melissa would look as a grownup, when she was first in love, or standing at the rim of the Grand Canyon.

"You mean the Townsends, Jan and Ed? What did they say?" The dog whirled his way to Melissa and wrapped his body around her thighs. The girl crouched down to get the full effect of his affection.

"The guy said they changed their minds, that's all. But the woman said they couldn't do right by Cooper and she wanted to make it right. She wanted to make it right with her daughter. Do you know what she was talking about? Look, they brought all this food and a new water dish and everything."

Rocky took her eyes off the dog long enough to see that the Townsends had delivered a fifty-pound sack of food and a food dish with little paw prints that looked far too poodle for Cooper. A blue nylon leash sat abandoned near the couch.

"Did you happen to tell the Townsends where I was?" said Rocky, her shoulders falling. The image of Ed and Jan staring at the broken glass on the backdoor mat suddenly bore down on her.

"Since I didn't really know who they were, I did what my Dad taught me to say. I said you were off on business, or doing business, I can't remember which I said. But my father said never give people who you don't know more information than they absolutely need."

Tess raised an eyebrow at the girl. "Let me guess, dear, your father is a lawyer."

"Yeah, he is. Did I say the right thing?"

Rocky sighed with relief. "You did great, Melissa. I don't know why they returned him, but I'm not going to argue with the best thing that has happened since I got to this island."

Tess slid her jacket on. "I leave this place for five days and the world gets turned upside down. I want to hear about everything that happened, but right now I have to check on a handful of summerhouses. Melissa filled me in on Cooper's odyssey, but I have a feeling that you have been through hell and back. You look dreadful, if you don't mind me saying so."

Rocky hugged the older woman as she left. "I need to talk to you, but I'm ready to drop. Will you come by tomorrow?"

"Tomorrow, late afternoon. I need to make a quick trip

into Portland to stock up on groceries." Tess turned to look at the two people and the dog. "This place is so filled up with good juju that I hate to leave."

Melissa stayed longer than she ever had at Rocky's. The exhausted, well-fed dog dozed on his side and fell into a dream. He whimpered in dream talk, his feet jerking as if he were trotting. Rocky and the girl stopped talking and watched him.

Melissa said, "I think animals dream like we do, but they can't tell us their dreams, so we'll never know."

Rocky paused and looked, really looked at Melissa. This was the first time that the girl had offered something that she had pondered. This was the first of a nest of pollywog thoughts that for some reason at this very moment, Melissa shared. One egg of her self dropped into the air and Rocky took it in. The fragility of the moment was not lost on her; anything that she could say now might be wrong. She tried to remember her old life, when she knew the right words to say to people to let them open up all the dark places on the inside. She stopped trying to think and just asked, "What do you think Cooper is dreaming?"

Melissa tucked one leg beneath her on the far corner of the couch. "Maybe he's dreaming about running before he got hurt. I heard that people who get their legs amputated always dream with their legs on."

"I never would have guessed that," said Rocky. "I would have said food or catching a stick. You're more complicated than I thought . . ." Rocky stopped. This could go wrong, she worried that Melissa would retreat again into her thinning bones.

"Melissa, I did something stupid when I was in Providence trying to find Cooper. I broke into the Townsend's house. I broke a window on their back door. I don't know what to do. I've never done anything like this before."

Melissa turned her head abruptly to Rocky. "That's like breaking and entering. You entered, right?"

"Yes, I broke and I entered. What would you do?" asked Rocky. She didn't want to lose the window that opened with Melissa and she was willing to brace open the portal with her entire body. And she believed that the girl might really know.

Melissa leaned toward Rocky. "Never tell them. Never."

For her entire career, Rocky had urged all who came to her to tell the truth, be brave, walk through the fear of emotional confrontation, and they would all be stronger for the effort.

Rocky nodded. "You're right. I can tell a lie in this case."

Chapter 30

Melissa was back at school for a full week before she noticed that she hadn't gone to the YMCA even once after school. Instead, she took the first ferry home and stopped to get Cooper for a walk. A fast winter storm had dumped six inches of snow and the dog rolled in it like a displaced polar bear.

Rocky had even taken to calling her Lissa and she let her. Nobody called her that except her old friend, Chris. Everything had changed with Rocky once Melissa had helped her through that rough spot. There was a moment when she knew that Rocky truly didn't understand how to bluff her way through a situation and that Rocky was programmed to confess the tiny little crime of breaking and entering that she had committed. Even the day after Melissa had plainly told Rocky to never, never tell the truth about smashing the Townsend's window, Rocky had a moment of doubt.

Rocky had said, "I should call the Townsends and confess that it was me who broke into their house. Nothing good can come of lying."

"No! No! Don't call them. They don't know it was you. They live in Providence. My history teacher said Providence is the crime center of the universe. Why would they think you'd broken into their house? Do not, repeat, do not tell them it was you."

Melissa couldn't believe that Rocky would risk losing Cooper again by letting the Townsends know she was a psycho lady crawling around in their backyard.

When Rocky asked Melissa for help, she had looked like some weird kind of kid, or a lost animal, or someone who doesn't get that being honest is not always the best answer. Before Melissa left Rocky and Cooper, she said, "Now promise me, no calling and making confessions."

Rocky had promised. And she looked ready to drop on the floor. She had dark circles under her eyes and looked like she was straight out of chemotherapy treatment. Melissa had checked out Rocky's kitchen before the big dog reunion. Rocky had no food in the house. Okay, two cans of tuna, a greenish loaf of bread, a jar of dill pickles, and milk that said it was best if consumed six days ago. Rocky had terrible eating habits. Didn't she know anything about nutrition? It had been weeks since she had logged on to the pro-Anna websites, but she remembered the caloric count of every food she had ever encountered.

Melissa rattled through the kitchen at home and found a brownie mix, read the directions, and with exacting measurements, produced a Pyrex pan of brownies. She didn't mind any of the ingredients except the oil, which if half the high school girls knew was in brownies, they wouldn't eat it.

Her mother returned home after dark. When she walked in the kitchen, she said, "This house smells unbelievable, Melissa. Did you make something?"

Her mother looked at the tray of brownies, then again at

Melissa and she seemed like she was going to say something, anything, which was going to be too much. Melissa cut her off before she could speak.

"Most of these are for Rocky. I don't think she knows how to cook. I'm worried about her."

Her mother sat down without taking off her coat. She slowly pulled off her fleece hat.

"I can't tell you how good this smells. It's like our house is beautiful again," she said quietly. Her mother didn't say any more and for that Melissa was grateful.

Chapter 31

Rocky knew she had been wrong about Isaiah's intention with Cooper and she left a phone message for him to call her when they returned. When Isaiah called her that night, he said their flight had been delayed from North Carolina.

"Does this mean you're speaking to me again?" he asked.

"Yes, and it means a lot more than that. It means I'm not going to quit my job, which I was going to do, and it means some really good things happened along with some moderately terrifying things. Can we be friends again? I'm sorry," she said. They agreed to meet at his office the next morning.

She told him everything, or mostly everything, leaving out the breaking and entering. And she didn't tell him how confused she had been when Hill said he had slept with Liz, that he had known her. She did say that she was done with her archery lessons.

Isaiah asked her why. "You worried about crossing the bay in bad weather? If the crossing is dangerous, the ferry doesn't run. And there's a place to practice in the winter. The VFW in Portland has a crappy banquet hall that they used to let people use for archery way back when. That's an indication of how bad the banquet hall was; they had one section with hay and targets."

Rocky considered telling him everything about Hill, and she knew Isaiah would be the perfect person to tell. He had heard everything when he was a minister, so she wasn't worried that she'd shock him or that he'd judge harshly. But to her surprise, she had already carved a space for Hill where she afforded him temporary protection. She had told no one about the paper target with Hill's mark on it that she had seen at Liz's old house in Orono. Tess had already guessed that Rocky was falling for her archery teacher. She told Rocky that her color was vastly diminished since she'd banned Hill from coming to visit. Rocky quickly switched the topic before Isaiah went down the same road.

"There's one more thing. Liz's old boyfriend probably has figured out that I have Cooper by now. I sent him on a false trail, and unless he's an idiot, he knows what I did. He sounded determined to get him. This guy has no right to Cooper, but he still sounds obsessed with Liz, and now that Liz is dead, Cooper has become his focus."

Rocky didn't tell Isaiah exactly how scared she was after Peter drove off. She already saw Isaiah's eyebrows moving together in a mountain of worry.

"What's his last name?" he asked.

"I don't know, but I might be able to find out. I met a friend of Liz's in Orono."

"Once you get his name, I can call the Portland police. They're used to me calling about ridiculous things. But I doubt there's anything they can do about a man with poor social skills who wants a dog that doesn't belong to him." The older man paused.

"Did he threaten you?"

"No, it wasn't me who he threatened. It was like he was still after Liz, or anything that belonged to her. I've worked with a few men who became obsessed with ex-girlfriends, and their ability to stay focused on one person was staggering," said Rocky.

"I've known them too, and I'll tell you what works with them; a slap on the head. They give men a bad name and we're skating on thin ice as it is."

Rocky had still not been able to find out Peter's last name. Shelly, the receptionist at the Orono Animal Clinic said she never knew it, and she only met him once. When Liz started up with Peter, she left everyone behind.

Peter's last name came from a surprising source. The Townsends called her to say that Peter had called them right after they got back to Providence. They also mentioned that their house had been broken into and they figured it was Peter. Jan said, "And the nerve of that guy. He called us the next day to see if we had Cooper. I told him he was one sorry son of a bitch and if he came anywhere near here, we'd call the police. He made like he was surprised and insulted."

Rocky felt queasy. "Well maybe it wasn't him who broke into your house. Could be a coincidence." She pressed her lips together to keep from confessing.

"I think you're right. The police said the same thing. They said the footprints were more like a young boy or a woman."

Footprints. Rocky decided to throw her running shoes away the next day and get another pair in Portland. She froze and didn't know what else to say.

Jan's voice got softer. "How is the dog?"

"He hasn't left my side except when his fan club is around. He's pretty popular around here. Thank you for bringing him back."

"I think Liz would like that. I've never been good with animals. That's probably a sign of me being a defective human being, but I've got to be honest with you, dogs give me the creeps. Got bit by one when I was a kid. Eighteen stitches on my thigh. Liz wanted a dog from the time she could speak, but I was terrified of them."

Rocky pictured Liz longing for the thing that most terrified her mother and she saw how mismatched the mother and daughter had been. And then she remembered that Jan had ostracized her own daughter and she wondered how she would live with that. Given all her options back then, Jan made a lousy choice.

"What made you decide to bring him back?" asked Rocky.

A long silence. Rocky waited, knowing that Jan was struggling with her emotions. "I made mistakes with Liz and I have to live with that. But you were right; she never would have hurt her dog. And he would have protected her at all costs. I can at least let Cooper live with someone who loves him. He deserves that." Jan's voice shook. "There's something missing in the picture about her death and I wish I knew what it was."

Rocky said, "I know what you mean. I haven't been able to stop thinking about it. Jan, did Peter say his last name?"

"I think he did. What the hell did he say it was? Ellis, yeah, like Ellis Island."

"Thanks. Sorry to hear about the break-in," said Rocky. She hoped that somewhere in the universe this counted as an apology.

Rocky waited for Peter's return. She had never seen obsession dissipate quickly, not with the laser focus that Liz's boyfriend had. Even a new relationship sometimes failed to dim the target. She locked her door at night and she never left Cooper alone. If she had to go places without him, she left him with Tess or Melissa.

And then there was the matter of Hill. She purchased her own archery equipment to replace what he had loaned her. She took Hill's equipment back to him. She went to his house midmorning when she knew he'd be teaching. At the last minute, she left him a note. "My dog is back."

Chapter 32

The first thing Tess noticed about the young man was his shimmering jaw muscle. The two of them were the only people standing outside on the ferry, headed for Portland. January had chased all the other passengers inside. Those bringing cars simply sat in them, hanging on to the last tendrils of heat.

Tess wore a large shearling hat, serious leather mittens that were lined with thick polyester, a sweater and a vest beneath her coat, and boots with wool socks. Winter was a fine time for her; it was the unfortunate people who didn't know how to dress for the cold who whined in misery until spring.

She guessed he was past a turning point, early thirties, where he imagined he would know something with certainty, and he looked angry that his life was not unfolding in a way befitting him. She glanced at his hands. They were red and sore from the cold. She jumped ahead to a conclusion, she imagined a lover saying to him, "It's cold out, wear some gloves." And in the beginning, in the blush of first lust, he'd take it as caring, and he'd say in a blustering way, "Nah, I don't feel the cold." Then weeks or months later when she stopped giving as much attention to him in a way that he was sure he deserved, he'd say, "Get the fuck off my back." And the lover would jerk in surprise and wonder what had changed.

She felt a tug, a draw to the young man and Tess had long since stopped wondering if what she felt was real. Synesthesia had opened up her world of options. She knew the sensation was true enough. She took a few steps closer to him and said, "At this time of year you can almost see my favorite building in Portland. Too overgrown in the summer." She pointed in the direction of a Victorian house that had emerged from the days of urban renewal unscathed. She knew her small size and her age kept him from being alarmed. Age especially gave her a stealth covering; he would neither feel compelled to strut as he would if she were a younger woman, or engage in territorial battle, if she were a man. Who knew that getting older was going to be this much fun?

She scanned his posture automatically. His head pronated forward as if his brain needed to arrive before his body. Oh, the anxious ones. In her practice, she could help people strengthen muscles, align their bodies into less tortuous postures, but she was frequently daunted by the toll that anxiety took on a person. Living with fear was exhausting. She remembered the days of fear when her husband smelled like oily liquor even when he sat bleary-eyed at the breakfast table with the children. She shook the memory away. Times had changed.

"Cold day to visit the island," she said. "Were you there for the day?" She hadn't seen him on the island before, but it was not uncommon to see strangers on the island. The fifteen-minute ferry ride from Portland opened them to the world.

"The cold doesn't bother me," he said, pulling his head back in line with his body. He wore a charcoal coat, zipped to the center of his chest. The filling of the coat exaggerated his size, giving him larger shoulders and arms.

"Not much open on the island in the winter, but Stan's Seafood is open until seven. Everything closes by then. I sometimes wonder what visitors do on the island in the winter," she said.

As she got one step closer, she thought she caught the scent of something metallic coming off him, the way aluminum tastes if you bite a scrunched up ball of it. She stepped back.

"Business," he said. "I had business to take care of." The hinge of his jaw locked shut. She could see his muscles tightening, starting at his jaw and spreading throughout his body. She glanced down and saw that both his hands formed into dry, chapped fists. Finally he said, "I'm working on one of the new houses in town. Lots of building going on there."

Tess relaxed a bit. Of course, there was a dreadful amount of construction going on. Before you knew it, a stoplight was going to show up one day. She hated being the old woman who groused about change and people moving in. Soon, all of Boston would move here and clog up the tiny roads with their oversized cars. She shook her arms and shoulders with a shudder.

"With every new house, something precious gets sacrificed," she said.

The man smiled for the first time, his lips spreading like a wet opening to a cave.

"That's right. Sometimes a sacrifice must be made."

The ferry jolted as it made first contact with the tire-lined pier. Tess put her hand on the railing to steady herself, looking at the dock. The man turned and walked quickly to the gangway. He stood in line with several people behind him. When the attendants opened the sturdy chain link barrier, he slipped off the ferry and disappeared before Tess could see where he went. She wanted to know, when is a sacrifice needed?

Tess walked to the restaurant to meet her ex-husband for dinner. She worried about hiding the illness from Len. His diagnostic skill had been brilliant when he was young and sober, and not all that bad even when he was in his drunken years. But that was long ago, and he was sober now, and long retired from medical practice. Would he notice that she carried herself differently? The family get-together at Christmas had been the greatest source of her worry, but she had passed through the holidays undetected, or almost.

"It's the skin," he once said to her. "And something about the eyes." He said that he could spot someone with cancer when he looked at them.

For the family visit, she made sure that she moisturized her skin, and at the last minute, she put Visine in her eyes until the sclera were parchment white. Only her little granddaughter, who she had suspected had received the thread of synesthesia through little knotted bunches of DNA, had noticed. She had taken Tess's hand and whispered in her ear, "Granny, your color has a dent in it. Why is that?" The girl was six and Tess did not want to lie to her.

"What you're seeing is a tummy ache. Thanks for noticing. I'll fix it when I go back home. Would you mind not telling the others? We're having a party, and no one wants to hear about bellyaches."

Tess did not want to make the child a co-conspirator in

silence. That was wrong. She would make it right later, some-how. If it was as bad as she imagined, she would tell the child, "You were the first to notice and you helped me." Lying to a child was the worst sin, the taste of it reeked of a dead car-cass. She would tell the child the truth when the time came. The child had to know that what she saw was real. Tess had to give her that.

Tess's mind jumped ahead to the dinner with Len. She pulled the flaps of her enormous hat over her ears and walked up the dark hill to the eatery. She'd agree only to surgery, not chemo, not radiation. Sacrifice, she would not sacrifice the end of her life to a drugged and hairless stupor.

Chapter 33

Rocky had purchased a bow with a thirty-pound draw. In the five weeks since Cooper's return, she had practiced almost daily. Now it was February, and on the few days that were both without wind and above freezing, she practiced behind Tess's house. On all the other days, she went to the boathouse. On Isaiah's advice, she asked the club if she could use their storage house. It was surprisingly spacious, with plenty of room down the center, between the boats. She hauled in some hay bales and set them between the rows of boats that sat stacked in neat formation. Rocky stood between the twenty- and thirty-foot rigs on one end and the piles of sea kayaks on the other. The cement floor drove the cold through her shoes after an hour. That was long enough for her. Once or twice Isaiah showed up, just to sit and watch, he said, but Rocky didn't like it when he was there. After two arrows skittered off a hull, she said, "This is like having someone watch you practice the piano or take a bath. I shoot lots worse when you're here."

Isaiah wore a leather bombardier hat with flaps over his ears.

"Well, if you're not going to bring your dog with you, I

thought you would like to have some company. I won't watch. I'll do some old man thing like whittle, which I'll have to learn to do eventually as I am getting older."

Since they'd had a fight and made up, it was like someone had scrubbed layers of varnish off them and Isaiah had grown larger and softer in her life.

"You don't need to look out for me," she said. "I think Liz's stalker ex-boyfriend is gone. It's been over five weeks. He's probably gone on to a new girlfriend and has a new set of obsessions. Give me some credit here; I know a few things about the strange entanglements of relationships."

She set an arrow, drew back, and released. Thwack. Outer ring. Rocky sighed.

Isaiah zipped his coat. "I can see your game is off when I'm here. Either that or you're just plain terrible all the time, and you're trying to blame it on me."

Rocky had her sights set on the forty-pound bow by spring. She felt her arms and back muscles firming. She had returned to swimming at the Y in Portland and her body was beginning to feel like hers again. Last night she had eaten a pile of spaghetti and meatballs.

She guided Isaiah to the big sliding metal door. "You're right, in a way. I'm not confident enough yet to let people watch me. If I was really focused in the way that I should be, I wouldn't even notice you sitting there," she said.

As Rocky watched her friend walk on the gravel path to the parking lot, Isaiah turned and said, "Go get yourself a tune-up with that archery teacher. That's what you need."

The door squealed as she pulled it shut. No, she did not want a tune-up from Hill. She wasn't sure if she trusted him about anything.

One of the overhead fluorescent lights flickered. The thought of spring was a bright speck of light drawing closer. As soon as she could stand it, she was going to start practicing outside again at Tess's. She looked at the offending light and wondered if she could haul a ladder inside and change the failing tube. The ceilings were twenty feet tall, maybe thirty.

Today was one of the days when Melissa came directly home from school and took Cooper for a walk. Rocky had started leaving Cooper alone for an hour or two; she had to get him used to being alone. She couldn't be with him constantly.

Melissa. Didn't she have any friends on the island? Rocky never saw her with another kid. She had seen her several times at the Y, and each time, Melissa had looked uncomfortable, as if she had been caught robbing a bank. Rocky had not said anything to cause a meltdown with the girl since Cooper came back. Could she broach the subject of friends? Was it any of her business? Melissa had looked alarmed when Rocky told her that she was a psychologist and that her husband had died on their bathroom floor.

"Why did you make up a big story?" Melissa had asked.

"Because I couldn't stand the truth. I couldn't stand the idea that people would expect me to know what I was doing because I was a therapist. And I knew CPR. When Bob died, it was like all of sudden I was handed a whole new set of skin that was sad and miserable and I didn't want to be that person. I was sad and miserable and I still am, but now I've got a couple of minutes each day when I don't think of death at the same moment that I'm thinking of my husband. I think of him the way he was, not him dying."

Melissa hadn't said anything, but later that night, Melissa returned with a plate of brownies and a note from Melissa's mother. *We are sad that your husband died and that it made you hide from us when you first came here. It is good to get to know you.*

Several days earlier Rocky learned Cooper's leg had gotten as good as it was going to get. His leg and shoulder were stiff when he first got up, and she suspected that the cold weather was tough on him in the site of his injury. She had asked Sam to take another look at the dog and he confirmed the diagnosis. Sam had offered to see Cooper at his house, where he offered vet services one morning per week.

"He's a good strong dog. Given the extent of his injuries, it's amazing that the only remaining result is a slight limp. This is where you tell me what a terrific vet I am," he said.

"You saved him," said Rocky.

Sam looked startled. "No sassy repartee? Don't tell me this big guy is improving your personality?"

"My personality needs more help than a canine can offer. But it's true, you're a good vet and you saved him."

Rocky and Sam stood in the entryway of Sam's house. He turned and yelled to his wife, "Honey, the dog warden is being too nice to me. Something must be wrong; help me. She gave me a direct compliment stripped of irony."

Rocky heard a rustling sound in another room.

"Don't get used to it," is what she thought she heard.

Sam turned up his hands and shrugged his shoulders. "You see what my world is like."

Rocky and Cooper loaded into the truck. The dog rode shotgun. "We're both going to be okay," Rocky had said, trying to be convincing. Cooper had looked over his left shoulder, giving her one of his stunning smiles, full of warm breath and contentment.

Rocky was home for a few moments when she saw Melissa and the dog coming up the road and was startled at their transformation. They both walked with abandon; the girl had dropped her tight control of every bone, muscle, and capillary in her thin body. Once when Cooper stopped abruptly, the girl didn't have time to catch herself and she tumbled over him. Rocky could swear they were old friends or playmates, apologizing to each other. The dog cringed for a moment and Melissa said something that must have been, "Hey, forget it, my fault." The black Lab then bounded around her legs and dove off the side of the road to roll in the last pile of snow in a shaded spot, kicking his legs into the air. Melissa squatted next to him, staying clear of his paws that punched the air.

Rocky watched with longing, wishing to ingest whatever it was that they had. They were happy. That was something she had not anticipated. If anything were to happen to her, Cooper would be fine. He'd spend the rest of his life with Melissa. Everybody loved him. Tess and Isaiah treated him like a good brother. Rocky couldn't stay here on this island forever; her leave from the college would be over at the end of the coming summer. She shook her head; that was the first time she'd thought about the next step, about going home and living her life without Bob, about her lonely bed, about wearing the mantle of widow.

Melissa and Cooper burst through the door. Melissa said, "He knew you were home. He can tell. How do they do that? How do dogs know when you're driving home even if it's a different time each day?"

A spigot had opened in Melissa, a faucet for her thoughts and ponderings that had previously been frozen. She didn't wait for Rocky to answer.

"Their noses are like one hundred times better than ours and their eyes reflect more light than ours do so they can see better at night, and they hear stuff at frequencies that we don't notice," she said.

Rocky gave Cooper several hearty thumps on his haunches that sent him into curls of delight. "You've been reading up on dogs."

Melissa stuck her hands in the front pouch of her sweatshirt.

"I've been reading about animal behavior on the Internet."

Rocky made a mental note to pick up a book about dogs for Melissa.

"It's like they have a different language, like dolphins or whales and we only want them to know our language but we never try to speak theirs."

The phone rang. Rocky had been mesmerized by the girl who was emerging out of the tight skin. Not that her musings were so extraordinary, but that she was sharing them, she was thinking about something aside from caloric intake and five hundred sit-ups. Rocky picked up the phone. It was the post office.

"You've got a box here, thought you might want it. It's from a sporting goods place."

Rocky paused and tilted her head to one side. "I didn't order anything from them. Must be a mistake."

"Well, you need to come and get it. Got your name on it."

She hung up and frowned. The call from the post office

rattled her. Who would send her something from a sporting goods store?

Melissa headed for the door. "I have calculus to do," she said. Rocky walked the girl to the deck. The girl leapt off, spread her arms wide and yelled, "I do calculus, therefore I am."

It was the first completely frivolous thing she had seen Melissa do. The leap was crooked and she landed awkwardly, yet she had a lightness that was untouched by the forces of gravity. The moment ended when Melissa caught herself and she resumed her exact and steel-clad posture. Rocky marveled at how swiftly she could go from spontaneous to rigid.

Rocky said, "See you later. Hey, my mother used to say the same thing except her version was 'I bitch, therefore I am.'"

Melissa gave Rocky a co-conspirator's glance for two seconds, three seconds, then she turned and sprang off on her young stick legs.

Rocky took the dog and walked the mile to the post office. The package was not from the sporting goods store in Portland, but from an archery company in Nebraska. Rocky checked the name, and yes it was addressed to her. The return address was unfamiliar. Hansen Bow Company, Traditional and Primitive Archery, Allen, Nebraska.

Rocky gave the package back to the postal clerk. "What should I do? I didn't order anything from them," she said.

"Could be a gift; maybe you have a secret admirer," said the postal clerk. The nametag said Marie. "You can always send it back as long as you don't open it."

Rocky kept the package. She carried it under one arm and walked slowly back to the house. Cooper left complicated urine messages on trees, fences, bushes, lampposts, telephone poles, and on one particularly alluring rock that had pushed its way up from the asphalt sidewalk. Cooper rationed out just enough urine for a round-trip from home to the downtown and back.

The package was light for its size, about three feet long. She pulled a tab that said "pull here" and a string eviscerated the package, cutting it in half. She pulled the cardboard apart and unrolled a Styrofoam blanket. Within its eternal protection was a group of arrows. The shafts were deep amber, the feathers notched tight. A flyer said, "Hansen's Traditional and Primitive Archery Equipment. These arrows are made of Osage orange and dried slowly in the open air of Nebraska."

She stopped reading. The arrows clattered to the table, the tips eyeing her with a husky glare. Nebraska. What had Sam said back when he first saw the arrow in the dog? He had told her that there was a place in Nebraska where they made something like these. Someone was sending her the same arrows that Liz used, the same type of arrow that someone had used to shoot Cooper.

Cooper. She looked over at him. He had carried his favorite stick into the house. It was about two feet long, and dotted with tooth marks. He dropped it with a clatter. She immediately thought of Peter. And in the next breath another name came up.

Chapter 34

Rocky pulled into Hill's driveway and as soon as she turned off the ignition, her throat grew dry and her hands went cold. All the blood galloped back to her torso for protection. Her heart pounded and she could hear her pulse thundering in her left ear. Was this what people heard before an aneurysm bursts loose, or a heart seizes up? No, she was terrified, not dying. If she could slow down her breathing and take deep breaths, she could regain enough control to get out of the car. She put her hands on the steering wheel and pushed her arms straight and took in a large gulp of air.

Beside her was the box with arrows from Hansen's in Nebraska, which she had not ordered, but had been sent to her nonetheless. She scooped up the box in one arm, opened the truck door, and walked up to Hill's house. She had never been in his house; all the lessons had taken place in his backyard. She hadn't seen him since the day he came out to Peak's Island.

He had called once and left a message but she had not returned his call. She knew he was not the kind of guy to call twice. But she imagined that every blinking light on her phone might be him, and she wondered what she would have done if he had called again. She had not erased his message.

"Rocky, what happened with Liz was long before you. You can't control the past, especially my past. I'd like to see what we've got here. Give me a call." Beep.

She hesitated at the fence to the backyard. No, she should just knock on the side door. Her hand was on the gate, and she stepped one foot into the backyard, the only part that she was familiar with. Then no, she turned and headed for the side door, and there he was. Hill stood at the door looking at her. He opened the door wide. "Nothing's easy with you, is it?" he said and stood aside to let her in.

He was just home from work. He wore khaki pants and a navy blue sweater. It never occurred to her that he ever wore different clothes than the ones he wore when he taught archery. Of course, archery was just one part of his life, and his livelihood was teaching high school kids. Rocky was startled by the picture that emerged of him teaching eleventh-grade English and not archery. This man graded papers, collected homework, and probably had to attend the spring prom. Her resolve at discovering the truth began to fray.

She held out the box to him. "I need to know one thing. Did you send this to me?" Her hands shook as she passed the box to him and she knew that he noticed.

"What? Send you what? I got the clear message from you that you weren't interested. I don't need a duplicate copy of the memo. I get it."

Rocky wanted very much to believe him, but she could not afford to be lied to. She watched his eyes and they met her straight on. She pulled an arrow out of the cardboard box. "These arrows are exactly the same as the one used to shoot

Cooper. There are only two people who I can think of who would send these to me: you and Liz's boyfriend, and I'm not feeling too great about either option."

Hill took the arrow from her and ran it between his thumb and forefinger.

"Before we speculate on the sender, do you mind if I admire these for about thirty seconds? These are beautiful. See that binding around the point? Deer gut. I bet this wood was cut by the same guy who made this arrow. Some guys go all the way when they become traditionalists. But I didn't send these. So I guess this would be a bad gift choice for you?"

She felt her calf muscles flicker, not knowing if they should spring like a cat or soften and stay.

"You look worried, if you don't mind me saying, and I want you to stay and tell me what's going on before you decide to bolt out of here. I can't believe you're standing in my house." He pulled out a chair and pushed aside his briefcase bulging with papers on the table. She sat down.

She watched him caressing the arrow shaft, turning it to look at the point. Then he picked up the flyer that had fallen out of the box. "I've heard of this guy. Nice work." He put the arrows down, folded up the piece of paper back into thirds and slid it into the box.

Rocky hadn't known what she wanted when she came to his house, or if she should believe him, no matter which way he answered.

"You swear that you didn't send these? You didn't order them and have them sent to me?"

Hill leaned against the sink and placed both palms on the edge. The kitchen was small enough that Rocky could see an angry hangnail on one thumb.

"I didn't send you this," he said and for the first time she really believed him. "I'd like an excuse not to read sixty essays. Why don't you stay and tell me what's happening," he said. He pulled two Mexican beers from the fridge and set one in front of Rocky. He slipped a knife from a drawer and cut a lime in half. Hill squeezed one lime into his beer and handed Rocky the other half. "Vitamin C. It's been a long winter," he said.

"Here's what's happening. I saw one of your paper targets at Liz's old house. I didn't know it was yours until you came out to the island and tacked up one of your targets."

She had a lot to tell him, but she wanted to say the worst part first. She saw the flicker of surprise on his face, the involuntary jump among a small group of forehead muscles, as he ran the whole story through his head, fast forward, and his eyes moved from lower left to upper right as if he was watching a video, then he met her gaze.

"You're wondering if I'm not telling you something, if I'm lying, if I kept seeing her after that one time, if I'm a psychopathic killer from the Maine woods."

"Yes, and in that exact order. If you're the psycho guy, save that part until last."

She wanted to rub her finger along his black eyebrows and she hoped he couldn't tell what she was thinking. She clubbed down the part of her that wanted to touch the perfect half spiral of his eyebrow near the middle and follow the dark hairs up and out to the edges where they ended with soft down.

Rocky told him about the house in Orono, and the meticulously sawn arrows that had been set aside by the carpenter and given to someone who sounded like Peter. Then she told him about Peter finding her at the old Hamilton place, about the way she lied to him about the dog to get the address of Liz's parents. He pushed his beer away and coiled tightly together. She watched him turn into the hunter.

"You've got what he wants," said Hill. "He could just be waiting for the right moment. Maybe you shouldn't stay out there."

"But that's where I live. Isaiah talked to the Portland police and they said there was nothing they could do without more information. Technically, he's done nothing wrong," said Rocky.

"Let me help you," Hill said. "I'm worried about you. A guy like this is bad news."

Rocky stood up and drew the box of arrows toward her. She wanted to stay. She wanted to put the box down and take off her shoes and toss her car keys on the table.

"When I went to Liz's house in Orono, she had one of your targets up in her backyard. That means that she hadn't forgotten you."

Hill started to speak and then rubbed one hand across his face in a way that far older men do.

"I am not going to lie about this. She was an amazing woman, sort of like a bolt of lightning. I wish I could have known her better, but I was married and it was just not going to happen. I tossed a roll of my targets into her car when I left. Stupid, huh?"

"You wanted her to remember you, and I guess she did," said Rocky. "Look, I'm glad I talked to you again." She tucked the box under her arm and slid her keys across the table into her fist. Hill might be separated, but he was still married, and Rocky suddenly felt foolish in his kitchen, talking about the time he had sex with Liz.

"You don't have to go. We don't have to keep skimming the surface," he said when he saw her grab her coat.

And Rocky saw herself floating on the surface of a pool, belly down, touching as lightly as a water strider.

"Sometimes the surface is the safest place to be," she said as she left.

Chapter 35

Rocky spent the next week practicing at the boathouse. By Friday afternoon she was deep into the rhythm of releasing the breath and the arrow when she heard a screech of metal against the door just as she plucked a round of arrows out of the target. Her first thought was that a tree had fallen. Had she been so engrossed with her archery practice that she hadn't noticed the wind? She went to the door and pulled on the handle, trying to slide open the massive door. The door held fast. It had never stuck before. The door had been stubborn, had wobbled in the groove, but never stuck. She worked at it, heaved her body against the cold metal. The door was huge, large enough to let in fat sailboats that were hibernating for the winter. There was little chance that her body was going to unstick the door. The last rays of daylight entered through the windows on the loft where kayaks were stacked. She climbed the ladder to the loft and peered out the window. There was no sight of anyone.

This was the hour of homecoming, a time to have a hot drink, have a beer, come in from the cold time of day. Cooper was with Tess. Rocky had dropped him off with her in the afternoon. Tess had looked a bit drawn and discolored. Rocky had said, "You look like you're sick. Do you have the bug that's going around? Melissa tells me half the school has it. Are you sure it's okay to leave Cooper with you?"

Tess kept one hand on her belly and said, "Must have been something I ate, an out-of-season crab cake. Cooper will keep me company while I nap on the couch."

So Tess was in no shape to come looking for her. Rocky would have to find a way out. The window in the loft was a crank window, but it only opened about four inches. She would not be able to get her head or her butt through. She went back down and searched for something to pry open the window a few more inches.

The building was remarkably devoid of anything but boats. She climbed the ladder again and found a kayak paddle and separated it into two halves and placed the fat end against the bottom edge of the window and pushed. She felt the window open one more inch. Encouraged, she pushed harder. The paddle slipped and met the glass full force before she could say breaking and entering, which is the first thought that ran through her, accompanied by the tinkle of glass.

"Jesus Christ!" she shouted as she stumbled forward with the momentum of the paddle.

Maybe this was breaking and exiting. But this time she could express remorse immediately; as soon as she got home she would call the boat guy and tell him exactly what happened and promise to pay for the replacement window. This was a chance for a re-do, a chance for complete honesty. She closed the windowless frame and stuck her head out to see how far down she'd have to jump. She had jumped this far before, back when she was in high school sneaking out of her girlfriend's house to meet boys. This second story looked much higher and less rewarding.

Rocky cleared the glass out of the sill with her boot, put on her leather gloves, and hung on to the window frame facing the building, edging her legs out the building. She dropped and crunched down on the broken glass. She felt nothing pierce her boots and she brushed the edges of them against a nearby tree, hoping to dislodge any glass fragments that might have hopped on.

Now she could take a look at the door around the front. She rounded the corner and stopped with icy awareness. Someone had wedged a two-by-four against the door, effectively locking it in place. The board was wedged so tightly that she finally had to kick it out with her foot. She ran inside and grabbed her equipment, tossing her arrows into the quiver. Slinging the bow over her arm with its bag dangling from her hand, she jogged to the truck.

It was Peter, she was sure of it. He'd come back after months of silence. If she'd had any doubts, when she opened her truck door, she saw a pile of neatly sawn arrow pieces stacked in a row on her dash. Rocky felt like the top of her head had opened, and the icy Atlantic water had filled her spine, grabbed her intestines and held them in a frozen fist.

How long had it taken her to get out of the building? Night was closing in, but the sky was clear and she could still easily see the outline of the nearby dock and leafless bushes.

He was bold, and somehow he knew everything. He knew where she was and he knew that she'd gone to Liz's house in Orono and talked to the carpenter remodeling the house. She should have listened to Hill; Peter was not going to go away without Cooper.

She had spent about thirty minutes getting out of the boat-house. That meant Peter had a thirty minute lead on her. He must think that he had plenty of time to go get Cooper. He had been waiting for the perfect time and he had taken his obsession to the next level. The dangerousness of his actions registered deep in her abdomen.

Thankfully, Cooper was with Tess at her house. Rocky got in the truck and slammed the door. She did not take the time to struggle with the old seat belt. She fishtailed out of the gravel drive and headed to Tess's house. Once she got there she'd call Isaiah and let him know that Peter was on the island and that he had tried to trap her in the boathouse. He'd never make it off the island; they'd stop him at the ferry.

In five minutes Rocky was in front of Tess's house where the faded prayer flags snapped in the wind. She jumped out and even before she got to the door, she saw the piece of paper attached to a clip. It said, "Rocky, I'm taking the big guy to your house. Feeling sick, heading to Portland."

Rocky felt the steady click, click, click of bad-luck dominoes falling over and she desperately needed to stop the fall. If Tess was already gone and had left the dog, then Rocky might be too late.

She got back in the truck and drove the two miles to her house. She passed one teenage boy on a bike, dressed completely in black and she almost hit him. She rolled down the window and shouted, "Get a light!" She passed Melissa's house and a warm, yellow light spilled from the windows. She wished that the dog warden's truck had a siren or a flashing light. No, she didn't want Peter to know that it was her. She pulled the truck as close to the house as she ever had, challenging the recent thaw and fresh mud.

She was out of the truck before it completely stopped. She heard Cooper barking in the house. He was still there, the dominoes could stop falling. But his bark was different. Rocky had only heard him bark like this one other time, with this explosive, split-open-the-sky sound.

"Cooper, Cooper, it's me," she said as soon as her feet hit the deck. She pushed open the door. Cooper stopped barking long enough to greet her, but he was clearly alarmed. His black ruff was raised along his back and he turned his head as if he heard a sound on the ocean side of the house. He boiled up a growl that raised the fine hairs on Rocky's arms.

What was the other sound? Rocky turned, followed the soft noise, and pushed open the bathroom door with the tip of her shoe. Cooper faced the kitchen windows, pulling his lips up, revealing the full danger of his teeth.

Rocky saw the small boots first, the legs folded on the floor, then she saw Tess's body heaved against the bathtub.

"Tess!"

She put her hand on Tess and the woman immediately stirred.

"Something's wrong," Tess whispered. "My stomach . . . I can't stand up, can't walk." She squeezed out the words as if the effort would kill her.

Rocky knelt on the linoleum floor and put one hand under the stricken woman. "I'm going to pull up, Tess, and get you out of the bathroom." An odd part of her brain demanded to change the variables, change the location of Tess, to fight off death and disaster. As soon as she put an arm around Tess's ribs, the woman shrieked, and Rocky knew a hot orange bolt of pain shot through the older woman. "I'm sorry, I'm sorry, but you are not dying in the bathroom. We're going to get

you out of here. I'll call Isaiah and he'll get the water ambulance." She dragged Tess to the hardwood floor in front of
the couch.

Rocky punched in Isaiah's number. Her hands shook. The
dog barked.

"Cooper, stop. I won't be able to hear."

After six rings, the answering machine came on and Rocky
said, "Tess is sick and needs to get to the hospital in Portland.
I'm calling nine-one-one right now."

She hoped that the volunteer squad was home. "We need
the water ambulance immediately. Isaiah's rental house."
She hung up without offering details. She had seen the small
fire truck go out on other calls. It was affectionately known
as the Tonka Truck. Now, she prayed to see it drive up. She
wanted to be ready for Peter if he tried to get in.

More than anything she wanted a weapon, and despite the
dog's unrelenting barking, she slipped out the front door, did
not turn on the outside light, and pulled her bow and arrows
from the truck. She left the terror of the unseen behind; this
was not the terror of going into a basement at night or having
a car go dead in a dim parking garage. This fear was about
Tess and the dog and losing what she had left. She wanted
to see Peter, and she was convinced that he was there in the
darkness. She wanted to run over him and flatten him like
a can. The adrenaline reservoir poured out and flooded her
body. Rocky slipped back in the house.

Cooper had barked so hard that foam pooled at the corners
of his black mouth and his body exploded with electricity.
He emitted a musky scent and his challenge of attack filled
the house.

Rocky grabbed her bow and notched an arrow. She held

the bow in her left hand with the arrow pointing to the floor. The dog stopped barking for a moment and she watched him. He tilted his head to one side and listened with heightened awareness. He turned his head slowly from the ocean side of the house to the front side. He growled again and faced the door. Headlights bounced into the windows.

"Take it easy, must be the fire crew. We're going to get Tess out of here." Rocky turned her head to yell back into the house. "Tess, they're here!"

She pulled aside the curtains of the front door and saw a familiar outline of a man. And there were no flashing lights. It was Hill, getting out of his truck. She immediately felt a twinge of relief. At the same moment Cooper went ballistic. Hill had parked at the far side of the drive fifty yards from the house. The dog threw himself at the door, claws digging at the wood, leaving jagged streams of exposed wood. Yes, it was Hill. She recognized the outline of his thick hair, his coat. What was he doing here?

"Down boy, it's a friend," she said.

She opened the door a few inches with her right hand, blocking the opening with her body so Cooper couldn't get out. Then she grabbed him by the collar and opened the door the rest of the way. The bow in her other hand clattered awkwardly against the doorframe as she stepped onto the deck.

Hill stopped when he saw Rocky and the dog. And at the same moment Rocky realized that Cooper had never seen Hill before. So why was the dog acting like this? Then the torrent of facts hit her. Hill was the one who knew every-thing because she had told him. He knew about the dog be-ing saved, about the house in Orono, about Cooper staying so often with Tess, about her friend Isaiah, oh God, Isaiah, he hadn't answered his phone.

"Stop! Stay there or I'll let him go," she shouted. Cooper strained against her like a bull.

Hill took another step and said, "Rocky, get inside, don't let the dog go!"

She didn't have time to pause. If he got closer, and if he had a weapon, neither of them could take him down. Everything was at stake. She had to do it quickly. She turned off all extraneous power routes in her body and nothing was left except the path from her brain to her arms, connected with a fiber optic line to her eyes. In one elongated moment she let the dog loose with her right hand, pulled the bow up with her left and pulled back with her right. She saw Hill jog to the right and her eye followed him like a missile. Breath exhaled and released. Hill dropped to the ground with a howl.

Cooper spent one moment barking on the deck, then burst off the planks. He was nearly even with Hill when the man fell to the ground. But the dog didn't stop. His muscled body lowered several inches as he ran. Rocky had seen other dogs run like this when they were in competition, either with themselves or with other dogs. They streamlined themselves, like jaguars or leopards in the final moments of running down prey. But Hill wasn't the prey. Cooper ran past Hill as if he were a tree stump and ran straight through the thicket of brush.

Rocky leapt off the deck, bow in hand, and came closer to Hill, keeping her legs flexed, not getting close enough to him that he could reach her. Hill lay in the dim light that ribboned out from the house. An arrow was embedded in his thigh and he grabbed his leg with both hands.

"Peter is out there," he said with a grimaced face. "Get the hell in the house. You don't know what you're dealing with. I found where he's been watching you."

Rocky turned and looked at the place where Cooper had entered the brush. She still heard him.

She cupped her hands around her mouth. "Cooper!"

She knew what she had to do. She took one step closer to Hill. "I was wrong. I'm sorry and I do know what I'm dealing with. You're not going to die." She reached into Hill's truck and saw what she prayed was there, his quiver of arrows. Thank God this man traveled with arrows. She hooked the bag around her left shoulder and ran into the brush, following the sound of the dog.

The darkness in the trail hummed with Cooper's scent. Rocky reached for the primitive part of her brain that operated on smell. She ran as if she could see in the tangle of dark and branches. Her lungs opened wide with the call of urgency from her legs to pound faster.

Two high shrieks, and a dog's scream cracked open the blackness. Then silence. Peter had hurt Cooper! He might have killed him. The sound came from the part of the trail closer to the ocean. Rocky stopped, notched an arrow, and let her body lead the way to the last sound that Cooper made. She no longer thundered through the brush; now she walked with soft steps, right hand on the string, arrow pulled halfway back, crouching, deadly. The wind was above her, unable to dip down into the dense tangle. She would not have to contend with the wind when she took her shot. There was nothing else but her heightened senses; she was no longer woman, but eyes, ears, nose . . . hunter. A dark coil of hair fell across her eye and she flicked her head to move it.

The scent of Cooper hit her first, the musk, his oily skin, and now another smell mixed in, urine, and a new scent carried to her by a tendril of moist air. Peter, he was close.

A voice from her right side said, "Drop what you're carrying or I'll give him a blast of this. And I don't think the combination of this Taser gun will mix well with the tranquilizer dart."

Rocky spun around and to her horror saw the dark outline of Cooper on the ground and Peter holding a Taser inches from the dog.

"I told you this dog was mine," he said.

Rocky considered her options, with Cooper's ability to withstand an assault from the Taser being her primary concern. She lowered the bow.

"Drop your little bow and arrow on the ground," he said and Rocky heard a hint of pleasure in his voice, a sort of satisfaction. The bow dropped to the ground and she measured its distance from her. She reached for the satisfaction that he got from bagging his prey. He would want to be noticed.

"How did you know I had him?" she started. She didn't care what the answer was; she only wanted him to talk.

"Are you kidding? I knew the day I talked with you. You were just like Liz. You thought I was stupid, didn't you? I saw it in your eyes. You were going to say anything to get rid of me. Didn't turn out so well for Liz either."

He stepped closer to her and kicked the bow to the edge of the trail. Rocky chanced a look at the dog. He was still. She prayed that Peter had not overdosed Cooper.

"He's alive. I want him alive. You and Liz aren't the only ones with silent weapons; a Taser gun is such a nice weapon. Do you know how it works? It shoots two little darts that deliver a wonderful bolt of electricity. I think it will work nicely on Cooper. This is one dog that needs to be trained. Liz wouldn't let me train him. If it wasn't for him, I'd still be with Liz."

Rocky had not moved, but she willed her body to relax; she and Cooper could not afford for her to freeze into fear. "She loved you. What happened?" she asked.

Come on, she thought, I know you can't think of anything else but Liz, talk to me.

"She was never going to find someone better than me, I told her that. And I had gotten her completely off that medicine she was taking. I was taking care of her. She was off all that junk for six months."

Rocky pictured Liz without her medication for six months: moods skyrocketing and plummeting, hallucinating if she had spiraled out far enough. An angry bile rose in her throat. She saw Cooper's front feet begin to twitch. She didn't have as much time as she had hoped.

"But she died from an overdose of meds. I thought you took all her medications away," she said.

Peter grabbed her arm securely and pulled her to the far edge of the small clearing. She judged his strength from the sharp points of pain where his fingers pressed flesh against bone. He tossed her a roll of duck tape.

"Here, take this and bind up his feet. Tight. I don't want anymore trouble from him."

"Where are you taking him?" Rocky knew if she kept him talking long enough, the island fire truck would arrive and Hill would tell them that she was in trouble. Then what? What would a crew of volunteer medics do?

"You think I'm leaving here on the ferry? I told you, I'm way ahead of you. Start wrapping his legs."

Rocky took the roll of tape and pulled out a two foot long strip. She held it up for Peter to cut it with the pocket knife that he took out of his jacket. She prayed for Cooper to stay dazed a bit longer. She wrapped his front legs together just above his feet.

"But how did she overdose?" Rocky asked again.

Peter snapped open what looked like a boat bag, the kind that kayakers use to keep their gear dry. He held the stun gun beneath one arm. "I had saved all of her medicine, kept it locked up in my truck. After she went nuts on me, after I brought her back from this island . . . that's when I said, 'Here, take all this shit. You want it, then take it!' And I dumped all her medicine at her house. We all make choices and Liz made hers."

Rocky wrapped Cooper's legs with as much care as she dared. Peter had not noticed the quiver that she carried. She let it fall quietly beside her. With one hand, she slipped out one of the arrows.

"She was in a manic phase and you gave her six months' worth of meds and then left her? Did you give up on her? No, wait, did she give up on you?" she asked.

Peter stood over her. "I'm telling you, if she had done everything I told her to do, she'd be here right now. 'Get rid of the damn dog,' I told her. No, she keeps the dog, treats him better than she treats me. When I found her on this island, she was fucking crazy, she thought I was the devil. She ran from me. Me! I ran after her and she had her archery stuff, pointing at me. I told her, 'Liz, it's me for Christ's sake!' Then

I hear the dog coming at me. The dog leaps at me. She shoots and hits the dog instead of me. Suppose I should be grateful to the dog."

Rocky slid the arrow part way up her jacket sleeve. She knew Peter hadn't told this saga to anyone, and it had been fermenting with acidic vapors since the fall and now he let his aggressive posture fall momentarily away as he talked.

"Here's what you're going to help me do. We're going to drag this dog down to the beach where I've got a boat," he said. "I've been slipping in and out of this island for weeks."

No, thought Rocky. This is all wrong; I needed someone to see us trying to leave on the ferry. I needed someone to help me. I can't do this alone; he's too strong. That's when she remembered Bob, when they first met, Bob sitting serenely at the bottom of the pool, waiting to be saved by her, trusting her with his life. He had smiled at her and blew out the remaining air in his lungs.

She felt her feet push off from the slick bottom of the pool, carrying the full weight of a man.

"And what about me?" she asked Peter. "I'm not coming with you."

He pulled the tranquilizer dart out of the dog's back leg and slipped the bag under Cooper's hindquarters. "Here, grab one side of this bag. We don't want our doggie to get wet on the crossing, do we? And you're coming with me, at least part way. Look like a good night for a swim?"

He crouched down and set the Taser beside him to stuff the dog into the bag. Rocky suddenly lay back on the ground and punched hard with both legs, hitting him in the chest. He fell sideways with a shout. "Fucking bitch!"

She fumbled with the arrow and pulled it out of her sleeve,

rolling onto her side. Peter reached for the stun gun; it was so close to him. Rocky rose up on her knees and drew her arm back, holding the arrow inches from the point and brought the arrow down on Peter's hand with the full weight of her body.

He screamed in shock. Rocky grabbed the stun gun and stood up. She pointed what she hoped was the front end of the gun at him.

"I will shoot you. I've already had a very bad day, and you are not the first person I've shot today. So don't move. Don't fooking move!" She had no idea if the gun had a lock, how it worked, but she had her fingers at what felt like a trigger.

Peter grabbed the protruding arrow with his free hand, and with a curdled howl he broke it in half. He rose up on one knee and stood up like a wrestler ready to lunge. Rocky knew that he was coming at her and this was her last chance. And Cooper, it was Cooper's last chance.

The man roared like a bear, opening his mouth, throwing both arms wide. Rocky squeezed the trigger, and the force of the charge from the two wires dropped him, convulsing to the ground. Keeping the Taser in one hand, she grabbed the bag that half-contained Cooper, dragging him onto the trail, far away from Peter.

"I've got you, I've got you."

Cooper whimpered. Rocky saw a light bounce around the corner of the trail, a huge flashlight, bouncing at an oddly familiar tempo. Then the light filled her eyes and she put her hands up to cover her face.

Melissa shouted, "I've found them! Isaiah, I've found them! Over here!"

The sudden presence of the girl both heartened and dismayed Rocky. She did not want Peter to harm Melissa if he recovered too quickly. "Lissa, toss me that roll of tape. Now help Cooper. Get that stuff off his legs."

Rocky saw Peter try to get up and she pulled the trigger again and prayed that the gun still held a charge. It did. Peter's body jerked into spasm. She ripped an arm's length of duct tape, placed one foot on his back, grabbed one arm, then the other, and circled his wrists with steel gray tape. Rocky stood up, panting and shaking.

Melissa's flashlight lay on the ground, offering an arc of light on the girl who crouched on the ground next to Cooper. Melissa's eyes were huge. She looked from Rocky to the man.

"You kick ass, therefore you are," said the girl slowly. Before Rocky could respond, the sound of Isaiah's voice boomed along the trail, calling her name.

Chapter 36

The ride to the mainland on the water ambulance was harrowing but brief. Tess and Hill were wrapped in thermal blankets and strapped to stretchers. Two volunteer firefighters sat on Peter, while Isaiah kept his arm around Rocky, who could not stop shivering. She was keenly aware of how small the boat was compared to the rumbling ferry. Every time it hit the top of a wave, she felt a jolt from her tailbone to her head. There was at least some comfort in the fact that Melissa and her mother were back at Rocky's house with Cooper, and they had promised to call Dr. Reynolds to see if the dog needed any medical attention after his ordeal. As they pulled into the dock in Portland, two police cars stayed to take Peter away and an ambulance waited with the rear doors open to take Hill and Tess to the hospital. Rocky impatiently answered the police officer's questions as she watched the ambulance pull away. Isaiah urged her to report every detail about Peter.

"We'll get to the hospital, but let's make sure Peter's stalking days are over first," he said.

By the time they arrived at the hospital, Tess was being

prepped and sedated for emergency surgery. Pre-op medications appeared to relieve Tess from the intensity of her pain. She grabbed Rocky's sleeve as the younger woman leaned over in concern.

"I might as well tell you, I've got cancer. I've known for months. It's been setting up shop in my abdomen. You better call Len; he understands hospitals and their language. His phone number is in my purse, in the address book. He'll call the children. I'm sorry, Rocky," said Tess, her eyes dreamy with medication.

"What! What do you mean, cancer? You're not dying, are you?" said Rocky as she collapsed in tears. Tess disappeared behind the automatic doors leading to the surgery unit.

Len did not live far from the hospital and was there in fifteen minutes. Isaiah had checked in on Hill, who was asking for Rocky. "He can wait," she insisted. "He's not dying, and I can only attend to one disaster at a time."

Rocky had never met Len before, and had only heard about him from Tess, who had regaled Rocky with stories about their weekly competition with darts. She did not expect the tall, handsome man with the searing blue eyes. Len moved easily in the hospital and was able to get a report from an obliging nurse. Tess had a ruptured appendix. Len shook his head. "The doctor said that she must have suffered with an inflamed appendix for weeks, even months. If she had just come in to be examined, they could have figured this out in fifteen minutes. Instead, her appendix ruptured. And on top of that, she had an obstructed bowel, and I can't honestly tell you where that came from, and neither can the docs."

Rocky said, "So she doesn't have cancer? She's going to live?"

"Cancer? Where did she get that idea? Did she think she was dying? And she wasn't going to tell me?" Len's eyes registered anger, but Rocky knew that the emotion was layered thick with years and that anger was just the surface.

Rocky reached for his hand. "Maybe it was one of those synesthesia things; maybe she thought she saw something. Maybe it was green or shaped funny or made a sound that the rest of us couldn't hear. But is she going to be OK?"

He squeezed her hand in return and sighed, relief pouring off him. "Yes. There's the infection to deal with, and the surgery, but yes, she'll recover."

"I've got one more emergency to handle. Will you excuse me?" asked Rocky. She located Hill's room as he waited for surgery. Someone had clipped the arrow so only several inches protruded from his upper thigh. An IV bag hung by his side, and just as Rocky walked in, a man in blue scrubs injected something into the line. "This should relax you. We'll come get you as soon as the last surgery is cleared out. See you in fifteen minutes."

Hill looked up at her and said, "You're not going to shoot me again, are you?" He held out his hand as she came closer to the gurney. "This is going to score so many points with my students in B Period English. We're studying Beowulf, and I brought a few bows to school for them to try. They're going to love this. Hey, that stuff he injected makes me feel like I just drank about four beers."

"What in the world were you doing on the island?" asked Rocky. She sat next to the wheeled stretcher.

"You had a very bad guy out there. I was hunting the bad guy." He smiled his crooked smile. "But the bad guy didn't know who he was up against. I'm not sure you needed me."

Rocky lifted his hand to her mouth and pressed her lips to his palm. "Not true, not true at all," she whispered.

Tess did not return to the island until March, after spending weeks recuperating at her daughter's home.

"Len hovered relentlessly. He also got more peeks at my poor belly than he'd had in decades. He said his interest was purely clinical, but I don't believe him," said Tess.

Rocky was thrilled to have Tess back again, as if everyone was finally back in the right place. It was an unseasonably warm day and Rocky followed Tess's instructions about uncovering her crocus from the winter debris so they could emerge unfettered. Tess watched her from a chair placed next to the garden. Cooper assisted by digging his own spot in the garden, until Rocky made him stop by throwing a stick for him.

"Len will be here again tomorrow. He said this is my penance for not telling him I was sick. He brought a dartboard and darts. He's beating me terribly while I'm compromised. Not fair."

Rocky knew that Len also came to walk with Tess. She had seen the two of them on the beach, the tall, white-haired Len, with Tess resting her hand lightly on his arm.

"Come inside. I'm done with your garden work. I've got some of Melissa's photos to show you," said Rocky.

Melissa had joined the photography club and Cooper was her number-one subject. Whenever Rocky noticed Melissa these days, a girl named Chris was with her. The two girls carried their cameras everywhere.

Rocky spread the photos of Cooper on the coffee table for Tess to see, but no sooner had Tess curled in her overstuffed

chair, than she dozed off, napping in the full tonic of sunshine like a cat. Cooper also decided to nap. Rocky picked up
one of the photos of Cooper.

In this one he was looking noble, his great chest expanded
without effort, offering the camera his best senatorial profile.
And here, in this one, Cooper and Tess were sitting on the
deck and he had one mighty paw on her foot. And in this
one, Melissa caught him in midflight, back legs extended,
head driving forward, all for the glory of catching a tennis
ball. There was not a hint of sadness in any of the photos.
When did he leave behind all the grief of losing his true
love? Where had it gone?

Rocky had gone over the scene again and again, knowing
only snippets from the police report, filling in the rest with
conjectures: Liz's sleep-deprived psychosis, her full-out non-
medicated mania, fleeing an obsessive boyfriend. Liz must
have bought the old Hamilton place as a refuge, and for a
brief moment in time it was, until the unexpected appearance of Peter.

Shouldn't Liz have known Cooper would try to protect her?
That the fur on this back would rise, a deep rumble would
erupt from this throat, that he would issue a last warning to
Peter to stay away? Liz would have faltered for a second, as she
stood with her weapon, her resolve crumbling just enough,
doubting her own perceptions, doubting the danger. The dog
leapt, following Peter's scent, leapt as high as he dared, to
pull him down, and Liz, at that very moment, pulled back
on her bow and took her shot. Liz had plucked her own dog
from the air.

Peter would not tell the police exactly how he dragged Liz
from the island. He did say that he told her over and over

again that she had killed her dog. And Cooper had been left behind. Rocky pictured the last days in Liz's life in Orono: the fragile structure of her mind unraveling, chewing away at itself as Peter drove her back to Orono and left her at her house, trying to teach her a lesson by tossing her bottles of stored medication at her, abandoning her. It would not take Liz long to saw her arrows and bows into tiny bits, stacking them on her table. It would not have taken her long to die by her own hand.

Rocky nudged Cooper with her foot. "Come on, you. Let's go home." She slipped quietly out of Tess's house. Her job still called and she had an important delivery to make today. But Cooper needed to go home first and she needed lunch.

As soon as Rocky and Cooper entered the house, Peterson began her new game of pouncing at the dog's tail and then dashing off. Cooper eyed her with the same level of interest as one might have for a fly, as if a dog of his standing could not possibly be interested in this type of inferior play. Yet just last night, Rocky noticed that Peterson had wedged herself behind Cooper as he lay gnawing on a stick. Cooper had peered over his backside as the once skittish cat curled against him and eyed her with surprise, then with an odd sigh, he returned to his slobbery stick.

Rocky made a ham and cheese sandwich and considered two letters that sat on her counter. One was from her boss at the university, asking her to verify her return date in the fall. The other was from Jan Townsend, who said they were coming out to the island soon to look at the house that was part of Liz's estate. And did Rocky know anyone on the island who might have an interest in buying the place before they contacted a real estate agent? The letters jostled for her attention. Rocky turned them facedown on the counter and placed her used plate on top of them. Not yet; she didn't have to decide anything yet. Right now she was still an animal control warden.

Ten days ago, a tomcat was discovered on the east side of the island, called in by a neighbor who said, "He's not exactly feral, but he's darn close. Guess you better come get him and bring him to the mainland before he starves to death."

Rocky had easily trapped the cat and kept him for a day at Isaiah's public works garage. The cat was black with three white paws and a white diamond on his face. His ears had been bitten and nicked from years of fighting with other toms and he had an abscess on his jaw. The cat hissed at her each time she came near. She waited twenty-four hours in case anyone called about a lost cat, then took him to the animal shelter in Portland. A sick and battered-up tom was the last cat anyone would adopt. She dropped him off at the shelter, knowing if the shelter was crowded, as they frequently were, he would be put down.

Yesterday, Rocky got a call. "This is Mrs. Hancock. My cat has been missing. He usually comes back after three days, but I'm afraid something has happened to him. He's black with white paws. Three of them, and a sweet white face."

Rocky rang up the shelter, fearing the worse. "Don't kill the tom I brought in! He's got an owner."

The receptionist said, "We've just finished all the procedures for the day. You're probably too late. I'll check and call you back."

Rocky dreaded telling Mrs. Hancock that she had delivered her cat to his doom. The shelter called back.

"You're not going to believe this. We made a mistake and

put him on the schedule for neutering. He's here. Do you hear that sound? He's not a happy boy. Come and get him tomorrow; I'll send someone down to the pier with him."

Rocky took the ferry over and was met at the pier by one of the shelter volunteers with a cat carrier.

"He's not happy about his missing testicles," she said.

Rocky got back on the ferry for the return trip. She delivered the cat to Mrs. Hancock, who opened the carrier and took out a suddenly sweet cat that pushed his tattered head into her hands. Rocky explained his shaved abdomen, with apologies. The women stroked him and the cat purred like an outboard motor.

"I know he's really as ugly as sin; I'm not blind. And he's a terror to other cats, but I don't know what I would do without him. There's no explanation for love. But love is all that matters, isn't it?"

Rocky felt her body rearrange itself; her bones slid into their sockets in a slightly different way, and a chunk of asphalt lifted off her heart. In its place, a space opened up that had been reserved for only Bob.

She left the reunited cat owner and drove home to get Cooper. They were going to visit Hill.

Chapter 37

At last, a pack of his own. With the First One, Liz, they had been a majestic pair and he had steadied her wild course. But they were cut off from others, isolated. Who can say why he had not been able to save her. He could no more answer that than know why the lives of dogs were a brief flash of light compared to the great expanse of human life.

How strange that humans live on and on while dogs move in and out of their lives like seasons. Even stranger is that humans cannot hear or smell all that surrounds them and all that they themselves announce through their hairless flesh.

He felt the formation of his pack grow daily. The cat pressing against his backside, the New One settling into this place muscle by muscle, the girl eating bits of food, the old one healing from the injury that he had long known was there from the scent of infection deep within her. And the others who circle his pack with the watchful eyes of friends: the man with the limp who looks at the New One with longing, or the old dark man who stands sentinel over the island.

But in this life, he is dog. His life is ocean, stick, ball, sand, grass, ride in the truck, sleep by the bed, look deep into the eyes of humans, lure them outdoors, greet them with a burst of joy when they come home, love them. Fill this brief life with more. And more.

A⁺

AUTHOR
INSIGHTS,
EXTRAS, &
MORE...

FROM

JACQUELINE
SHEEHAN

AND

AVON A

ABOUT THE BOOK

Inspiration for *Lost & Found*

Lost & Found is a profound departure from my first book, *Truth*, a novel about Sojourner Truth, the courageous nineteenth-century slave and abolitionist. It took five years to write *Truth* because of the enormous amount of research that I had to do and in order to present the true essence of her character. Because I admired Sojourner Truth so deeply, I felt like my feet were constantly held to the fire. During this time period, I periodically took breaks from my historical novel to give voice to the wonderfully flawed and irreverent Rocky and the character for my next book was born. In the stories and snippets that I wrote about Rocky, she was always drawn to bow hunting and she was always in love with her husband. At some point I asked the heartless question that authors often ask about their characters, which is, what if Rocky lost the thing that was most important to her? And for Rocky, that was her husband.

Truth required that I dive into another culture, another time. I wanted Rocky to come primarily from my own experiences and from our contemporary world. My world has been driven by psychology; it is a rich and satisfying world that gives me endless insight into the motivation of people and the resilience of the human spirit. Psychology was my training ground for fiction, and likewise, I often urge clients in counseling to use writing as a way to tap into a deeper and wiser side of themselves.

Is this autobiographical?

No and yes. No, this is fictional, and yes, Rocky is a psychologist and so am I. Yes, I was once a lifeguard, but only for one summer and I wasn't a terribly good one. And, yes, I was called on to perform CPR and the victim did not survive. And yes, I have known and loved two of the most extraordinary dogs, both of whom would have stood in front of a racing train to save the ones they loved.

Do your life experiences with loss influence the tragedy in Rocky's life?

Death is a major character in this book and death has been a major character in my life. When I was nine years old, my father died suddenly from a massive heart attack. People did not talk much about the impact of loss back then and I was simply expected to go back to school and continue on as if nothing had happened. He died in mid-June and I don't recall the summer at all except that the sky was constantly gray. In the fall, I started fourth grade with a wonderful teacher, Mrs. Vivien Tarbox. She informed us that we would be studying science and the arts. I selected an unlikely author, Edgar Allan Poe, and spent the year reading everything he ever wrote. He was my maudlin grieving partner; he knew about parental loss and sadness and he and I were sad together. He understood losing someone to the thief of death and he took grief to the farthest, most macabre level in his writing. His mother died when he was two years old and his father before that. He brooded over the mystery of death and I brooded right along with him.

It was not until years later when I was in graduate school studying about grief that I fully understood my year with Poe.

As odd as it must have looked for a young child to cozy up to Poe, no one in my family even noticed because everyone was so shattered by my father's death. But once the year was over, I put my friend aside. He had taken me through a year of grieving.

Readers have said to me that they are startled and horrified at Rocky's behavior after her husband's death, particularly when she disposes of his ashes in such a spectacular, yet gruesome manner. Yes, Rocky is a bit over the top, but in dealing with grief there are infinite ways that people choose to make a statement to the dead. Her behavior tells us just how far off center she is blown. I have known people who wear their lover's ashes in a vial hung around their neck. When my ex-husband was killed in a motorcycle accident while I was writing this book, I knew immediately what I had to do. I took a dear friend to a bar, ordered a shot of Jack Daniels and a cigar. I did not leave the bar until both the cigar and several more shots were consumed. These were potent symbols of my former spouse and I felt connected to him as I rolled the powerful smoke in my mouth and the Jack Daniels scorched my throat and belly.

What we believe about death determines how we live. Billy Collins, the former poet laureate of the United States, often warns students as they enter his poetry classes, "Welcome to the school of death." Poets so often write about death and loss, and fiction writers are not far behind.

Cardio-pulmonary resuscitation (CPR) is widely taught as a lifesaving technique. Why do you present a case where it doesn't work?

When I began to write about Rocky, I knew she would have her world shattered by the death of her young husband, and that she would feel betrayed when her iron-clad belief in CPR is ripped away from her. She completely believed that she possessed a skill that would save her husband.

My own experience with CPR made its way into the novel. I have known CPR since I was a lifeguard at age 23. I was never called on to perform CPR during my one summer as a lifeguard, despite working with handicapped and medically fragile people. It was not until years later when I had just started a job at a college in Massachusetts that my old training was tragically needed. As I walked up a flight of stairs in the student center, a man flew down the stairs and said, "There's a guy in the men's room who's not breathing." I ran into the men's room and there was a young man wedged between the urinal and the corner of the room; his skin was already blue, his lips an alarming shade of purple. As soon as a student and I got him on the floor, I knelt next to his head and began CPR. I never hesitated for a second and part of me assumed he would be revived; he would open his eyes at any moment because we were going to save him through CPR. Within moments the head of the athletic club arrived and took over compressions, then the campus police arrived and all of us took turns doing everything we could to convince his heart to start. We were undaunted; we continued until the EMTs arrived with defibrillators. I imagined that we were breathing for him and squeezing his heart into action until the medical professionals could make his heart start for real. I believed that much in CPR. The young man never revived. I was devastated and so were all the people who tried to save him.

Less than a year later I was walking in a park with a friend and saw that a man had fallen on the asphalt and two women stood over him. Once again, the man was not breathing and the stubborn lifeguard in me responded. One of the women was a nurse and we immediately began CPR. I remember thinking; we've got this one. Once again the man did not survive; a massive heart attack had left his heart damaged beyond reach.

CPR remains a lifesaving technique, and particularly for drowning accidents, the rate of success is very good. But like many people, I had placed an inordinate amount of faith into a technique that simply can't compete with the assault of some cardiac disasters. I held on to the sense of despair for nine years before I transformed it by turning it into fiction.

Animals play a large role in this book. Did you know that a dog would become a major character?

Although I had grown up with dogs and cats, it was not until I was 25 and living in Chicago, working with street kids, that I met my first extraordinary dog. He arrived with my future husband. The dog was a gorgeous golden retriever mix. He never wore a leash or a collar; he heeled so perfectly that people often imagined that he had a leash on. It wasn't long before I realized that I could walk anywhere in Chicago, at any time of day or night, and feel perfectly safe if I had Poncho with me. His full name was Poncho Rafaelo Jesus Gonzales. He blissfully pranced the sidewalks with a tennis ball in his jaws, but if he didn't like someone, he'd drop the ball and get between the person he had profiled and me. I once wandered into a deserted industrial area of the city and as we walked under a trestle, a man suddenly appeared out of the shadows and demanded to walk with me. He made the mistake of trying to shoo Poncho away by stomping his feet. Poncho lunged at him, growling and displaying every impressive fang. The man fled and Poncho covered his fangs once again with his golden retriever smile. Something changed for me in that moment. This dog would fight for me and protect me in a way that was immediate and non-negotiable. I had not trained him to do this. He had chosen me and I was his. My heart grew larger that day as dusk set and we emerged from the most desolate stretch of Chicago. He never bit anyone, but I knew that if he had to, he would.

We moved from Chicago to Oregon and Poncho was my constant companion for hiking, running through Douglas fir forests, and camping. My husband accompanied me for most camping adventures, but I felt perfectly secure camping only with Poncho. He taught me about loyalty, forgiveness, and the pure joy of reveling in the moment. There were times, as he and I followed animal trails in the foothills of the Cascade Mountains, when I became more dog and he led and I followed. And there were times when he became more human, learning the human rules of an Easter egg hunt and following the traditions perfectly, eating the collected eggs only when I said so. I tried to learn his language: a raised eyebrow, a dropped tail, rear end up, a slight turn of the head, a two-wag instead of a three-wag greeting. And he made every effort to learn my language. He forgave me when I came home cranky and unloving and I forgave him for eating a freshly baked peach pie. We were both contrite, ashamed of our bad behavior. He mended and expanded a part of me. I threw a lot of balls and sticks for him.

The second exceptional dog was a great barrel-chested black lab named Spud that belonged to my sister and brother-in-law. He played soccer amazingly well with my three nephews, visited (on his own initiative) a home day care center to the delight of the children, and as he matured, exhibited what I could only call a heroic personality. Spud weighed over 90 pounds and was clearly a powerful animal, yet he never fought with other dogs, instead he calmed them. He once escorted two ferocious Rottweilers from my sister's yard by simply herding them in the most congenial manner. He looked like a good-humored bouncer guiding the drunks out to the sidewalk. He continually stayed between my sister and any unknown visitor. He also knew how to be careful around our fragile mother in her later years. Our mother regarded him as the ultimate hero after he deflected the above-mentioned Rottweilers when she was out walking an antagonistic ankle biter sort of dog.

In my stories, and in this novel, animals are a presence and a personality. They are a part of the plot. They may be hero, martyr, or rascal, and in the case of the dog that Rocky finds and saves, they often have their own say. It is understandably risky to give a dog a point of view in fiction. It could potentially go so badly. We hear several chapters from the point of view of this dog, and we get a taste of his inner world and the depth of his emotional sensations. Early readers told me that I simply should not, could not do this. But I could no more deny this dog a point of view that I could refuse the invitation to hurl myself along animal trails with my old dog Poncho. The viewpoint was there all along.

But did I imagine that the dog would take such a front and center role? Absolutely not. Much as dogs do in real life, this dog brazenly walked into this novel and persistently revealed his personality until I paid attention.

READ ON

Have You Read?

Truth, a novel based on the life of Sojourner Truth

"Truth rings as true as the original words of the incomparable Sojourner Truth on which this novel is based. It made the hairs stand up on the back of my neck!"

Christiane Northrup, M.D., author of
Women's Bodies, Women's Wisdom

Born a slave, survived a free bondswoman, reborn an outspoken abolitionist, Sojourner Truth died a heroine of graceful proportions. But the story of her inner struggles is as powerful and provocative as her accomplishments and could only be captured in fiction. This emotionally searing novel beautifully infuses the historical atrocities of the 1800s with the psychological speculation of who Sojourner Truth really was, beyond her social and political persona.

In a feat of literary ventriloquism, Sheehan puts the story back in Sojourner's voice, lending the telling a naked, crystalline quality that transport the reader to a time when survival could mean sacrificing little pieces of one's soul.

Women Writing in Prison, **an anthology**
Edited by Jacqueline Sheehan

"If courage is grace under pressure, then these poems are graceful expressions under the real pressures of confinement. Poetry's acclaimed power to liberate is vividly exemplified in Women Writing in Prison; *each poem is at once a private act of escape and confrontation."*

Billy Collins, former U.S. Poet Laureate

After working with women in prison teaching writing workshops, Sheehan edited an anthology of their work. The project is run by Voices From Inside, a group designed to bring creative writing to incarcerated women and to bring their voices to the outside world to increase awareness about the human cost of incarceration.

What do women in prison write about? They write about food, home, family, planting gardens, the men who have beat them, the smell of grandmother's hair. They make funny rhymes, laugh at old boyfriends, long to pee in a bathroom with a door, and breathe fresh air. They write with honesty and freshness that is only lightly edited to maintain their unique voices. Part of the bondage that many incarcerated women face is drug addiction, and they write about this with searing frankness. The purchase of this anthology funds continuing writing programs for women in prison.

Jacqueline Sheehan

I grew up in Connecticut and live in Massachusetts today, where I divide my time between writing, teaching writing workshops and yoga, and running a small psychotherapy practice. But I spent twenty years living in western states: California, Oregon, and New Mexico. For most of my childhood, I lived in a single-parent home, after the early death of my father left my mother with five kids. My siblings were 8 to 13 years older than I was at the time, so they really had a different childhood, complete with two parents. My mother was a nurse by day, but she had the spirit of an artist. My first memory of her was watching her paint at her easel on her day off. She was one of the most fascinating people I've ever met and even as a child, I was aware of my good fortune to have landed in her nest.

Which is not to say that childhood or my teen years were easy. They were not. I was impulsive and wild, slipping out of my bedroom window at night to meet friends, smoke Newport cigarettes, and drive with boys in fast cars. After unsuccessfully attempting to rein me in, she wisely took another approach and gave me a very long leash, which was what I needed. At the end of my second year of college, a girlfriend and I hitchhiked across the country and to her amazing credit, my mother actually drove us to our first highway entrance and dropped us off.

At college in Colorado, I studied anthropology and art, preparing me for few jobs. During the summer I worked at an institution in Connecticut for people with mental retardation. This was truly the Dark Ages in how we regarded people with developmental delays and we clumped them all together under the umbrella of mental retardation. People of all ages were warehoused in large buildings in awful conditions. College students who worked there in the summer were acutely aware of the injustices done to residents and we plotted many small and not so small rebellions on behalf of the residents.

My career path after college did not lead straight to writing, but instead took a sometimes dizzying route. Among my more illustrious job choices were: director of a traveling puppet troupe, roofer, waitress, recreation worker and lifeguard for handicapped kids, health-food clerk, freelance photographer (the low point was taking pictures of kids with Santa, the high point was photographing births), substance-abuse counselor with street kids in Chicago, freelance newspaper writer, and something about baiting sewers for rats in Oregon, but that one is always too hard to explain. After the birth of my daughter, I returned to graduate school to study psychology, eventually earning my Ph.D. and working at university counseling centers.

As soon as I settled in with psychology, I began to write fiction. Short stories, long stories, novellas, novels, essays. I woke at five A.M. to write before I left for work, spent part of every weekend writing, most holidays, and parts of every vacation that I could squeeze out of my very full life. I have now switched the balance; writing is my primary occupation and private practice is my part-time job.

When people ask me how I find time to write, I am always puzzled, because finding time is not a huge problem. Pat Schneider, a wise writing teacher, once said, "You would find time for a lover, wouldn't you? That is how you find time for writing." And possibly the image of my mother, happily painting at her easel on her day off made an imprint on me that said, here is what you do with your life, do those things you love.

I have a backlog of stories and novels that are yammering to come out and I am doing my best to keep them in an orderly line. I am currently working on a novel that came to me in nearly complete form while I sat daydreaming on a ferry from the Isle of Skye to the mainland of Scotland.

www.jacquelinesheehan.com